Jessica's First Prayer

Palgrave Macmillan Classics of Children's Literature

This series brings back into print some of the most important works in children's literature first published before 1939. Each volume, edited by a leading scholar, includes a substantial introduction, a note on the text, suggestions for further reading, and comprehensive annotation. While these full critical editions are an invaluable resource for students and scholars, the series is also designed to appeal to the general reader. *Classics of Children's Literature* presents wonderful stories that deserve a place in any adult's or child's library.

Series Editors:
M. O. Grenby, University of Newcastle, UK
Lynne Vallone, Rutgers University, USA

Jessica's First Prayer
and
Froggy's Little Brother

Hesba Stretton (*Jessica's First Prayer*)

Brenda (*Froggy's Little Brother*)

Edited with an Introduction by

Elizabeth Thiel

Formerly Senior Lecturer, University of Roehampton, UK

First published 2013 by
PALGRAVE MACMILLAN

Palgrave Macmillan in the UK is an imprint of Macmillan Publishers Limited, registered in England, company number 785998, of Houndmills, Basingstoke, Hampshire RG21 6XS.

Palgrave Macmillan in the US is a division of St Martin's Press LLC, 175 Fifth Avenue, New York, NY 10010.

Palgrave Macmillan is the global academic imprint of the above companies and has companies and representatives throughout the world.

Palgrave® and Macmillan® are registered trademarks in the United States, the United Kingdom, Europe and other countries

ISBN: 978–0–230–36054–9 paperback

This book is printed on paper suitable for recycling and made from fully managed and sustained forest sources. Logging, pulping and manufacturing processes are expected to conform to the environmental regulations of the country of origin.

A catalogue record for this book is available from the British Library.

A catalog record for this book is available from the Library of Congress.

Contents

Acknowledgements

A number of people have generously given their time and shared their knowledge of Hesba Stretton and Brenda to assist in the production of this volume. Thanks are owed, in particular, to Elaine Lomax for help with my research on Stretton and to Brenda's great granddaughter who has so willingly provided me with invaluable access to Brenda's texts and memorabilia and who entrusted me with a signed first edition of *Froggy's Little Brother* for this project. Much gratitude is also due to Joanne Noble, who gallantly and enthusiastically helped with the task of comparing editions and to whom this volume is dedicated, and to my colleagues at the University of Roehampton for their encouragement. Finally, my thanks to series editors Matthew Grenby and Lynne Vallone for the opportunity to be a part of this important series.

Introduction

Our perceptions of mid- to late-nineteenth century children's literature have been shaped largely by the period's canonical texts; as historical artefacts, they have also informed and extended our understanding of the past, exposing the ideologies and preoccupations of the period in which they were written. However, knowledge gleaned solely in this way is limited. To achieve a more accurate comprehension of Victorian life and culture, it is vital to access children's literature beyond the canon and it is through the popular, non-canonical literature of the nineteenth century, in texts such as Hesba Stretton's *Jessica's First Prayer* (1867) and Brenda's *Froggy's Little Brother* (1875), that additional insights into the Victorian world can be gained.[1] The 'street arab' genre,[2] to which both texts belong and which they exemplify, offers images of childhood

---

[1] To avoid confusion, Sarah Smith will be referred to throughout as Hesba Stretton and Georgina Castle Smith as Brenda.

[2] The term 'street arab', used extensively in nineteenth-century social commentary and retained as common parlance into the twentieth century, was apparently coined by Lord Shaftesbury to describe the children of the streets. In *Street Arabs and Guttersnipes*, George Needham offers a description of the nomadic Arab as 'uncertain, vindictive and selfish ... the source of apprehension to every traveller ... living in clans or hordes, for self-protection' before stating that 'it was with acute discernment that ... Lord Shaftesbury discovered the resemblance. To this noble Earl ... we are indebted for the epithet, so unique and suggestive, of STREET ARAB [sic]'. George Needham (1884) *Street Arabs and Guttersnipes: The Pathetic and Humorous Side of Young Vagabond Life in the Great Cities, with Records of Work for their Reclamation* (Boston: Guernsey, 1884), p.22. As Kimberley Reynolds comments, 'street arab' is a telling label, 'it exposes a way of thinking about poor city children that refused to see them either as part of British society or as children. It marked these street children as outcasts ...'. Kimberley Reynolds, '*Froggy's Little Brother*: Nineteenth-Century Evangelical Writing for Children and the Politics of Poverty', in *The Oxford Handbook of Children's Literature*, ed. by Julia Mickenberg and Lynne Vallone (Oxford: Oxford University Press, 2011), pp.255–74 (p.257).

that differ to those of many canonical works; its focus is rarely the middle-class child of, for example, Robert Michael Ballantyne or Lewis Carroll, although a middle-class reader and middle-class mores may be implied, but the child of the inner-city streets who is parentless and destitute, or whose home conditions are presented as a travesty of the nineteenth-century domestic ideal.[3]

While there were hundreds of street arab tales, *Jessica's First Prayer* was undoubtedly the most commercially successful and is commonly acknowledged as the archetype; street arab tales typically focus on a poor and potentially endangered child who is rescued from the streets and destitution and relocated to a safe, Christian and, frequently, middle-class environment. In Stretton's story, Jessica, the young daughter of a destitute and wayward mother, is left alone to wander through London. Appearing one day at the coffee stall of churchwarden Daniel, Jessica befriends the elderly man who grudgingly provides her with coffee and food. Jessica secretly follows Daniel to his church, meets the minister and his daughters, and so learns about Christ and prayer. She is finally rescued and adopted by Daniel after he visits her dilapidated home and finds her abandoned and near to death.

It is for *Jessica's First Prayer* that Stretton is best remembered, although she was the author of some 60 books, as well as stories and articles for journals, including Charles Dickens' *Household Words*. Born Sarah Smith in 1832 in Shropshire and taking the initials of her siblings' names and the village of All Stretton in her home county to create her pseudonym, Stretton helped to found

---

[3] Anna Davin notes that 'in their religious aspect waif stories belong to the "tract fiction" discussed by Nancy Cutt in *Ministering Angels* (1979) and to the "Sunday School literature" about which Gillian Avery and J.S. Bratton have written.' The concerns of waif stories had been heralded in Puritan writings and more recent models existed in early nineteenth-century didactic writing for children. She suggests that authors influencing waif fiction include Mrs Sherwood, Mary Howitt, Charlotte Tucker and Maria Charlesworth and that the Religious Tract Society, through publication of fiction in *The Sunday at Home*, was 'a major player in the production of the genre, while the multiplying Sunday Schools were an important part of its market'. Anna Davin, 'Waif Stories in Late Nineteenth-Century England', *History Workshop Journal*, 52 (2001), pp.67–98 (p.67).

the organisation that was to become the National Society for the Prevention of Cruelty to Children. An extensive traveller, both at home and overseas, Stretton remained unmarried, living with her sister, Elizabeth, and dying in Ham, Richmond in 1911 after a long illness.

By the time of Stretton's death, some two million copies of *Jessica's First Prayer* are believed to have been printed and the tale was translated world-wide within five years of publication.[4] There were magic lantern slides, a Service of Song – an adaptation featuring both narrative and songs for Sunday school perform- ance – and two silent film versions produced in 1909 and 1921, the latter by the Seal Film Company. A memoir on Stretton in *The Sunday at Home* of December 1911 'records "strong men" reduced to tears and rough sailors "choking red eyed" over *Jessica*' and Lord Shaftesbury 'declared the story unrivalled for its "simplicity, pathos, and depth of Christian feeling" '.[5] In the Literary Gossip section of *The Athenaeum* on 14 October 1911, the unnamed author commented that the success of the book had been 'imme- diate and astonishing'.[6]

There are no surviving publisher's records for *Froggy's Little Brother* and so only limited information about its publishing his- tory is available, but Brenda's text, the most renowned of her 23 novels, was widely read by different social classes and new edi- tions continued into the twentieth century; sold as a Sunday school prize and for Sunday reading, it was admired by middle- and upper-class readers.[7] Protagonists Froggy and Benny, raised as Christians by their mother, are orphaned early in the novel – their mother dies from illness and their father is fatally injured.

---

[4] Nancy Cutt, *Ministering Angels: A Study of Nineteenth-Century Evangelical Writing for Children* (Wormley: Five Owls Press, 1979), pp.135–6.

[5] Elaine Lomax, *The Writings of Hesba Stretton: Reclaiming the Outcast*, (Farnham and Burlington: Ashgate, 2009), p.57.

[6] Anon, 'Literary Gossip', *The Athenaeum*, 14 October 1911, p.460.

[7] *Froggy's Little Brother* was also made into a film by Oswald Stoll in 1921, but Benny did not die in this version and Brenda was reportedly upset by the changes. Liz Thiel, 'The Woman Known as Brenda', in *A Victorian Quartet: Four Forgotten Women Writers*, ed. by Liz Thiel, Elaine Lomax, Bridget Carrington and Mary Sebag-Montefiore (Lichfield: Pied Piper Publishing, 2008), pp.147–208 (p.163).

Froggy strives to support himself and his sibling, Benny, and resists becoming a thief as he struggles to earn money for food and fruitlessly petitions the Queen for help, but Benny weakens and dies. However, Froggy is rescued from poverty and is finally settled safely in a home for boys.

Like Stretton, Brenda adopted a pseudonym for her writing; she was born Georgina Meyrick in London in 1845 and took a *nom de plume* chosen by her mother. Her first publication, the street arab story *Nothing to Nobody*, was produced in 1873 by John F. Shaw and Company, who published the majority of her texts. Married to solicitor Castle Smith in 1875, Brenda raised her five children in London as she continued to write and publish, but she and her husband left the city during the early 1900s and lived on the Isle of Wight before moving to Lyme Regis in Dorset, where Brenda died in 1933. Her writing career spanned some 59 years and while her texts often explored social issues, her work extended beyond street arab stories to include domestic narratives for children.

However, and despite the breadth of her oeuvre, it was for *Froggy's Little Brother* that Brenda was consistently acclaimed. Arthur Gore, writing to Brenda's husband after her death, commented, 'I do not think that anything in English literature – even that written by Dickens – can equal the pathos of "Benny's" life and death', while for Beatrice Rochdale, wife of Colonel George Kemp, Baron of Rochdale, the book was 'beloved by countless people'.[8]

Although *Jessica's First Prayer* and *Froggy's Little Brother* display the characteristic formula adhered to by numerous other authors of street arab tales, they differ in their religious emphases. Stretton's text centres on the spiritual conversion of the child and Jessica's influence on the hypocritical Daniel, while Brenda's novel, although imbued with Christian doctrine and replete with hymns, seeks salvation for Froggy and his brother primarily through the philanthropic interventions of existing charitable institutions. However, both reflected the nineteenth-century axiom that children and adults, however wretched, might be 'saved' if they turned to God and so each text echoed the religious theme prevalent in many earlier texts for children, albeit

---

[8] Thiel, 'The Woman Known as Brenda', in *A Victorian Quartet*, ed. by Thiel et al., pp.160–1.

less dogmatically. James Janeway's *A Token for Children* (1672) had forcefully proclaimed God and repentance as the only route to heaven, an exhortation mirrored over 100 years later in Mary Martha Sherwood's *History of the Fairchild Family* (1818) with its hint of damnation for those who did not repent. The nineteenth-century rise in Evangelical Christianity, coupled with concern for the urban poor, resulted in a literature that again urged the reader to look to their own redemption through God, but also to work for the salvation of those less fortunate than themselves. The evangelical Religious Tract Society, founded in 1799, was particularly productive in the second half of the nineteenth century, with publications for children by a number of popular authors, including Stretton.

Stretton's and Brenda's narratives are located within the general context of nineteenth-century evangelicalism, child poverty and mid-century London, although *Froggy's Little Brother*, published eight years after Stretton's text, incorporates numerous contemporary references (detailed in the footnotes to the text) and thus self-consciously and continuously strives for additional realism. As Kimberley Reynolds comments, in the final section of the text the narrator's question, 'You will like to know what became of poor little Froggy, will you not?', answered in the present tense and explaining that Froggy is in a home, learning to be a carpenter 'gives the impression that the story is both absolutely current and based on events from life.... The immediacy it provides helps Brenda keep the pathos of her story at a high pitch while simultaneously assuring readers that changes for the better in the way the poor were cared for are in hand'.[9]

It is inevitable, perhaps, that the two texts are sometimes compared in scholarly discourse and this is not always to Brenda's advantage. In *The Impact of Victorian Children's Fiction* (1981), Jacqueline Bratton praises Stretton's work: 'it is a skilfully constructed narrative whose strength lies in its apparent simplicity...she has achieved the transformation of the available materials, both in terms of current social problems and specific

---

[9] Reynolds , *'Froggy's Little Brother'*, in *The Oxford Handbook of Children's Literature*, p.268.

motifs in which they are embodied, into a pattern which was to become archetypal.'[10]

She is, however, less complimentary about Brenda's text and is particularly critical of what she sees as the self-validation of the middle-class reader:

> Froggy and little Benny... pull with such determination at the reader's heart-strings that they lose all artistic decorum.... The whipped-up emotion is then, at the end of the book, turned into fuel for a homily to the reader... [and] [t]hese passages highlight the other artistic pitfall of her work. Their assumption is that the reader is well-off, comfortable, completely insulated from the story; Froggy and his brother, therefore, and all the detail of their lives, are a display put on to prove our tears and our generosity, to each other and especially to them.[11]

Stretton's *Jessica's First Prayer* is undoubtedly a skilfully written, spare but effective narrative and Bratton comments that it is 'one of the first books in which one can imagine the Sunday School reader fully understanding and accepting the moral notions the author has to convey, and, moreover, not feeling threatened or diminished by those notions'.[12] Her judgement is justified; Stretton's narrative is never patronising and the street child is endowed with intelligence and agency and Bratton's criticism of sentimentality in Brenda's text is similarly fair. For Bratton, *Froggy's Little Brother* is 'a very long way ... from *Jessica's First Prayer*', but her assertion that it 'is difficult to imagine a ragged school child finding Froggy anything but a sham, indeed an insult'[13] fails to take account of Brenda's intended readership. A ragged school child might certainly have experienced such feelings, but the implied reader of Brenda's text is not a ragged school child and so marketing of the text to Sunday Schools for the poor may well have been inappropriate (if profitable for the publishers). *Froggy's*

---

[10] Jacqueline Bratton, *The Impact of Victorian Children's Fiction* (London: Croom Helm, 1981) pp.85–6.

[11] Bratton, *The Impact of Victorian Children's Fiction*, pp.99–100.

[12] Bratton, *The Impact of Victorian Children's Fiction*, p.86.

[13] Bratton, *The Impact of Victorian Children's Fiction*, p.100.

Little Brother is explicitly addressed throughout to the more affluent classes, often through use of an intrusive narrator, and this is
particularly evident in its closing paragraphs: 'Parents and little
children, you especially who are rich, remember it is the Froggys
and Bennys of London for whom your clergyman is pleading,
when he asks you to send money and relief to the poor East End!'[14]
In this way Brenda's text urged the monied reader to embrace her
cause and like Stretton's *Jessica's First Prayer*, and perhaps because
of its sentimentality, clearly engendered concern for the plight
of destitute children in England's inner-city slums among upper-
class readers such as Gore and Rochdale (see p.x).

The children of the streets

Although *Jessica's First Prayer* and *Froggy's Little Brother* are set
in London, the plight of its child characters was evident in cities throughout the country. As Nancy Cutt comments, 'Hesba
Stretton's picture of slum life ... tiny in scale, is essentially true.
Surrounding the situation in the book was the whole complex
matter of slum poverty, worst in Manchester, Liverpool and
London – the poverty described by Engels and Mayhew, inter-
preted by Dickens and Mrs Gaskell, analysed by Charles Booth.'[15]

Dickens was the most celebrated writer who emphasised the pitiful condition of London's poor and 'was both a model and sup-
porter of many of those who wrote street arab fiction'.[16] Stretton's
and Brenda's protagonists are certainly in the Dickensian mould
and Froggy's story, in particular, would seem to pay homage to
both *Oliver Twist* (1837–8) and *Bleak House* (1853) with Froggy's
unwitting involvement with pickpockets and his work as a crossing sweeper, the latter reminiscent of Dickens' Jo. However, Jessica
and Froggy are also fictional and sympathetic representations of
the thousands of children who lived on the city streets in the
mid- to late-nineteenth century.

---

[14] Brenda, *Froggy's Little Brother* (London: John F. Shaw, 1875), p.169.

[15] Cutt, *Ministering Angels*, p.136.

[16] Reynolds , '*Froggy's Little Brother*', in *The Oxford Handbook of Children's
Literature*, p.267.

In reality, sympathy for such children was not always unqualified. James Greenwood, writing in *The Seven Curses of London* in 1869, asserted that

> daily, winter and summer within the limits of our vast and wealthy city of London, there wander, destitute of proper guardianship, food, clothing or employment, *a hundred thousand* boys and girls in fair training for the treadmill and the oakum shed, and finally for Portland and the convict's mark.[17]

His subsequent assertion locates the street child not as a victim, but as a social contaminant, fecund and uncontrolled:

> There is no present fear of the noble annual crop of a hundred thousand diminishing. They are so plentifully propagated that a savage preaching 'civilization' might regard it as a mercy that the localities of their infant nurture are such as suit the ravening appetites of cholera and typhus. Otherwise they would breed like rabbits in an undisturbed warren, and presently swarm so abundantly that the highways would be over-run, making it necessary to pass an Act of Parliament, improving on the latest enacted for dogs, against the roaming at large of unmuzzled children of the gutter.[18]

In his introduction to Greenwood's text, Jeffrey Richards comments that Greenwood 'settled on the exploitation of children' as his primary explanation for the situation, although modern research suggests that the 'armies of neglected' children were the result of high birth and death rates, family break-up through hardship, death and homelessness, migration within and into cities and a shortage of work for children.[19] Whatever the explanation for such numbers of children, Greenwood's declaration exposes a common anxiety that clearly existed in parallel with the agenda

---

[17] James Greenwood, *The Seven Curses of London* (Oxford: Blackwell, 1981), p.3.

[18] Greenwood, *The Seven Curses of London*, p.5.

[19] Jeffrey Richards, 'Introduction', in Greenwood, *The Seven Curses of London* (Oxford: Blackwell, 1981), p.xii.

to 'save' such children from degeneration and that in many ways exemplified the numerous paradoxes within Victorian society; as *The Times* remarked, 'This Metropolis certainly is the strangest place in the world. It is a place where extremes meet, and where splendour is next door to misery.'[20] The work of social reformers such as Lord Shaftesbury had resulted in a reduction in child labour and the establishment of Ragged Schools in the cities, but as the London *Daily News* noted:

A Ragged School may, at its first institution, include a good many of the perishing and dangerous class; but in a little while the character of the attendance rises, and the most wretched class drops out at the bottom. The young creatures are off in their wildness to prey upon their kind – the girls to haunt fairs and markets ... and the boys forming gangs, and drawing in and training little children of half their own age.[21]

Inherent in the *News* commentary is the notion that the child of the streets is prey to corruption, a notion that, at its roots, invests wholeheartedly in the concept of the innocent child. For both social commentators and writers of street arab stories, the child was vulnerable and at risk from the influence of degenerate parents and companions. Within these dangerous environments, the once innocent creature would become sullied and, as the *News* suggests, would then infect younger, vulnerable children. George Needham's *Street Arabs and Guttersnipes: The Pathetic and Humorous Side of Young Vagabond Life in the Cities with Records of their Work for their Reclamation* (1884) was, he wrote, 'a plea on behalf of neglected and destitute children ... too often educated in crime by unnatural parents or vicious guardians; or who, through the stress of circumstances, are forced into a course of life which tends to the multiplication of criminals and the increase in the dangerous classes'.[22]

---

[20] Anon, 'Juvenile Mendicancy – Lord Shaftesbury's Bill', *Ragged Schools Union Magazine*, 6, 61 (1854), p.165.

[21] Anon, 'Juvenile Mendicancy', *Ragged School Union Magazine*, p.167.

[22] George Needham, *Street Arabs and Guttersnipes: The Pathetic and Humorous Side of Young Vagabond Life in the Great Cities, with Records of Work for their Reclamation* (Boston: Guernsey, 1884), p.iii.

Needham, writing of both England and America, emphasised the dangers of allowing children to remain in what he perceived as 'sinful' environments:

> Go into the low quarters of Glasgow, the filthy back streets of Liverpool, the foul fever-slums of almost any of our great cities, and there you will see bright-eyed, tattered, ill-fed children growing up amid the reek of gin and amid scenes of blasphemy, in low, infamous rooms, and in low, infamous streets, dirty, dissolute and depraved – the very seed-plot of our future criminals... many a drunkard's child in England is being trained up deliberately in the habits of sin.[23]

Thus it was imperative that the inherently innocent child of both fact and fiction be rescued and relocated far from such influences, whether this was at home or overseas. The child emigration programme that climaxed in the second half of the nineteenth century and that saw thousands of children sent to Canada and South Africa, among other places, served to control, through practical means, the ragged, seemingly unmanageable children that roamed the streets. It was however vaunted primarily as a rescue mission of innocents and so the idealised, nineteenth-century image of childhood was effectively maintained while the problem was, to some degree, resolved.[24]

---

[23] Needham, *Street Arabs and Guttersnipes*, p.464.

[24] The dual purpose of the emigration programme as both rescuer and eradicator of street children is explicit in a poem from *Our Waifs and Strays*, 1887, entitled 'The Departure of the Innocents', cited in Pamela Horn, *The Victorian Town Child* (New York: New York University Press, 1997), n.p.

Take them away! Take them away!
Out of the gutter, the ooze and the slime,
Where the little vermin paddle and crawl,
Till they grow and ripen into crime.

Take them away from the jaws of death,
And the coils of evil that swaddle them round
And stifle their souls in every breath
They draw on the foul and fetid ground.

The innocent child, an image derived from Rousseau and Romanticism and epitomised in William Wordsworth's Ode on *Intimations of Immortality from Recollections of Early Childhood* (1807), was invariably the construct that predominated in street arab fiction. Sometimes depicted as a means of salvation for others – Jessica 'saves' Daniel when she guides him to an authentic, rather than a superficial Christianity – the child protagonist generally displays an inherent goodness that validates him as worthy of rescue; Brenda's Froggy resists corruption because of his moral sensibilities and is horrified when he realises that he is in the company of thieves: '...oh! what would father and mother think if they were looking down at him from their home in heaven?'[25] Indeed, parents are significant within many street arab tales and are depicted very occasionally as a positive force for the child, as is seemingly the case in *Froggy's Little Brother*. More commonly, however, they are portrayed as inept or degenerate individuals whose failures impact dangerously on the development and potential future of the young boy or girl.[26]

Take them away! Away! Away!
The bountiful earth is wide and free,
The New shall repair the wrongs of the Old –
Take them away o'er the rolling sea!
Monica Flegel discusses the tension between the street child and Victorian ideologies of the child, commenting that '[a]s the construction of childhood as properly a sanctified, protected space became increasingly dominant in England...the "savage" child primarily elicited concern. When writers were confronted with the animalistic child of the streets, their response was therefore often one of horror: "Can these be *children*?".... A child that was allowed to be unrestrained and unlawful, was a child that questioned the sanctified space of childhood itself'. Monica Flegel, *Conceptualising Cruelty to Children in Nineteenth-century England: Literature, Representation and the NSPCC* (Farnham: Ashgate, 2009), pp.53–4.

[25] Brenda, *Froggy's Little Brother*, p.96.

[26] See Elizabeth Thiel, *The Fantasy of Family: Nineteenth-century Children's Literature and the Domestic Ideal* (London and New York: Routledge, 2008) for a more detailed discussion of parenting and family in nineteenth-century children's texts.

The sins of the parents

Family life in *Jessica's First Prayer* and *Froggy's Little Brother* is presented as in striking opposition to the idealised, sacrilised domestic state perpetuated in much nineteenth-century discourse; John
Ruskin's 'place of Peace; the shelter, not only from all injury, but
from all terror, doubt and division' bears little resemblance to
Jessica's hayloft or Froggy's attic.[27] Froggy's family live

> in a very bare garret, at the top of a dark, dingy house, the upper
> part of which was scorched and blackened from the effects of a
> fire which had occurred several years ago, on the opposite side
> of the way, and which had damaged more or less all the panes
> of glass in the neighbouring windows.[28]

Jessica, whose mother is often 'out on a spree',[29] returns to 'a single room, which had once been a hayloft over the stable of an
old inn … . The mode of entrance was by a wooden ladder, whose
rungs were crazy and broken … . The interior of the home was as
desolate and comfortless as that of the stable below … . Everything
that could be pawned had disappeared long ago'.[30] Both dwell-
ings are potentially highly dangerous; the Shoreditch garret displays the effects of a neighbouring fire, while Jessica is obliged
to climb a 'crazy' and 'broken' ladder to access her hayloft. The
neighbours are similarly undesirable. Froggy and Benny are not
explicitly abused by others in the building, although Benny is
often left with landlady Mrs Ragbon who is rumoured to beat
her own children when she is drunk.[31] Jessica, however, claims
to be subject to frequent physical abuse; she tells Daniel, ' "It's
Jess here, and Jess there … And they think nothing of giving me
smacks, and kicks, and pinches. Look here!" Whether her arms

---

[27] John Ruskin, 1865. 'Of Queen's Gardens', in *Sesame and Lilies, the Two
Paths and the King of the Golden River* (London: J.M.Dent, 1901), pp.48–79
(p.59).

[28] Brenda, *Froggy's Little Brother*, p.44.

[29] Hesba Stretton, *Jessica's First Prayer* (London: Religious Tract Society,
1867), p.28.

[30] Stretton, *Jessica's First Prayer*, p.11.

[31] Brenda, *Froggy's Little Brother*, p.52.

were black and blue from the cold, or from ill-usage, ... [Daniel] could not tell.'[32] Daniel is shown to doubt the veracity of Jessica's statement, although her later, honest response to his test of leaving a penny on the pavement suggests that her claim of abuse may have been true.

Moreover, the children's situation is depicted as the direct result of parental failure. Jessica's mother is the more explicitly culpable and is entirely in contravention, of the idealised image of womanhood and the natural mothering tendencies that Victorian ideology attributed to the female. Finally abandoning her sick child because Jessica's illness may be contagious – '[t]he neighbour informed ... [Daniel] that the child's mother had gone off some days before, fearing that she was ill of some infectious fever'[33] – Jessica's mother has consistently neglected Jessica and has denied her a childhood by forcing her to beg, scantily clad, on the streets. Her former identity as an actress, known as 'The Vixen', and her predilection for 'always get[ting] very drunk of a Sunday'[34] is further evidence of Jessica's mother's failure as a parent, while her attempt to involve Jessica in the then often notorious theatre world by permitting her to play 'a fairy in the pantomime' consolidates her degeneracy.[35] The trope of the drunken mother is a familiar one in street arab narratives and Lomax notes that

> [t]he image of drunken irresponsibility which attaches to the mother in the *Jessica* narratives ... mirrors stereotypical perceptions which find increasing expression in novels, 'melodramatic' temperance tracts, journalistic articles and visual texts, as the period progresses. Associated with the transmission of solely negative values, it represents the antithesis of feminine respectability, maternal propriety and nurturing qualities.

Lomax also observes that although such figures may lack individual identity, Jessica's parent is given a voice in the sequel, *Jessica's*

---

[32] Stretton, *Jessica's First Prayer*, p.6.

[33] Stretton, *Jessica's First Prayer*, p.34.

[34] Stretton, *Jessica's First Prayer*, p.28, 26.

[35] Stretton, *Jessica's First Prayer*, p.20.

Mother (1867), although, ultimately excluded from the story, she is 'destined to be renounced and "cast out" from the narrative'.[36] In this way she is silenced and metaphorically denied any further opportunity to impede Jessica's transition from waif to respectability, or to serve as a catalyst for conversion.

The failure of Froggy's parents, Jeanie and Harry, while less explicit than that of Jessica's mother, is nevertheless the catalyst for Froggy and Benny's destitution. Indicative of what might be perceived as the passive approach to parenting displayed by the poor, Jeanie has little to offer her sons as she lies on her deathbed, other than her preoccupation with 'the Better Land';[37] her primary legacy to Froggy is his enforced adoption of her maternal role as he struggles to care for his younger sibling. Father Harry's fragile income with the Punch and Judy show, the family's sole means of survival, is destroyed when Harry dies beneath the wheels of a drag cart and the show is 'smashed to pieces. Poor Froggy! his heart sank at this. Without the friendly old Punch and Judy, which had kept the wolf from the door and fire in the grate all these years, what was to be done? How was he to get food for Benny?'[38] Thus Harry bequeaths nothing of practical use to Froggy and Benny and the destruction of the Punch and Judy show assures their impoverishment. However, and significantly, *Froggy's Little Brother* also suggests that poor children with parents fare little better than Froggy and Benny. Mac Ragbon, the son of a violent, neglectful mother who drinks and consequently has been

---

[36] Lomax, *The Writings of Hesba Stretton*, p.141. Lomax contextualises the image of the drunken woman within a broader range of historical references: '[Jessica's] … mother's fate evokes the downward spiral associated with the evils of drink represented in images ranging from the inebriate, negligent mother of Hogarth's much earlier "Gin Lane" (1751) to the dramatic sequences of Cruikshank's *The Black Bottle* (1847) and *The Drunkard's Children* (1848). The "fall" and apparent drowning [Jessica's] mother falls from a bridge] are reminiscent of Cruikshank's caricature of a woman throwing herself from a bridge – one of many artistic and literary or journalistic evocations of the "river suicide", among them Thomas Hood's "The Bridge of Sighs" (1844) and the engravings of Gustave Doré, which respond to the actuality and bolster the myth of the fallen woman' (pp.141–2).

[37] Brenda, *Froggy's Little Brother*, p.50.

[38] Brenda, *Froggy's Little Brother*, p.57.

deserted by her husband, turns pickpocket and is finally arrested in connection with a jewel robbery. Other children die and there is a sentiment akin to laissez-faire in the attitudes of the mothers and fathers who gather at Debbie Blunt's coffin:

'Oh my dear, I wouldn't fret about it overmuch if I was you,' said one poor woman [to Mrs Blunt]…. 'Life's a sad business, take it altogether from cradle to grave and it's worse I ses for women than for men. We don't likes to lose 'em when we've got 'em; no more we does, bless their innocent hearts, but depend upon it children's best out of it all!'

'Yes, that they be,' said an older neighbour mournfully. 'Robert and me, we've had seven, and we've buried 'em all, and we thank the Lord for it now, though we grieved terrible at first!'[39]

A similar image of the poor as ineffectual and incapable parents had appeared two years previously in Stretton's *Lost Gip* (1873). Protagonist Sandy attempts to keep his new sister healthy, aware that the other babies produced by his overly-fecund mother have died:

He had a vague notion that there was someone, somewhere, who could save the new-born baby from dying…. In the streets he had seen numbers of rich babies, who did not want for anything and whose cheeks were fat and rosy…. But how it happened, whether it was simply because they were rich, or because there was somebody who could keep them alive, and cared more for them than the poor, he could not tell.[40]

This suggestion that the poor cannot care for their children is echoed in the fatalistic approach of Mrs Blunt and her neighbours in *Froggy's Little Brother* and evident in the comment that 'children's best out of it all'. Those who live in poverty are shown to be inadequate parents and although the influence of Froggy's mother is displayed in the boys' dedication to prayer and in Froggy's nursing of

---

[39] Brenda, *Froggy's Little Brother*, p.120.
[40] Hesba Stretton, *Lost Gip* (London: Religious Tract Society, 1873), p.11.

Benny, albeit with the ineffective Keating's Elixir, Jeanie remains little more than a shadow of the ideal mother whose influence in life and after death provides inadequate support for her children. The narrative may strive to present her as the iconic dead mother of nineteenth-century fiction – her 'sacred' Sunday bonnet is kept reverentially in 'the old deal box' with the Bible and '[does]...the work of "the rich boy's photograph" for Froggy.'[41] However the bonnet is apparently forgotten when Froggy leaves the garret; it is rendered redundant as he begins life with a new 'family'.[42]

A safe haven

The necessity of extricating the destitute child from the slums is a constant theme in street arab stories, whether removal is engendered via the emigration programme, or by relocation of the child to a morally-sound, implicitly middle-class 'home' environment.[43] It is evident that neither Jessica nor Froggy will ever flourish in their hayloft and garret, and it is consequently imperative that they are removed, if they are to have a chance of survival. In both texts, however, the impetus for this change of location is not merely poverty and destitution, but sickness; Jessica almost dies before being taken from her hayloft and Benny's fatal illness instigates the intervention that cannot save the dying boy, but provides aid for his brother. It may be that these episodes are designed to increase the tales' dramatic thrust and overall pathos, but they also represent a forceful and persuasive demand for

---

[41] Brenda, *Froggy's Little Brother*, p.108.

[42] For further discussion of the iconic dead mother in Victorian fiction, see Carolyn Dever, *Death and the Mother from Dickens to Freud: Victorian Fiction and the Anxiety of Origins* (Cambridge: Cambridge University Press, 1998).

[43] Significantly, Lord Shaftesbury, writing of the Ragged Schools in 1880, draws on family imagery in his discussion of the movement: '[w]e adopted and followed the parental system, and rescued from the streets and placed in honest employment full three hundred thousand children that would have otherwise been the pests and dangers of society'. Lord Shaftesbury, 'Jessica's Second Prayer', *Ragged School Union Quarterly Record*, January 1881, p.4.

greater expediency in rehoming such children and enabling their subsequent development into useful adults.

Jessica's 'near death' is doubly purposeful; not only is she removed from her hayloft, but the episode also serves to emphasise her innate spirituality and so further validates her rescue. Having wept instinctively when she first hears church organ music,[44] Jessica now becomes confessor to and instigator of change for Daniel. As Daniel kneels by her side, she prays for him and it is through Jessica's influence that Daniel is reformed. Thus both Jessica and Daniel are 'saved' and while Daniel begins life afresh as a committed Christian, Jessica is physically tended and ultimately created anew. Daniel wraps 'the poor deserted Jessica in his coat, and bearing her tenderly in his arms down the ladder, ... carried her to a cab, which the neighbour brought to the entrance of the court. It was to no other than his own solitary home that he had resolved to take her.'[45] Prior to Jessica's full recovery, Daniel rents 'a little house for himself and his adopted daughter to dwell in',[46] assuring her physical wellbeing and simultaneously nurturing her spiritual development by employing her to join him in tending the chapel: '... her great delight being to attend to the pulpit and the vestry, and the pew where the minister's children sat, while Daniel and the woman he employed cleaned the rest of the building'.[47] Furthermore, Jessica contributes to the household by '[taking] ... her place behind the [coffee] stall, and soon [learning] to serve the daily customers'.[48] Relocated and renewed, Jessica becomes a useful and Godly member of society and while Daniel is evidently working class, his servitude to the minister and his daughters suggests that he also embraces the middle-class ideologies that will be internalised by his 'daughter'.[49]

---

[44] Stretton, *Jessica's First Prayer*, p.15.

[45] Stretton, *Jessica's First Prayer*, p.34.

[46] Stretton, *Jessica's First Prayer*, p.36.

[47] Stretton, *Jessica's First Prayer*, p.37.

[48] Stretton, *Jessica's First Prayer*, p.36.

[49] Jessica's relocation to a middle-class family environment is explicit in Stretton's sequel, *Jessica's Mother*. Hesba Stretton, *Jessica's Mother* (London: Religious Tract Society, 1867). When the minister suffers a stroke, Jessica stays with his daughters who see her as 'one who could help and counsel them' (p.8). The minister recovers and tells Jessica's mother that he 'loves

Benny's death is less religiously didactic than Jessica's sick-bed episodes, but utilises the trope of the 'beautiful death', employed by numerous nineteenth-century writers such as Mary Martha Sherwood and Florence Montgomery, to beatify the child as he slips away:[50]

> 'Yes, Froggy, I can hear the angels singing' again!' said Benny faintly, and a peculiar light shone over his face…. 'Then it's near evening – everybody's going home,' murmured little Benny, and Froggy heard him sigh deeply, but that was all! There was nothing else to tell that in London's sorrowful army of starving, struggling people, another little sufferer had fallen out of the ranks, because there seemed no room for it here, and had gone with its pitiful face and bleeding heart to lay its head down, and to be consoled and comforted for ever more in the bosom of the Saviour! A look of unspeakable rest and satisfaction settled on his features.[51]

However, and unlike the 'beautiful' deaths of Sherwood and Montgomery, Benny's demise is only partly compensated for by the notion that he will now be 'comforted in the bosom of the Saviour'. The passage, emphasising that *another* child has 'fallen out of the ranks' of those who fight for survival, implies that while

---

[the child] almost like one of his own little girls' (p.26), later declaring to the dying Daniel that 'Jessica shall come home to me' (p.30). However, it is unlikely that Jessica will be adopted; the minister's comment that he loves the child 'almost' as much as his own daughters is significant and it may be that Jessica is destined to be a companion or servant, rather than of equal status to Jane and Winny.

[50] In Sherwood's *History of the Fairchild Family* (1818), little Charles Trueman's demise exemplifies the beautiful death: 'The manner of his breathing changed; he looked round the room eagerly; then, suddenly looking upwards, and fixing his eyes on one corner of the room, the appearance of his countenance changed to a kind of heavenly and glorious expression, the like of which no one present ever before had seen'. Mary Martha Sherwood, *History of the Fairchild Family* (London: James Nesbit and Co., 1818), pp.294–5. See also Florence Montgomery's (in) famous text, *Misunderstood* (1869) and the 'in death' reunion of Humphrey and his mother.

[51] Brenda, *Froggy's Little Brother*, p.159.

Benny may now be safe in heaven there should have been 'room for him' on earth. Nevertheless, it is through Benny's death that Froggy is saved and Benny's 'pitiful face' and 'bleeding heart', descriptions reminiscent of the crucifixion of Christ, sanctify the child who dies so that his brother can live.

Through Benny's illness, Froggy is rescued and ultimately relocated to a quasi-familial environment, a 'Home for little boys' in the city.[52] His philanthropic rescue is effected by clergyman Mr Wallace, parish doctor, Dr Brown, and Miss Goff, the undermatron at the orphanage where Froggy is first taken, and the clear familial resonances in the descriptions of these individuals indicate their eligibility as replacement parents. Dr Brown speaks kindly to Froggy and, laying 'a friendly' hand on the boy's shoulder tells him that 'God has sent you friends at last' while Mr Wallace, in similar fatherly fashion, speaks 'soothingly' to Froggy, 'laying his small gentleman-like hand on Froggy's little shoulder'.[53] Miss Goff, described by Dr Brown as 'a very kind good lady … accustomed to nursing and sickness … [who] will do for your brother all that his mother would have done',[54] provides physical and emotional nourishment, bringing food and warm wraps and, after Benny's death, tells Froggy, 'you must come home with me'.[55] Her 'home' is a clean building near to a church and is 'very noisy and very happy'; while it is not a traditional home environment, it nevertheless offers a comforting and sheltering space and the large letters above the door, 'Suffer the little children to come unto Me',[56] emphasise its spiritual rectitude and allegiance to Froggy's final spiritual home in Heaven. Eventually, Froggy is sent 'through the kindness of Dr Brown and Mr Wallace' to a home for boys 'where he is learning the trade of a carpenter'[57] and where he is tended by the 'kind, motherly' Mrs Holt.[58] It is here that Froggy's alternative family is made complete when Billy,

---

[52] Brenda, *Froggy's Little Brother*, p.163.

[53] Brenda, *Froggy's Little Brother*, p.149.

[54] Brenda, *Froggy's Little Brother*, p.153.

[55] Brenda, *Froggy's Little Brother*, p.161.

[56] Brenda, *Froggy's Little Brother*, p.162.

[57] Brenda, *Froggy's Little Brother*, p.163.

[58] Brenda, *Froggy's Little Brother*, p.166.

soon to be an orphan and 'somethink' like Benny,[59] is given into
Froggy's care. Mrs Holt even suggests renaming Billy to replicate
Froggy's lost brother – 'Would you like to call him *Benny*, Froggy?'
asked the matron kindly – although Froggy declines.[60]

Froggy's new situation promises a future that his parents failed
to provide in their Shoreditch slum. It is implied that the middle-
class clergyman, doctor and matron will nurture him towards an
eminently preferable, viable and useful adulthood and that Froggy
will become a respectable member of society, schooled in appropriate behaviour and endowed with a strong work ethic in his training
as a carpenter. In addition, these new 'parents' are shown to be the
likely facilitators of at least a semblance of the childhood denied to
Froggy in his East End home. The reader's final glimpse of Froggy
(and Billy) is of them 'wondering anxiously whether enough
money would come into the Home this year to give them a treat
in the country',[61] a 'treat' that echoes the Romantic link between
child and nature and the healing and inspiriting propensity of the
natural world. Yet this passage simultaneously affirms the enduring effects of the deprivation that the boys have suffered; Froggy
and Billy await the decision 'with several other pale-faced, sorrowful-eyed little boys'.[62] While the children have been rehomed, it
would seem that the legacy of their former lives remains imprinted
on their faces; they may never resemble the rosy-cheeked, bright-
eyed idealised image of childhood, whatever their future brings.

Philanthropy and the woman writer

A concern for the future of inner-city children is clearly the impetus for both Stretton's and Brenda's narratives and each text pro-
poses that street children can and should be saved. Jessica and
Froggy, safely relocated beyond the corrupting influences of dubi-
ous individuals and immersed in religion and the middle classes,
represent what might be achieved through philanthropic endeavour and social reform. As Lomax comments, Stretton's first-hand

[59] Brenda, *Froggy's Little Brother*, p.168.
[60] Brenda, *Froggy's Little Brother*, p.168.
[61] Brenda, *Froggy's Little Brother*, p.169.
[62] Brenda, *Froggy's Little Brother*, p.169.

knowledge of slum life in Manchester and London and of Ragged Schools, orphanages and refuges resulted in a 'commitment to social amelioration and consciousness-raising, find[ing] expression in her writings ... and in the key role she played in campaigning for the formation of the London Society for the Prevention of Cruelty to Children (later the NSPCC) of which she became a founder member in 1884'.[63]

Stretton was celebrated by Lord Shaftesbury, among many others, and composed a fund-raising article for the Ragged Schools entitled 'Jessica's Second Prayer' which was published in *Sunday at Home* and in *The Ragged School Union Quarterly Record* of 1881. Stretton's essay is essentially a plea for continuing and additional support for the schools. Although Board Schools were available, she stresses that these are not free, but Ragged Schools are

> open to the very poor, as well as to the most abandoned .... The lowest, the most needy and most miserable can creep in, and sit down on the benches of the Ragged School with no fear of the scholars shrinking away from their touch, or the teacher's face clouding over at the sight of their wretchedness. All are penniless here; all out at elbows; all pinched more or less in the same fast clutch of poverty.[64]

There is no evidence that Brenda was actively involved in social reform campaigns, but it is likely that she too had experienced the slums of London. She and her sister Augusta performed penny readings to raise money for charity and personal knowledge would seem to be evident in her swingeing criticism of the middle-class visitor of the poor that appears in *A Saturday's Bairn* (1877):

> [The] nerves [of the poor] are often strung at a painful tension from a hundred worries and anxieties that we know nothing

---

[63] Elaine Lomax, 'Writing Other Lives: The Outcast Narratives of Hesba Stretton', in *A Victorian Quartet: Four Forgotten Women Writers*, ed. by Liz Thiel, Elaine Lomax, Bridget Carrington and Mary Sebag-Montefiore (Lichfield: Pied Piper Publishing, 2008), p.10.

[64] Hesba Stretton, 'Jessica's Second Prayer', *Ragged School Union Quarterly Record*, 6 (1881), pp. v–vii (p.v).

about, and makes them keenly sensitive to all outward influences. Without intention, it is easy to ruffle them.... I have
seen people...go into the homes of the poor and pick their way
about, with silk dresses caught up...as if they were treading
on hot bricks all the while...and then I have heard them wonder...why the poor are always such a grumpy, unget-at-able
set.[65]

Moreover, *Froggy's Little Brother* evidently appealed to the affluent
classes and may well have drawn substantial financial support for
various charitable institutions. Lord Arran, an enthusiastic admirer
of Brenda's work, later became the treasurer of the Children's
Country Holiday Fund and among Brenda's memorabilia are letters of gratitude praising her writing from Lord Shaftesbury and
Victoria of Hesse, granddaughter of Queen Victoria; Victoria's
sister Alix, later to become Alexandra Feodorovna, wife of Tsar
Nicholas II, also apparently enjoyed Brenda's work. In 'Children's
Classics' in *Quiver* of 1906, Bella Sidney Woolf notes that 'a rich
Lancashire cotton merchant' read the book and the next morning sent a £100 cheque to a boys' home.[66] She also reports that
Queen Victoria, after hearing the story, enquired whether Froggy
and Benny were known personally to Mrs Castle Smith, a somewhat ironic question, perhaps, given Froggy's failure to secure
help from the Queen.

Stretton and Brenda were born into middle-class families –
Stretton's father was a bookseller and Brenda's a solicitor – yet each
engaged purposefully with the destitute class and child poverty in
their writings, as did many other women authors of the time. As I
have discussed elsewhere (see Thiel, *The Fantasy of Family*, 2008),
the subject of child rescue was an area undoubtedly deemed
appropriate for women writers who were 'naturally' maternal and
the woman author of street arab tales thus metaphorically became
the mother of the poor, campaigning to save the children of the
streets. Stretton's narrative avoids an explicitly maternal tone and
is delivered through a third-person voice, although descriptions

---

[65] Brenda, *A Saturday's Bairn* (London: John F. Shaw, 1877), p.251.

[66] Bella Sydney Woolf, 'Children's Classics', *Quiver* (Jan. 1906), pp.
672–9 (p.678).

of Jessica as she stands, wan and ragged by Daniel's coffee stall and her tearful reaction to the church music certainly encourage an emotional response from the reader. However, maternal sorrow resounds through *Froggy's Little Brother*, most notably as Froggy returns to the garret after his experience with Mac, Dandy and Chickabiddy:

> He made his way to a doorstep, where he sat down to recover himself...[and] he fell fast asleep and dreamed that he was a little boy again...taken care of by his mother and father.... He dreamed he was in his little night-shirt sitting on his mother's knee, and she was rocking him to sleep with her arms round him, and singing to him a soft lullaby, as she used often to do. Froggy woke up with a little sob, because he knew it was all a dream.[67]

The pathos of this episode is excessive and the narrator unequivocally beseeching. Froggy can only dream of a mother's embrace – although this caress is his fundamental right as a child – and the passage demands a response from the mother who may be reading the text or, perhaps, from her listening daughter, already 'naturally' possessed of embryonic maternal instincts. However, and although the narrative is unashamedly complicit with nineteenth-century gender ideology, it simultaneously urges the female reader to take action, albeit within the appropriately womanly sphere of caring for children.

As writers of gender-appropriate fiction, it is perhaps unsurprising that Stretton and Brenda were publicly vaunted as exemplary Victorian women within nineteenth-century discourse, although Stretton was apparently complicit in this idealisation. As Cutt comments, 'a sentimental legend grew up about...[Stretton] which she did nothing to dispel' and a reporter, interviewing her in 1892, 'described her as having "a grave sweet face, large grey eyes and silvering curls"'. Stretton discouraged the reporter from a character sketch, but to no avail; he produced a description of 'so truly good and strong and womanly a woman, who, notwith-

---

[67] Brenda, *Froggy's Little Brother*, p.100.

standing a world-wide reputation of over thirty years as one of the most talented and most helpful writers of the time has remained so perfectly natural and sincere'.[68]

There is no comparable evidence of complicity from Brenda, but others certainly sought to elevate her to iconic status after her death. Her obituary in *The Times* praised Brenda for her 'deep insight and reverence to all those who serve in the Kingdom of God on earth for the very poor', while Lord Arran, writing to Castle Smith after his wife's death, claimed that '[n]obody could have written "Froggy's Little Brother" who did not possess the heart of an angel of the Almighty'.[69] The patriarchal Victorian predilection for valorising women as angels is clearly in evidence, but Stretton was also a 'socially aware and politically engaged' woman, an energetic and vigorous campaigner whose 'writings reflect, expose and challenge a range of dominant nineteenth-century anxieties, prejudices and inequalities'.[70] Brenda does not appear to have campaigned beyond her writing, but she, like Stretton, was a Victorian woman, rather than an angelic cipher. She was also a working mother whose authorship supplemented an ageing parent's income and who published her last novel at the age of 87 years.

The legacy of the past

Although *Jessica's First Prayer* and *Froggy's Little Brother* were first published well over a hundred years ago, they remain of significance to contemporary readers and continue to attract scholarly interest, as do their authors. Representative of many other women writers of the period whose works and names have been overlooked and often forgotten, these non-canonical authors form a valuable contribution to literary and social history. As popular writers, Stretton and Brenda were widely read and their images of childhood imbibed by those who encountered their work; their texts are historical relics of a significant social problem that confronted

---

[68] Cutt, *Ministering Angels*, p.116.

[69] Arthur Gore, Sixth Earl of Arran. Letter 'To Castle Smith', 3 January 1934. Castle Smith family memorabilia.

[70] Lomax, 'Writing Other Lives', in *A Victorian Quartet*, p.4.

Victorian society and that was prominent in non-fictional discourse for much of the second half of the nineteenth century.

Ironically, although popular opinion appeared to idealise female authors who engaged with child poverty, it was perhaps Stretton's and Brenda's characterisation as laudable images of womanhood that helped to ensure the survival of *Jessica's First Prayer* and *Froggy's Little Brother*. Historically, women writers have been marginalised, as have writers for children, and so nineteenth-century women writing for children are likely to have suffered manifold disadvantages. However, Stretton and Brenda, writing within a genre deemed appropriate for women and on a subject that was perceived as worthy, were simultaneously empowered to contribute to the debates on child welfare reform and to voice their messages to new generations. Children's literature remains a powerful tool in the acculturation of the child and *Jessica's First Prayer* and *Froggy's Little Brother* not only informed the child reader, and perhaps his or her parents, but also issued an invitation to action to those who might, in future years, engender social change.

The numerous changes in welfare provision and education that began in the nineteenth century and continued into the twentieth century sought to ensure that the appalling poverty depicted by social commentators and authors like Stretton and Brenda were forever eradicated. Slum clearance programmes erased the tenements occupied by Froggy's non-fictional counterparts, while charitable organisations and, later, social welfare reforms attempted to provide adequate homes and viable futures for disadvantaged children. Yet in contemporary Britain, seemingly far distant from the nineteenth-century world of Jessica and Froggy, child poverty is once again in the public arena. A 2012 website page by 'End Child Poverty', a campaign group comprising over 150 civic organisations, states that 'four million children – one in three – are currently living in poverty in the UK, one of the highest rates in the industrial world' and that '[p]overty can have a profound impact on the child, their family, and the rest of society'.[71] A Save the Children organisation

---

[71] End Child Poverty, 'Jobs, Growth and Poverty Reduction: An End Child Poverty Briefing for Budget', (2012) www.endchildpoverty.org.uk [accessed 7 April 2012].

report on 'Bringing Families and Schools Together' asserts that 'young children face a number of risk factors or disadvantaging conditions, including poverty, parenting behaviour, home environment and nutrition that can have profound effects on physical and mental well-being, cognitive function, educational attainment and later life outcomes'.[72] A social worker of the second half of the nineteenth century, had there been such an individual, might well have made similar observations about Jessica and Froggy.

While we remain late Victorians, as it were, the inheritors of the numerous ideologies and social and industrial transformations wrought by our nineteenth-century ancestors, social deprivation is seemingly also a part of that legacy. Today, popular children's writers such as Jacqueline Wilson are still engaging with the issue of child neglect and poor parenting, although without the strength of public reaction engendered by Stretton's and Brenda's texts.[73] *New Internationalist Magazine* writer David Hewitt points out that the visible effects of child poverty have changed since the Victorian period: '[w]hile some children live in obvious squalor, others may look like they are fine, even though their parents are struggling to buy food or clothing'. But as he also observes, the key social issues addressed by Dickens are the 'same issues still dominat[ing] the news agenda in modern day Britain.[74]

---

[72] Save the Children, 'Severe Child Poverty: Nationally and Locally', (2011) www.savethechildren.org.uk/assets/images/Severe_Child_Poverty_Nationally_And_Locally_February2011.pdf [accessed 4 April 2012].

[73] Award-winning children's author Wilson has addressed a range of social issues, from divorce to adoption. Her novel *The Story of Tracey Beaker* (1991) is possibly the best-known of her publications and focuses on children in care homes. Other titles include *The Illustrated Mum* (1999) featuring a depressive single mother and *Dustbin Baby* (2001), the tale of a girl abandoned as a baby.

[74] David Hewitt, 'Rich London, Poor London – A Tale of Two Cities', *New Internationalist Magazine*, (February 2012) www.newint.org/features/web-exclusive/2012/02/07/london-inequality-what-would-charles-dickens-think [accessed 2 April 2012].

Like the works of Dickens and the writings of numerous Victorian social commentators, Stretton's *Jessica's First* Prayer and Brenda's *Froggy's Little Brother* are enduring indicators of the social changes that have occurred since the nineteenth century. They are also, however, historical texts that clearly have relevance for a reader of the twenty-first century.

Note on the Texts

The texts of *Jessica's First Prayer* by Hesba Stretton (Sarah Smith, 1832–1911) and *Froggy's Little Brother* by Brenda (Georgina Castle Smith, 1845–1933) are those of the first editions to be published in volume form.

Stretton's story was initially serialised in four parts in the Religious Tract Society's *The Sunday at Home, A Family Magazine for Sabbath Reading* (7 July 1866–28 July 1866) and was credited to 'the author of "Fern's Hollow"'. The first volume edition, published by the Religious Tract Society in 1867, is an almost square octavo, with a plain spine and gilt bordered title and is again credited to 'the author of "Fern's Hollow"'. There are six full page and three vignette illustrations by A.W. Bayes. Jeanette White notes that an Edwardian edition featured four colour plates by W. S. Stacey and the volume in print at the time of Stretton's death included twenty illustrations by G. Browne.[1] The novel was also included in the Penny Stories series, as was its sequel, *Jessica's Mother* (first published 1867). The transition of *Jessica's First Prayer* from periodical to volume is marked by a number of significant textual alterations which are discussed in the footnotes to the text. For this edition, the punctuation of Stretton's first volume edition has been retained. The introductory letters of each chapter were illuminated in the first volume edition, as they were in Brenda's *Froggy's Little Brother*.

Froggy's Little Brother was published as a volume by John F. Shaw and Co. with a gilt front and spine title and an image of the Punch and Judy show, Froggy's mother with Benny in her arms, and Froggy, cap held out for money, on the cover. The title page accreditation is 'by Brenda, Author of "Nothing to Nobody." With Illustrations by Cas.'. 'Cas.' was Brenda's husband Castle Smith and there are eight full-page illustrations. Later editions have

---

[1] Jeanette White, 'Further Notes on Children's Best Sellers', in *Children's Books History Society Newsletter*, 29 (1984), pp. 3–4 (p.4).

additional illustrations by M. Irwin for chapter title pages and a colour frontispiece of Froggy at Buckingham Palace (illustrator unknown) appears in early twentieth-century editions.

Although *Froggy's Little Brother* is generally noted as being published in 1875, it was advertised (as duodecimo) in *The Athenaeum* of 5 December 1874.[2] Corroboration comes from an inscription, in a copy of the first edition, to 'Castle Smith Esq With Brenda's Kind Regards' which is dated 'Dec. 21 1874.' A second inscription, 'Castle Smith with Brenda's love October 75', is written in ink below. It may be that Brenda's was an advance copy, but the date of her first inscription and the fact that the book was advertised pre-Christmas suggest that it may have been published late in 1874, although no records for John F. Shaw and Co. remain and so the publication date cannot be verified. Consequently, the generally advertised publication date of 1875 will be used in this volume. It is the first edition (and actually the copy bearing Brenda's inscriptions) that has been used as the copy-text for this new edition.

Comparison of this first edition with a later print (c.1886) and with the Gollancz Revivials edition, edited by Gillian Avery (1968), reveals several changes to the original text and these are itemised in the footnotes for *Froggy's Little Brother*. As with Stretton's text, first-edition punctuation has been retained throughout and full-page illustrations as per the first editions of both texts are included in this edition. Page references for the primary texts in the Introduction and footnotes relate to the texts within this edition.

---

[2] Anon, 'List of New Books', *The Athenaeum*, 2458 (December), p.750.

Further Reading

Bratton, Jacqueline. *The Impact of Victorian Children's Fiction.* (London: Croom Helm, 1981).

Cunningham, Hugh. *The Children of the Poor: Representations of Childhood Since the Seventeeth Century.* (Oxford: Blackwell, 1991).

Cutt, Nancy. *Ministering Angels: A Study of Nineteenth-Century Evangelical Writing for Children.* (Wormley: Five Owls Press, 1979).

Davin, Anna. *Growing Up Poor: Home, School and Street in London 1870–1914.* (London: Rivers Oram Press, 1996).

Flegel, Monica. *Conceptualising Cruelty to Children in Nineteenth-Century England: Literature, Representation and the NSPCC.* (Farnham and Burlington: Ashgate, 2009).

Hillel, Margot. '"She Faded and Drooped as a Flower": Constructing the Child in the Child-Rescue Literature of Late Victorian England' in *The Child in British Literature: Literary Constructions of Childhood, Medieval to Contemporary.* (Basingstoke: Palgrave Macmillan, 2012), pp.146–61.

Hollingshead, John. *Ragged London in 1861.* Introduction and Notes Anthony S. Wohl. (London: Dent, 1986).

Lomax, Elaine. *The Writings of Hesba Stretton: Reclaiming the Outcast* (Farnham and Burlington: Ashgate, 2009).

Rickard, Suzanne. '"Living By the Pen": Hesba Stretton's Moral Earnings' in *Women's History Review*, 5,2 (1996), pp.219–38.

Thiel, Elizabeth. *The Fantasy of Family: Nineteenth-Century Children's Literature and The Myth of the Domestic Ideal.* (London: Routledge, 2008).

JESSICA'S FIRST PRAYER

Figure 1   Frontispiece
Jessica's First Prayer, 1867. A.W.Bayes. London: The Religious Tract Society.

Contents

Illustrations

CHAPTER I.[1]

THE COFFEE-STALL AND ITS KEEPER.[2]

IN a screened and secluded corner of one of the many railway-bridges which span the streets of London, there could be seen, a few years ago, from five o'clock every morning until half-past eight, a tidily set out coffee-stall, consisting of a trestle and board, upon which stood two large tin cans, with a small fire of charcoal burning under each, so as to keep the coffee boiling during the early hours of the morning when the work-people were thronging into the city, on their way to their daily toil.[3] The coffee-stall was a favourite one, for besides being under shelter, which was of great consequence upon rainy mornings, it was also in so private a niche that the customers taking their out-of-door breakfast were not too much exposed to notice; and moreover, the coffee-stall keeper was a quiet man, who cared only to serve the busy workmen, without hindering them by any gossip. He was a tall, spare, elderly man, with a singularly solemn face, and a manner which was grave and secret. Nobody knew either his name or dwelling-place; unless it might be the policeman who strode past the coffee-stall every half-hour, and nodded familiarly to the solemn man behind it. There were very few who cared to make any enquiries about him; but those who did could only discover that he kept the furniture of his stall at a neighbouring coffee-house, whither he wheeled his trestle and board and crockery every day, not later than half-past eight in the morning; after which he was wont to glide away with a soft footstep, and a mysterious and fugitive air, with many backward and sidelong glances, as if he dreaded observation, until he was lost among the crowds which thronged the streets. No one had ever had the persevering curiosity to track him all the way to his house, or to find out his other means of gaining a livelihood; but in general his stall was surrounded by customers, whom he served with silent seriousness, and who did not grudge to pay him his charge for the refreshing coffee he supplied to them.

For several years the crowd of work-people had paused by the coffee-stall under the railway-arch, when one morning, in a partial lull of his business, the owner became suddenly aware of a pair of very bright dark eyes being fastened upon him and the slices of bread and butter on his board, with a gaze as hungry as that of a mouse which has been driven by famine into a trap.[4] A thin and meagre face belonged to the eyes, which was half hidden by a mass of matted hair hanging over the forehead, and down the neck; the only covering which the head or neck had, for a tattered frock, scarcely fastened together with broken strings, was slipping down over the shivering shoulders of the little girl. Stooping down to a basket behind his stall, he caught sight of two bare little feet curling up from the damp pavement, as the child lifted up first one and then the other, and laid them one over another to gain a momentary feeling of warmth. Whoever the wretched child was, she did not speak; only at every steaming cupful which he poured out of his can, her dark eyes gleamed hungrily, and he could hear her smack her thin lips, as if in fancy she was tasting the warm and fragrant coffee.

"Oh, come now!" he said at last, when only one boy was left taking his breakfast leisurely, and he leaned over his stall to speak in a low and quiet tone, "why don't you go away, little girl? Come, come; you're staying too long, you know."

"I'm just going, sir," she answered, shrugging her small shoulders to draw her frock up higher about her neck; "only it's raining cats and dogs outside; and mother's been away all night, and she took the key with her; and it's so nice to smell the coffee; and the police has left off worriting me while I've been here. He thinks I'm a customer taking my breakfast." And the child laughed a shrill little laugh of mockery at herself and the policeman.

"You've had no breakfast, I suppose," said the coffee-stall keeper, in the same low and confidential voice, and leaning over his stall till his face nearly touched the thin, sharp features of the child.

"No," she replied, coolly, "and I shall want my dinner dreadful bad afore I get it, I know. You don't often feel dreadful hungry, do you, sir? I'm not griped yet, you know; but afore I taste my dinner it'll be pretty bad, I tell you. Ah! very bad indeed!"[5]

She turned away with a knowing nod, as much as to say she had one experience in life to which he was quite a stranger; but before she had gone half a dozen steps, she heard the quiet voice calling to her in rather louder tones, and in an instant she was back at the stall.

"Slip in here," said the owner, in a cautious whisper; "here's a little coffee left and a few crusts. There, you must never come again, you know. I never give to beggars; and if you'd begged, I'd have called the police. There; put your poor feet towards the fire. Now, aren't you comfortable?"

The child looked up with a face of intense satisfaction. She was seated upon an empty basket, with her feet near the pan of charcoal, and a cup of steaming coffee on her lap; but her mouth was too full for her to reply, except by a very deep nod, which expressed unbounded delight. The man was busy for a while packing up his crockery; but every now and then he stopped to look down upon her, and to shake his head gravely.

"What's your name?" he asked, at length; "but there, never mind! I don't care what it is. What's your name to do with me, I wonder?"

"It's Jessica", said the girl: "but mother and everybody calls me Jess.[6] You'd be tired of being called Jess, if you was me. It's Jess here, and Jess there; and everybody wanting me to go errands. And they think nothing of giving me smacks, and kicks, and pinches. Look here!"

Whether her arms were black and blue from the cold, or from ill-usage, he could not tell; but he shook his head again seriously, and the child felt encouraged to go on.

"I wish I could stay here for ever and ever, just as I am!" she cried. "But you're going away, I know; and I'm never to come again, or you'll set the police on me!"

"Yes," said the coffee-stall keeper, very softly, and looking round to see if there were any other ragged children within sight; "if you'll promise not to come again for a whole week, and not to tell anybody else, you may come once more. I'll give you one other treat. But you must be off now."[7]

"I'm off, sir," she said, sharply; "but if you've a errand I could go on, I'd do it all right, I would. Let me carry some of your things."

"No, no," cried the man; "you run away, like a good girl; and mind! I'm not to see you again for a whole week."

"All right!" answered Jess, setting off down the rainy street at a quick run, as if to show her willing agreement to the bargain; while the coffee-stall keeper, with many a cautious glance around him, removed his stock-in-trade to the coffee-house near at hand, and was seen no more for the rest of the day in the neighbourhood of the railway-bridge.[8]

* * *

CHAPTER II.
JESSICA'S TEMPTATION.

JESSICA kept her part of the bargain faithfully; and though the solemn and silent man under the dark shadow of the bridge looked out for her every morning as he served his customers, he caught no glimpse of her wan face and thin little frame. But when the appointed time was finished, she presented herself at the stall, with her hungry eyes fastened again upon the piles of buns and bread and butter, which were fast disappearing before the demands of the buyers. The business was at its height, and the famished child stood quietly on one side watching for the throng to melt away. But as soon as the nearest church clock had chimed eight, she drew a little nearer to the stall, and at a signal from its owner she slipped between the trestles of his stand, and took up her former position on the empty basket. To his eyes she seemed even a little thinner, and certainly more ragged, than before; and he laid a whole bun, a stale one which was left from yesterday's stock, upon her lap, as she lifted the cup of coffee to her lips with both her benumbed hands.[9]

"What's your name?" she asked, looking up to him with her keen eyes.

"Why?" he answered, hesitatingly, as if he was reluctant to tell so much of himself; "my christened name is Daniel."

"And where do you live, Mr. Dan'el?" she enquired.

"Oh, come now!" he exclaimed, "if you're going to be impudent, you'd better march off. What business is it of yours where I live? I don't want to know where you live, I can tell you."

"I didn't mean no offence," said Jess, humbly; "only I thought I'd like to know where a good man like you lived. You're a very good man, aren't you, Mr. Dan'el?"

"I don't know," he answered, uneasily; "I'm afraid I'm not."

"Oh, but you are, you know," continued Jess. "You make good coffee; prime![10] And buns too! And I've been watching you hundreds of times afore you saw me, and the police leaves you alone, and never tells you to move on. Oh, yes! you must be a very good man."

Daniel sighed, and fidgeted about his crockery with a grave and occupied air, as if he were pondering over the child's notion of goodness. He made good coffee, and the police left him alone! It was quite true; yet still as he counted up the store of pence which had accumulated in his strong canvas bag, he sighed again still more heavily. He purposely let one of his pennies fall upon the muddy pavement, and went on counting the rest busily, while he furtively watched the little girl sitting at his feet. Without a shade of change upon her small face, she covered the penny with her foot, and drew it in carefully towards her, while she continued to chatter fluently to him. For a moment a feeling of pain shot a pang through Daniel's heart; and then he congratulated himself on having entrapped the young thief. It was time to be leaving now; but before he went he would make her move her bare foot, and disclose the penny concealed beneath it, and then he would warn her never to venture near his stall again. This was her gratitude, he thought; he had given her two breakfasts and more kindness than he had shown to any fellow-creature for many a long year; and, at the first chance, the young jade turned upon him, and robbed him![11] He was brooding over it painfully in his mind, when Jessica's uplifted face changed suddenly, and a dark flush crept over her pale cheeks, and the tears started to her eyes. She stooped down, and picking up the coin from amongst the mud, she rubbed it bright and clean upon her rags, and laid it upon the stall close to his hand, but without speaking a word. Daniel looked down upon her solemnly and searchingly.

"What's this?" he asked.

Figure 2   Jessica at the coffee-stall
Jessica's First Prayer, 1867. A.W.Bayes. London: The Religious Tract Society.

"Please, Mr. Daniel," she answered, "it dropped, and you didn't hear it."

"Jess," he said, sternly, "tell me all about it."

"Oh, please," she sobbed, "I never had a penny of my very own but once; and it rolled close to my foot; and you didn't see it; and I hid it up sharp; and then I thought how kind you'd been, and how good the coffee and buns are, and how you let me warm myself at your fire; and please, I couldn't keep the penny any longer. You'll never let me come again, I guess."

Daniel turned away for a minute, busying himself with putting his cups and saucers into the basket, while Jessica stood by trembling, with the large tears rolling slowly down her cheeks. The snug, dark corner, with its warm fire of charcoal, and its fragrant smell of coffee, had been a paradise to her for these two brief spans of time; but she had been guilty of the sin which would drive her from it.[12] All beyond the railway arch the streets stretched away, cold and dreary, with no friendly faces to meet hers, and no warm cups of coffee to refresh her; yet she was only lingering sorrowfully to hear the words spoken which should forbid her to return to this pleasant spot. Mr. Daniel turned round at last, and met her tearful gaze, with a look of strange emotion upon his own solemn face.

"Jess," he said, "I could never have done it myself.[13] But you may come here every Wednesday morning, as this is a Wednesday, and there'll always be a cup of coffee for you."

She thought he meant that he could not have hidden the penny under his foot, and she went away a little saddened and subdued, notwithstanding her great delight in the expectation of such a treat every week; while Daniel, pondering over the struggle that must have passed through her childish mind, went on his way, from time to time shaking his head, and muttering to himself, "I couldn't have done it myself: I never could have done it myself."

* * *

CHAPTER III.[14]
AN OLD FRIEND IN A NEW DRESS.

WEEK after week, through the three last months of the year, Jessica appeared every Wednesday at the coffee-stall, and after waiting patiently till the close of the breakfasting business, received her pittance from the charity of her new friend. After a while Daniel allowed her to carry some of his load to the coffee-house, but he never suffered her to follow him farther, and he was always particular to watch her out of sight before he turned off through the intricate mazes of the streets in the direction of his own home. Neither did he encourage her to ask him any more questions; and often but very few words passed between them during Jessica's breakfast time.

As to Jessica's home, she made no secret of it, and Daniel might have followed her any time he pleased. It was a single room, which had once been a hayloft over the stable of an old inn, now in use for two or three donkeys, the property of costermongers dwelling in the court about it. The mode of entrance was by a wooden ladder, whose rungs were crazy and broken, and which led up through a trap-door in the floor of the loft. The interior of the home was as desolate and comfortless as that of the stable below, with only a litter of straw for the bedding, and a few bricks and boards for the furniture. Everything that could be pawned had disappeared long ago, and Jessica's mother often lamented that she could not thus dispose of her child. Yet Jessica was hardly a burden to her. It was a long time since she had taken any care to provide her with food or clothing, and the girl had to earn or beg for herself the meat which kept a scanty life within her. Jess was the drudge and errand-girl of the court; and what with being cuffed and beaten by her mother, and over-worked and ill-used by her numerous employers, her life was a hard one. But now there was always Wednesday morning to count upon and look forward to; and by and by a second scene of amazed delight opened upon her.

Jessica had wandered far away from home in the early darkness of a winter's evening, after a violent outbreak of her drunken mother, and she was still sobbing now and then with long-drawn sobs of pain and weariness, when she saw, a little way before her, the tall, well-known figure of her friend Mr. Daniel. He was dressed in a suit of black, with a white neckcloth, and he was pacing with brisk yet measured steps along the lighted streets. Jessica felt afraid of speaking to him, but she followed at a little distance, until presently he stopped before the iron gates of a large building, and, unlocking them, passed on to the arched doorway, and with a heavy key opened the folding-doors and entered in. The child stole after him, but paused for a few minutes, trembling upon the threshold, until the gleam of a light lit up within tempted her to venture a few steps forward, and to push a little way open an inner door, covered with crimson baize, only so far as to enable her to peep through at the inside. Then, growing bolder by degrees, she crept through herself, drawing the door to noiselessly behind her. The place was in partial gloom, but Daniel was kindling every gaslight, and each minute lit it up in more striking grandeur. She stood in a carpeted aisle, with high oaken pews on each side, almost as black as ebony. A gallery of the same dark old oak ran round the walls,[15] resting upon massive pillars, behind one of which she was partly concealed, gazing with eager eyes at Daniel, as he mounted the pulpit steps and kindled the lights there, disclosing to her curious delight the glittering pipes of an organ behind it. Before long the slow and soft-footed chapel-keeper disappeared for a minute or two into a vestry; and Jessica, availing herself of his short absence, stole silently up under the shelter of the dark pews until she reached the steps of the organ loft, with its golden show. But at this moment Mr. Daniel appeared again, arrayed in a long gown of black serge; and as she stood spell-bound gazing at the strange appearance of her patron, his eyes fell upon her, and he also was struck speechless for a minute, with an air of amazement and dismay upon his grave face.

"Come, now," he exclaimed, harshly, as soon as he could recover his presence of mind, "you must take yourself out of this. This isn't any place for such as you. It's for ladies and gentlemen; so you must run away sharp before anybody comes. How ever did you find your way here?"

He had come very close to her, and bent down to whisper in her ear, looking nervously round to the entrance all the time. Jessica's eager tongue was loosened.

"Mother beat me," she said, "and turned me into the streets, and I see you there, so I followed you up. I'll run away this minute, Mr. Daniel; but it's a nice place.[16] What do the ladies and gentlemen do when they come here? Tell me, and I'll be off sharp."

"They come here to pray," whispered Daniel.

"What is pray?" asked Jessica.

"Bless the child!" cried Daniel, in perplexity. "Why, they kneel down in those pews;[17] most of them sit, though; and the minister up in the pulpit tells God what they want."

Jessica gazed into his face with such an air of bewilderment that a faint smile crept over the sedate features of the pew-opener.[18]

"What is a minister and God?" she said; "and do ladies and gentlemen want anything? I thought they'd everything they wanted, Mr. Daniel."

"Oh!" cried Daniel, "you must be off, you know. They'll be coming in a minute, and they'd be shocked to see a ragged little heathen like you. This is the pulpit, where the minister stands and preaches to 'em; and there are the pews, where they sit to listen to him, or to go to sleep, may be; and that's the organ to play music to their singing. There, I've told you everything, and you must never come again, never."

"Mr. Daniel," said Jessica, "I don't know nothing about it. Isn't there a dark little corner somewhere that I could hide in?"

"No, no," interrupted Daniel, impatiently; "we couldn't do with such a little heathen, with no shoes or bonnet on. Come now, it's only a quarter to the time, and somebody will be here in a minute. Run away, do!"

Jessica retraced her steps slowly to the crimson door, casting many a longing look backwards; but Mr. Daniel stood at the end of the aisle, frowning upon her whenever she glanced behind. She gained the lobby at last, but already some one was approaching the chapel door, and beneath the lamp at the gate stood one of her natural enemies, a policeman.[19] Her heart beat fast, but she was quickwitted, and in another instant she spied a place of concealment behind one of the doors, into which she crept for safety until the path should be clear, and the policeman passed on upon his beat.

The congregation began to arrive quickly. She heard the rustling of silk dresses, and she could see the gentlemen and ladies

Figure 3   Jessica and Daniel
Jessica's First Prayer, 1867. A.W.Bayes. London: The Religious Tract Society.

pass by the niche between the door and the post. Once she ventured to stretch out a thin little finger and touch a velvet mantle as the wearer of it swept by, but no one caught her in the act, or suspected her presence behind the door. Mr. Daniel, she could see, was very busy ushering the people to their seats; but there was a startled look lingering upon his face, and every now and then he peered anxiously into the outer gloom and darkness, and even once called to the policeman to ask if he had seen a ragged child hanging about. After a while the organ began to sound, and Jessica, crouching down in her hiding-place, listened entranced to the sweet music. She could not tell what made her cry, but the tears came so rapidly that it was of no use to rub the corners of her eyes with her hard knuckles; so she lay down upon the ground, and buried her face in her hands, and wept without restraint. When the singing was over, she could only catch a confused sound of a voice speaking. The lobby was empty now, and the crimson doors closed. The policeman, also, had walked on. This was the moment to escape. She raised herself from the ground with a feeling of weariness and sorrow; and thinking sadly of the light, and warmth, and music that were within the closed doors, she stepped out into the cold and darkness of the streets, and loitered homewards with a heavy heart.

* * *

CHAPTER IV.
PEEPS INTO FAIRY-LAND.

It was not the last time that Jessica concealed herself behind the baize-covered door.[20] She could not overcome the urgent desire to enjoy again and again the secret and perilous pleasure; and Sunday after Sunday she watched in the dark streets for the moment when she could slip in unseen. She soon learned the exact time when Daniel would be occupied in lighting up, before the policeman would take up his station at the entrance, and again, the very minute at which it would be wise and safe to take her departure.[21] Sometimes the child laughed noiselessly to herself, until she shook with suppressed merriment, as she saw Daniel standing unconsciously in the lobby, with his solemn face and grave air, to receive the congregation, much as he faced his customers at the coffee-stall. She learned to know the minister by sight, the tall, thin, pale gentleman, who passed through a side door, with his head bent as if in deep thought, while two little girls, about her own age, followed him with sedate yet pleasant faces. Jessica took a great interest in the minister's children. The younger one was fair, and the elder was about as tall as herself, and had eyes and hair as dark; but oh, how cared for, how plainly waited on by tender hands! Sometimes, when they were gone by, she would close her eyes, and wonder what they would do in one of the high black pews inside, where there was no place for a ragged, barefooted girl like her;[22] and now and then her wonderings almost ended in a sob, which she was compelled to stifle.

It was an untold relief to Daniel that Jessica did not ply him with questions, as he feared, when she came for breakfast every Wednesday morning; but she was too shrewd and cunning for that.[23] She wished him to forget that she had ever been there, and by and by her wish was accomplished, and Daniel was no longer uneasy, while he was lighting the lamps, with the dread of seeing the child's wild face starting up before him.[24]

But the light evenings of summer-time were drawing near apace, and Jessica foresaw with dismay that her Sunday treats would soon be over. The risk of discovery increased every week, for the sun was later and later in setting, and there would be no chance of creeping in and out unseen in the broad daylight. Already it needed both watchfulness and alertness to dart in at the right moment in the grey twilight; but still she could not give it up; and if it had not been for the fear of offending Mr. Daniel, she would have resolved upon going until she was found out. They could not punish her very much for standing in the lobby of a chapel.

Jessica was found out, however, before the dusky evenings were quite gone. It happened one night that the minister's children, coming early to the chapel, saw a small tattered figure, bareheaded and barefooted, dart swiftly up the steps before them and disappear within the lobby. They paused and looked at one another, and then, hand in hand, their hearts beating quickly, and the colour coming and going on their faces, they followed this strange new member of their father's congregation. The pew-opener[25] was nowhere to be seen, but their quick eyes detected the prints of the wet little feet which had trodden the clean pavement before them, and in an instant they discovered Jessica crouching behind the door.

"Let us call Daniel Standring," said Winny, the younger child, clinging to her sister;[26] but she had spoken aloud, and Jessica overheard her, and before they could stir a step she stood before them with an earnest and imploring face.

"Oh, don't have me drove away," she cried; "I'm a very poor little girl, and it's all the pleasure I've got. I've seen you lots of times, with that tall gentleman as stoops, and I didn't think you'd have me drove away. I don't do any harm behind the door, and if Mr. Daniel finds me out, he won't give me any more coffee."

"Little girl," said the elder child, in a composed and demure voice, "we don't mean to be unkind to you; but what do you come here for, and why do you hide yourself behind the door?"

"I like to hear the music," answered Jessica, "and I want to find out what pray is, and the minister, and God. I know it's only for ladies and gentlemen, and fine children like you; but I'd like to go inside just for once, and see what you do."

"You shall come with us into our pew," cried Winny, in an eager and impulsive tone; but Jane laid her hand upon her outstretched arm, with a glance at Jessica's ragged clothes and matted hair. It was a question difficult enough to perplex them. The little outcast was plainly too dirty and neglected for them to invite her to sit side by side with them in their crimson-lined pew, and no poor people attended the chapel with whom she could have a seat. But Winny, with flushed cheeks and indignant eyes, looked reproachfully at her elder sister.

"Jane," she said, opening her Testament, and turning over the leaves hurriedly, "this was papa's text a little while ago. 'For if there come into your assembly a man with a gold ring, in goodly apparel, and there come in also a poor man in vile raiment; and ye have respect to him that weareth the gay clothing, and say unto him, Sit thou here in a good place; and say to the

Figure 4   Jessica and the Minister's daughters
Jessica's First Prayer, 1867. A.W.Bayes. London: The Religious Tract Society.

poor, Stand thou there, or sit here under my footstool; are ye not then partial in yourselves, and are become judges of evil thoughts?' If we don't take this little girl into our pew, we have the faith of our Lord Jesus Christ, the Lord of glory, with respect of persons.' "[27]

"I don't know what to do," answered Jane, sighing; "the Bible seems plain; but I'm sure papa would not like it. Let us ask the chapel-keeper."

"Oh, no, no!" cried Jessica, "don't let Mr. Daniel catch me here. I won't come again, indeed; and I'll promise not to try to find out about God and the minister, if you'll only let me go."

"But, little girl," said Jane, in a sweet but grave manner, "we ought to teach you about God, if you don't know him. Our papa is the minister, and if you'll come with us, we'll ask him what we must do."

"Will Mr. Daniel see me?" asked Jessica.

"Nobody but papa is in the vestry," answered Jane, "and he'll tell us all, you and us, what we ought to do. You'll not be afraid of him, will you?"

"No," said Jessica, cheerfully, following the minister's children as they led her along the side of the chapel towards the vestry.

"He is not such a terrible personage," said Winny, looking round encouragingly, as Jane tapped softly at the door, and they heard a voice saying "Come in."

* * *

CHAPTER V.[28]
A NEW WORLD OPENS.

THE minister was sitting in an easy chair before a comfortable fire, with a hymn-book in his hand, which he closed as the three children appeared in the open doorway. Jessica had seen his pale and thoughtful face many a time from her hiding-place, but she had never met the keen, earnest, searching gaze of his eyes, which seemed to pierce through all her wretchedness and misery, and to read at once the whole history of her desolate life. But before her eyelids could droop, or she could drop a reverential curtsey, the minister's face kindled with such a glow of pitying tenderness and compassion, as fastened her eyes upon him, and gave her new heart and courage. His children ran to him, leaving Jessica upon the mat at the door, and with eager voices and gestures told him the difficulty they were in.

"Come here, little girl," he said; and Jessica walked across the carpeted floor till she stood right before him, with folded hands, and eyes that looked frankly into his.

"What is your name, my child?" he asked.

"Jessica," she answered.

"Jessica," he repeated, with a smile; "that is a strange name."

"Mother used to play 'Jessica' at the theatre, sir," she said, "and I used to be a fairy in the pantomime, till I grew too tall and ugly.[29] If I'm pretty when I grow up, mother says I shall play too; but I've a long time to wait. Are you the minister, sir?"

"Yes," he answered, smiling again.

"What is a minister?" she enquired.

"A servant!" he replied, looking away thoughtfully into the red embers of the fire.

"Papa!" cried Jane and Winny, in tones of astonishment; but Jessica gazed steadily at the minister, who was now looking back again into her bright eyes.

"Please, sir, whose servant are you?" she asked.

"The servant of God and of man," he answered, solemnly. "Jessica, I am your servant."

The child shook her head, and laughed shrilly as she gazed round the room, and at the handsome clothing of the minister's daughters, while she drew her rags closer about her, and shivered a little, as if she felt a sting of the east wind, which was blowing keenly through the streets. The sound of her shrill, childish laugh made the minister's heart ache, and the tears burn under his eyelids.

"Who is God?" asked the child. "When mother's in a good temper, sometimes she says 'God bless me!' Do you know him, please, minister?"

Figure 5 Jessica meets the Minister

Jessica's First Prayer, 1867. A.W.Bayes. London: The Religious Tract Society.

But before there was time to answer, the door into the chapel was opened, and Daniel stood upon the threshold. At first he stared blandly forwards, but then his grave face grew ghastly pale, and he laid his hand upon the door to support himself until he could recover his speech and senses. Jessica also looked about her, scared and irresolute, as if anxious to run away or to hide herself. The minister was the first to speak.

"Jessica," he said, "there is a place close under my pulpit where you shall sit, and where I can see you all the time. Be a good girl and listen, and you will hear something about God. Standring, put this little one in front of the pews by the pulpit steps."

But before she could believe it for very gladness, Jessica found herself inside the chapel, facing the glittering organ, from which a sweet strain of music was sounding.[30] Not far from her Jane and Winny were peeping over the front of their pew, with friendly smiles and glances. It was evident that the minister's elder daughter was anxious about her behaviour, and she made energetic signs to her when to stand up and when to kneel; but Winny was content with smiling at her, whenever her head rose above the top of the pew. Jessica was happy, but not in the least abashed. The ladies and gentlemen were not at all unlike those whom she had often seen when she was a fairy at the theatre; and very soon her attention was engrossed by the minister, whose eyes often fell upon her, as she gazed eagerly, with uplifted face, upon him. She could scarcely understand a word of what he said, but she liked the tones of his voice, and the tender pity of his face as he looked down upon her. Daniel hovered about a good deal, with an air of uneasiness and displeasure, but she was unconscious of his presence. Jessica was intent upon finding out what a minister and God were.

* * *

CHAPTER VI.
THE FIRST PRAYER.

WHEN the service was ended, the minister descended the pulpit steps, just as Daniel was about to hurry Jessica away, and taking her by the hand in the face of all the congregation, he led her into the vestry, whither Jane and Winny quickly followed them. He was fatigued with the services of the day, and his pale face was paler than ever, as he placed Jessica before his chair, into which he threw himself with an air of exhaustion; but bowing his head upon his hands, he said in a low but clear tone, "Lord, these are the lambs of thy flock.[31] Help me to feed thy lambs!"

"Children," he said, with a smile upon his weary face, "it is no easy thing to know God. But this one thing we know, that he is our Father – my Father and your Father, Jessica. He loves you, and cares for you more than I do for my little girls here."

He smiled at them and they at him, with an expression which Jessica felt and understood, though it made her sad. She trembled a little, and the minister's ear caught the sound of a faint though bitter sob.

"I never had any father," she said, sorrowfully.

"God is your Father," he answered, very gently; "he knows all about you, because he is present everywhere. We cannot see him, but we have only to speak, and he hears us, and we may ask him for whatever we want."

"Will he let me speak to him, as well as these fine children that are clean, and have got nice clothes?" asked Jessica, glancing anxiously at her muddy feet, and her soiled and tattered frock.[32]

"Yes," said the minister, smiling, yet sighing at the same time; "you may ask him this moment for what you want."

Jessica gazed round the room with large, wide-open eyes, as if she were seeking to see God; but then she shut her eyelids tightly, and bending her head upon her hands, as she had seen the minister do, she said, "O God! I want to know about you. And please pay Mr. Dan'el for all the warm coffee he's give me."

Jane and Winny listened with faces of unutterable amazement; but the tears stood in the minister's eyes, and he added "Amen" to Jessica's first prayer.

* * *

CHAPTER VII.
HARD QUESTIONS.

DANIEL had no opportunity for speaking to Jessica; for, after waiting until the minister left the vestry, he found that she had gone away by the side entrance. He had to wait, therefore, until Wednesday morning, and the sight of her pinched little face was welcome to him, when he saw it looking wistfully over the coffee-stall. Yet he had made up his mind to forbid her to come again, and to threaten her with the policeman if he ever caught her at the chapel, where for the future he intended to keep a sharper look-out. But before he could speak, Jess had slipped under the stall, and taken her old seat upon the up-turned basket.

"Mr. Dan'el," she said, "has God paid you for my sups of coffee yet?"

"Paid me?" he repeated, "God? No."

"Well, he will," she answered, nodding her head sagely; "don't you be afraid for your money, Mr. Dan'el; I've asked him a many times, and the minister says he's sure to do it."

"Jess," said Daniel, sternly, "have you been and told the minister about my coffee-stall?"

"No," she answered, with a beaming smile, "but I've told God lots and lots of times since Sunday, and he's sure to pay in a day or two."

"Jess," continued Daniel, more gently, "you're a sharp little girl, I see; and now mind, I'm going to trust you. You're never to say a word about me or my coffee-stall; because the folks at our chapel are very grand, and might think it low and mean of me to keep a coffee-stall. Very likely they'd say I mustn't be chapel-keeper any longer, and I should lose a deal of money."

"Why do you keep the stall then?" asked Jessica.

"Don't you see what a many pennies I get every morning?" he said, shaking his canvas bag. "I get a good deal of money that way in a year."

"What do you want such a deal of money for?" she enquired; "do you give it to God?"

Daniel did not answer, but the question went to his heart like a sword thrust. What did he want so much money for? He thought of his one bare and solitary room, where he lodged alone, a good way from the railway-bridge, with very few comforts in it, but containing a desk, strongly and securely fastened, in which was his savings' bank book and his receipts for money put out at interest, and a bag of sovereigns, for which he had been toiling and slaving both on Sundays and week-days. He could not remember giving anything away, except the dregs of the coffee and the stale buns, for which Jessica was asking God to pay him. He coughed, and cleared his throat, and rubbed his eyes; and then, with nervous and hesitating fingers, he took a penny from his bag, and slipped it into Jessica's hand.

"No, no, Mr. Dan'el," she said; "I don't want you to give me any of your pennies. I want God to pay you."

"Ay, he'll pay me," muttered Daniel; "there'll be a day of reckoning by and by."

"Does God have reckoning days?" asked Jessica. "I used to like reckoning days when I was a fairy."

"Ay, ay," he answered, "but there's few folks like God's reckoning days."

"But you'll be glad, won't you?" she said.

Daniel bade her get on with her breakfast, and then he turned over in his mind the thoughts which her questions had awakened. Conscience told him he would not be glad to meet God's reckoning day.

"Mr. Dan'el," said Jessica, when they were about to separate, and he would not take back his gift of a penny, "if you wouldn't mind, I'd like to come and buy a cup of coffee to-morrow, like a customer, you know: and I won't let out a word about the stall to the minister next Sunday, don't you be afraid."

She tied the penny carefully into a corner of her rags, and with a cheerful smile upon her thin face, she glidedfrom under the shadow of the bridge, and was soon lost to Daniel's sight.

* * *

CHAPTER VIII.
AN UNEXPECTED VISITOR.

WHEN Jessica came to the street into which the court where she lived opened, she saw an unusual degree of excitement among the inhabitants, a group of whom were gathered about a tall gentleman, whom she recognised in an instant to be the minister. She elbowed her way through the midst of them, and the minister's face brightened as she presented herself before him. He followed her up the low entry, across the squalid court, through the stable, empty of the donkeys just then, up the creaking rounds of the ladder, and into the miserable loft, where the tiles were falling in, and the broken window-panes were stuffed with rags and paper. Near to the old rusty stove, which served as a grate when there was any fire, there was a short board laid across some bricks, and upon this the minister took his seat, while Jessica sat upon the floor before him.

"Jessica," he said, sadly, "is this where you live?"

"Yes," she answered, "but we'd a nicer room than this when I was a fairy, and mother played at the theatre; we shall be better off when I'm grown up, if I'm pretty enough to play like her."

"My child," he said, "I'm come to ask your mother to let you go to school in a pleasant place down in the country. Will she let you go?"

"No," answered Jessica, "mother says she'll never let me learn to read, or go to church;[33] she says it would make me good for nothing. But please, sir, she doesn't know anything about your church, it's such a long way off, and she hasn't found me out yet. She always gets very drunk of a Sunday."

Figure 6   The Minister visits Jessica
Jessica's First Prayer, 1867. A.W.Bayes. London: The Religious Tract Society.

The child spoke simply, and as if all she said was a matter of course; but the minister shuddered, and he looked through the broken window to the little patch of gloomy sky overhead.

"What can I do?" he cried mournfully, as though speaking to himself.

"Nothing, please, sir," said Jessica, "only let me come to hear you of a Sunday, and tell me about God.[34] If you was to give me fine clothes like your little girls, mother 'ud only pawn them for gin. You can't do anything more for me."

"Where is your mother?" he asked.

"Out on a spree," said Jessica, "and she won't be home for a day or two.[35] She'd not hearken to you, sir. There's the missionary came, and she pushed him down the ladder, till he was nearly killed. They used to call mother the Vixen at the theatre, and nobody durst say a word to her."[36]

The minister was silent for some minutes, thinking painful thoughts, for his eyes seemed to darken as he looked round the miserable room, and his face wore an air of sorrow and disappointment. At last he spoke again.

"Who is Mr. Daniel, Jessica?" he enquired.

"Oh," she said cunningly, "he's only a friend of mine as gives me sups of coffee. You don't know all the folks in London, sir!"

"No," he answered, smiling, "but does he keep a coffee-stall?"

Jessica nodded her head, but did not trust herself to speak.

"How much does a cup of coffee cost?" asked the minister.

"A full cup's a penny," she answered, promptly; "but you can have half a cup; and there are halfpenny and penny buns."

"Good coffee and buns?" he said, with another smile.

"Prime," replied Jessica, smacking her lips.

"Well," continued the minister, "tell your friend to give you a full cup of coffee and a penny bun every morning, and I'll pay for them as often as he chooses to come to me for the money."

Jessica's face beamed with delight, but in an instant it clouded over as she recollected Daniel's secret, and her lips quivered as she spoke her disappointed reply.

"Please, sir," she said, "I 'm sure he couldn't come; oh! he couldn't. It's such a long way, and Mr. Daniel has plenty of customers. No, he never would come to you for the money."

"Jessica," he answered, "I will tell you what I will do. I will trust you with a shilling every Sunday, if you'll promise to give it to your friend the very first time you see him. I shall be sure to know if you cheat me." And the keen, piercing eyes of the minister looked down into Jessica's, and once more the tender and pitying smile returned to his face.

"I can do nothing else for you?" he said, in a tone of mingled sorrow and questioning.

"No, minister," answered Jessica, "only tell me about God."

"I will tell you one thing about him now," he replied. "If I took you to live in my house with my little daughters, you would have to be washed and clothed in new clothing to make you fit for it. God wanted us to go and live at home with him in heaven, but we were so sinful that we could never have been fit for it. So he sent his own Son to live amongst us, and die for us,[37] to wash us from our sins, and to give us new clothing, and to make us ready to live in God's house. When you ask God for anything, you must say 'For Jesus Christ's sake.' Jesus Christ is the Son of God."

After these words the minister carefully descended the ladder, followed by Jessica's bare and nimble feet, and she led him by the nearest way into one of the great thoroughfares of the city, where he said good-bye to her, adding, "God bless you, my child," in a tone which sank into Jessica's heart. He had put a silver sixpence into her hand to provide for her breakfast the next three mornings, and, with a feeling of being very rich, she returned to her miserable home.

The next morning Jessica presented herself proudly as a customer at Daniel's stall, and paid over the sixpence in advance. He felt a little troubled as he heard her story, lest the minister should endeavour to find him out; but he could not refuse to let the child come daily for her comfortable breakfast. If he was detected, he would promise to give up his coffee-stall rather than offend the great people of the chapel; but unless he was, it would be foolish of him to lose the money it brought in week after week.

* * *

CHAPTER IX.³⁸
JESSICA'S FIRST PRAYER ANSWERED

EVERY Sunday evening the barefooted and bareheaded child might be seen advancing confidently up to the chapel, where rich and fashionable people worshipped God; but before taking her place she arrayed herself in a little cloak and bonnet, which had once belonged to the minister's elder daughter, and which was kept with Daniel's serge gown, so that she presented a somewhat more respectable appearance in the eyes of the congregation. The minister had no listener more attentive, and he would have missed the pinched, earnest little face if it were not to be seen in the seat just under the pulpit. At the close of each service he spoke to her for a minute or two in his vestry, often saying no more than a single sentence, for the day's labour had wearied him. The shilling, which was always lying upon the chimney-piece, placed there by Jane and Winny in turns, was immediately handed over, according to promise, to Daniel as she left the chapel, and so Jessica's breakfast was provided for her week after week.

But at last there came a Sunday evening when the minister, going up into his pulpit, did miss the wistful, hungry face, and the shilling lay unclaimed upon the vestry chimney-piece. Daniel looked out for her anxiously every morning, but no Jessica glided into his secluded corner, to sit beside him with her breakfast on her lap, and with a number of strange questions to ask. He felt her absence more keenly than he could have expected. The child was nothing to him, he kept saying to himself; and yet he felt that she was something, and that he could not help being uneasy and anxious about her. Why had he never enquired where she lived? The minister knew, and for a minute Daniel thought he would go and ask him, but that might awaken suspicion. How could he account for so much anxiety, when he was supposed only to know of her absence from chapel one Sunday evening? It would be running a risk, and, after all, Jessica was nothing to him. So he went home and looked over his savings' bank book, and counted his money, and he found to his satisfaction that he had gathered together nearly four hundred pounds, and was adding more every week.

But when upon the next Sunday Jessica's seat was again empty, the anxiety of the solemn chapel-keeper overcame his prudence and his fears. The minister had retired to his vestry, and was standing with his arm resting upon the chimney-piece, and his eyes fixed upon the unclaimed shilling, which Winny had laid there before the service, when there was a tap at the door, and Daniel entered with a respectful but hesitating air.

"Well, Standring?" said the minister, questioningly.

"Sir," he said, "I'm uncomfortable about that little girl, and I know you've been once to see after her; she told me about it; and so I make bold to ask you where she lives, and I'll see what's become of her."

"Right, Standring," answered the minister; "I am troubled about the child, and so are my little girls. I thought of going myself, but my time is very much occupied just now."

"I'll go, sir," replied Daniel, promptly; and, after receiving the necessary information about Jessica's home, he put out the lights, locked the door, and turned towards his lonely lodgings.

But though it was getting late upon Sunday evening, and Jessica's home was a long way distant, Daniel found that his anxiety would not suffer him to return to his solitary room. It was of no use to reason with himself, as he stood at the corner of the street, feeling perplexed and troubled, and promising his conscience that he would go the very first thing in the morning after he shut up his coffee-stall. In the dim, dusky light, as the summer evening drew to a close, he fancied he could see Jessica's thin figure and wan face gliding on before him, and turning round from time to time to see if he were following. It was only fancy, and he laughed a little at himself; but the laugh was husky, and there was a choking sensation in his throat, so he buttoned his Sunday coat over his breast, where his silver watch and chain hung temptingly, and started off at a rapid pace for the centre of the city.

It was not quite dark when he reached the court, and stumbled up the narrow entry leading to it; but Daniel did hesitate when he opened the stable door, and looked into a blank, black space, in which he could discern nothing. He thought he had better retreat while he could do so safely; but as he still stood with his hand upon the rusty latch, he heard a faint, small voice through the nicks of the unceiled boarding above his head.

"Our Father," said the little voice,[39] "please to send somebody to me, for Jesus Christ's sake, Amen."

"I'm here, Jess," cried Daniel, with a sudden bound of his heart, such as he had not felt for years, and which almost took away his breath as he peered into the darkness, until at last he discerned dimly the ladder which led up into the loft.

Very cautiously, but with an eagerness which surprised himself, he climbed up the creaking rounds of the ladder and entered the dismal room, where the child was lying in desolate darkness. Fortunately he had put his box of matches into his pocket, and the end of a wax candle, with which he kindled the lamps,[40] and in another minute a gleam of light shone upon Jessica's white features. She was stretched upon a scanty litter of straw under the slanting roof where the tiles had not fallen off, with her poor rags for her only covering; but as her eyes looked up into Daniel's face bending over her, a bright smile of joy sparkled in them.

"Oh!" she cried, gladly, but in a feeble voice, "it's Mr. Dan'el![41] Has God told you to come here, Mr. Dan'el?"

"Yes," said Daniel, kneeling beside her, taking her wasted hand in his, and parting the matted hair upon her damp forehead.[42]

"What did he say to you, Mr. Dan'el?" said Jessica.

"He told me I was a great sinner," replied Daniel. "He told me I loved a little bit of dirty money better than a poor, friendless, helpless child, whom he had sent to me to see if I would do her a little good for his sake. He looked at me, or the minister did, through and through, and he said, 'Thou fool, this night thy soul shall be required of thee: then whose shall those things be which thou hast provided?' And I could answer him nothing, Jess. He was come to a reckoning with me, and I could not say a word to him."

"Aren't you a good man, Mr. Dan'el?" whispered Jessica.

"No, I 'm a wicked sinner," he cried, while the tears rolled down his solemn face. "I've been constant at God's house,[43] but only to get money; I've been steady and industrious, but only to get money; and now God looks at me, and he says, 'Thou fool!' Oh, Jess, Jess! You're more fit for heaven than I ever was in my life."

"Why don't you ask him to make you good for Jesus Christ's sake?" asked the child.

"I can't," he said. "I've been kneeling down Sunday after Sunday when the minister's been praying, but all the time I was thinking how rich some of the carriage people were. I've been loving money and worshipping money all along, and I've nearly let you die rather than run the risk of losing part of my earnings. I'm a very sinful man."

"But you know what the minister often says," murmured Jessica. " 'Herein is love, not that we loved God, but that he loved us, and sent his Son to be the propitiation for our sins.' "

"I've heard it so often that I don't feel it," said Daniel. "I used to like to hear the minister say it, but now it goes in at one ear and out at the other. My heart is very hard, Jessica."

By the feeble glimmer of the candle Daniel saw Jessica's wistful eyes fixed upon him with a sad and loving glance; and then she lifted up her weak hand to her face, and laid it over her closed eyelids, and her feverish lips moved slowly.

"God," she said, "please to make Mr. Dan'el's heart soft, for Jesus Christ's sake, Amen."

She did not speak again, nor Daniel, for some time.[44] He took off his Sunday coat and laid it over the tiny, shivering frame, which was shaking with cold even in the summer evening; and as he did so he remembered the words which the Lord says he will pronounce at the last day of reckoning, "Forasmuch as ye have done it unto one of the least of these my brethren, ye have done it unto me." Daniel Standring felt his heart turning with love to the Saviour, and he bowed his head upon his hands, and cried in the depths of his contrite spirit, "God be merciful to me, a sinner."

* * *

CHAPTER X.
THE SHADOW OF DEATH.

THERE was no coffee-stall opened under the railway arch the following morning, and Daniel's regular customers stood amazed as they drew near the empty corner, where they were accustomed to get their early breakfast. It would have astonished them still more if they could have seen how he was occupied in the miserable loft. He had intrusted a friendly woman out of the court to buy food, and fuel, and all night long he had watched beside Jessica,[45] who was light-headed and delirious, but in the wanderings of her thoughts and words often spoke to God,[46] and prayed for her Mr. Dan'el. The neighbour informed him that the child's mother had gone off some days before, fearing that she was ill of some infectious fever,[47] and that she, alone, had taken a little care of her from time to time. As soon as the morning came he sent for a doctor, and, after receiving permission from him, he wrapped the poor deserted Jessica in his coat, and bearing her tenderly in his arms down the ladder, he carried her to a cab, which the neighbour brought to the entrance of the court. It was to no other than his own solitary home that he had resolved to take her; and when the mistress of the lodgings stood at her door with her arms a-kimbo, to forbid the admission of the wretched and neglected child, her tongue was silenced by the gleam of a half-sovereign, which Daniel slipped into the palm of her hard hand.

By that afternoon's post the minister received the following letter: –

"REVEREND SIR,

"If you will condescend to enter under my humble roof, you will have the pleasure of seeing little Jessica, who is at the point of death, unless God in his mercy restores her. Hoping you will excuse this liberty, as I cannot leave the child, I remain with duty,

"Your respectful Servant,
"D. STANDRING.

"P.S. Jessica desires her best love and duty to Miss Jane and Winny."

The minister laid aside the book he was reading, and without any delay started off for his chapel-keeper's dwelling. There was Jessica lying restfully upon Daniel's bed, but the pinched features were deadly pale, and the sunken eyes shone with a waning light.[48] She was too feeble to turn her head when the door opened, and he paused for a minute, looking at her and at Daniel, who, seated at the head of the bed, was turning over the papers in his desk, and reckoning up once more the savings of his lifetime. But when the minister advanced into the middle of the room, Jessica's white cheeks flushed into a deep red.

"Oh, minister!" she cried, "God has given me everything I wanted except paying Mr. Dan'el for the coffee he used to give me."

"Ah! but God had paid me over and over again," said Daniel, rising to receive the minister. "He's given me my own soul in exchange for it. Let me make bold to speak to you this once, sir. You're a very learned man, and a great preacher, and many people flock to hear you till I'm hard put to it to find seats for them at times; but all the while, hearkening to you every blessed Sabbath, I was losing my soul, and you never once said to me, though you saw me scores and scores of times, 'Standring, are you a saved man?' "[49]

"Standring," said the minister, in a tone of great distress and regret, "I always took it for granted that you were a Christian."

"Ah," continued Daniel, thoughtfully, "but God wanted somebody to ask me that question, and he did not find anybody in the congregation, so he sent this poor little lass to me. Well, I don't mind telling now, even if I lose the place;[50] but for a long time, nigh upon ten years, I've kept a coffee-stall on week-days in the city, and cleared, one week with another, about ten shillings:[51] but I was afraid the chapel-wardens wouldn't approve of the coffee business,[52] as low, so I kept it a close secret, and always shut up early of a morning. It's me that sold Jessica her cup of coffee, which you paid for, sir."

"There's no harm in it, my good fellow," said the minister, kindly; "you need make no secret of it."

"Well," resumed Daniel, "the questions this poor little creature has asked me have gone quicker and deeper down to my conscience than all your sermons, if I may make so free as to say it.

She's come often and often of a morning, and looked into my face, with those dear eyes of hers, and said, 'Don't you love Jesus Christ, Mr. Dan'el?' 'Doesn't it make you very glad that God is your Father, Mr. Dan'el?' 'Are we getting nearer heaven every day, Mr. Dan'el?' And one day says she, 'Are you going to give all your money to God, Mr. Dan'el?' Ah, that question made me think indeed, and it's never been answered till this day. While I've been sitting beside the bed here, I've counted up all my savings: 397*l*. 17*s*. it is; and I've said, 'Lord, it's all thine; and I'd give every penny of it rather than lose the child, if it be thy blessed will to spare her life.'"

Daniel's voice quavered at the last words, and his face sank upon the pillow where Jessica's feeble and motionless head lay. There was a very sweet yet surprised smile upon her face, and she lifted her wasted fingers to rest upon the bowed head beside her, while she shut her eyes and shaded them with her other weak hand.

"Our Father,"[53] she said, in a faint whisper which still reached the ears of the minister and the beadle,[54] "I asked you to let me come home to heaven; but if Mr. Dan'el wants me, please to let me stay a little longer, for Jesus Christ's sake, Amen."

For some minutes after Jessica's prayer there was a deep and unbroken silence in the room, Daniel still hiding his face upon the pillow, and the minister standing beside them with bowed head and closed eyes, as if he also were praying. When he looked up again at the forsaken and desolate child, he saw that her feeble hand had fallen from her face, which looked full of rest and peace, while her breath came faintly but regularly through her parted lips. He took her little hand into his own with a pang of fear and grief; but instead of the mortal chillness of death,[55] he felt the pleasant warmth and moisture of life. He touched Daniel's shoulder, and as he lifted up his head in sudden alarm, he whispered to him, "The child is not dead, but is only asleep."

Before Jessica was fully recovered, Daniel rented a little house[56] for himself and his adopted daughter to dwell in. He made many enquiries after her mother, but she never appeared again in her old haunts, and he was well pleased that there was nobody to interfere with his charge of Jessica. When Jessica grew strong enough, many a cheerful walk had they together, in the early mornings, as they wended their way to the railway bridge, where the little girl took her place behind the stall, and soon learned to serve the daily customers; and many a happy day was spent in helping to sweep and dust the chapel, into which she had crept so secretly at first, her great delight being to attend to the pulpit and the vestry, and the pew where the minister's children sat, while Daniel and the woman he employed cleaned the rest of the building.[57] Many a Sunday also the minister in his pulpit, and his little daughters in their pew, and Daniel treading softly about the aisles, as their glance fell upon Jessica's eager, earnest, happy face, thought of the first time they saw her sitting amongst the congregation, and of Jessica's first prayer.

FROGGY'S LITTLE BROTHER

Figure 1   Frontispiece: ' "Give me Benny, Mudder," said Froggy gently.'
Froggy's Little Brother, 1875. Cas. London: John F. Shaw.

CONTENTS

ILLUSTRATIONS

CHAPTER I.
THE BETTER LAND.

In the neighbourhood of Shoreditch, a part of the East End of London inhabited mostly by very poor, hard-working people, and seldom visited by the grand West End folk, there lived some years ago a father and mother and two little boys. The father had a Punch and Judy show, which supported the family, and kept them all employed except little Benny, the baby boy. While the father was showing off Punch inside the green curtain, and making those funny nasal noises which all London children know so well, the mother used to stand by with Benny asleep in her arms, watching that no inquisitive ones should come too close, and peep into the mysteries behind the green curtain. Then Froggy, the elder boy, who was not much more than a baby either in size, but was very wise beyond his years, used to stand by the drum, keeping shrewd watch on all the windows from which people could see the performance, so that when it was ended, and the time came for collecting the money, he could tell mother exactly where to go for it. This little boy's real name was Tommy, but his father had always called him *Froggy*, because he was so often cold, and croaked sometimes when he had a cough, like those little creatures who live in the ditches, and have such very wide mouths and large goggle eyes.

It was a very hard life that these poor people led. Every morning they used to sally forth from their home in Shoreditch to go to wealthier neighbourhoods, where people could afford the luxury of Punch. No matter what the weather was, whether hail, rain, snow, or sunshine, in summer or winter, they went; and, as a rule, I believe, the worse the weather was, the richer they returned at night. On rainy, bad days, when the little children living in the squares and terraces towards the rich West End could not go out, as soon as they heard the familiar sound of the drum, and the shrill "Oy! oy!" coming round the corner, they would run off, and entreat mammas and papas and indulgent grandmammas, to let them set up Punch *just* this once, as it was so dull indoors, and they had nothing to amuse them! And this

43

generally ended in two or three little beaming faces appearing at the dining-room window, nodding "Yes!" frantically to the Punch and Judy party, who were standing out in the cold and rain waiting anxiously for the first nod as a signal to let down the green curtain, and to open the mysterious box. Then out would come Punch with his funny nose and red cheeks, and the Judy, and the beadle, and doctor, and ghost, and all the rest of the things.[1]

It was a sad sight sometimes to see the family returning home after the day's work was done; – the father in front, carrying the Punch show, now and then walking, alas! very unsteadily, from the effects of a visit to the public-house;[2] – and behind – saddest of all – the poor mother, with her thin face and consumptive cough, carrying little Benny, and cheering on Froggy at her side, who would often look up into her face and say –

"I are so tired, Mudder! I wish I was little, like Benny, to be carried!"

"Froggy, be good, and walk out brave, and he shall soon have his nice supper, and enjoy it ever so!" the mother would say soothingly; and at the sound of her voice Froggy gained fresh courage, and would never complain again till they reached the place in Shoreditch which these poor people called home.

Home did they call it? Ah well! home is home whatever it is like, isn't it? But theirs was a peculiarly wretched one; – only a very bare garret, at the top of a dark, dingy house, the upper part of which was scorched and blackened from the effects of a fire, which had occurred several years ago, on the opposite side of the way, and which had damaged more or less all the panes of glass in the neighbouring windows. These windows afforded a considerable amount of ventilation, which was felt severely by the occupants on bitter winter nights; and in consideration of this fact, the landlady, who was given to drinking, and could never make up her mind to spend the money to have fresh glass put in, had consented to let the garret to the Punch and Judy man and his family at a very reduced rate. The careful mother had pasted sheets of brown paper over some of these broken panes, and stopped up small holes in others with such rags as she could spare; – even *rags*, my little readers, are precious things in some homes! On Saturdays she always tried to come home an hour or two earlier, that she might clean up and tidy this desolate room for Sunday; for she loved God's holy Sabbath, and she liked to have all clean and bright to welcome the resting-day of the week – God's own good gift to the toilers of this world, which only He could have given them as their *birthright*, however their fellow-men may sometimes rob them of it. Do we ever think enough of its preciousness to weary workers when sometimes Sundays are called *dull* days in luxurious homes by people who are idle, or only idly busy, all the week?

One night, late in December, there was a sadder pilgrimage homewards than there had ever been before, and one which little Froggy will never forget, even when he grows up and becomes a man. It had been raining and snowing all day at the West End, and though they had been trudging about the streets and squares as usual, they had done very little business, and were returning with scarcely any more money in their pockets than they had started out with in the morning. The father, sullen and angry as he was apt to be when he had done a bad day's business, stalked doggedly on in front with the Punch and Judy show, making no room for anybody, but making everybody make room for him; and following behind in the pitiless rain, with their clothes hanging wet and limp about them, came the poor mother with Froggy and Benny. Benny was asleep as usual, with a smile on his little white face as he nestled close to his mother, evidently in happy oblivion of the dark, rainy world through which he was being carried. But not so with Froggy; he was wide awake, and fully alive to everything that was going on around him. He could not tell what it was, but he felt certain there was something terribly wrong with mother to-night. So deep was his conviction of this, that he never once thought of looking up into her face, as he generally did, to tell her he was so tired, and to ask her if they would soon be home. He felt that somehow *he* must be the comforter to-night.

"What made mother look so ghastly pale when they passed under the gas-lamps? Why did she totter and walk so crooked? What made her hold Benny so loose in her arms? Why didn't she speak to him? And why did she linger so far behind, and never hurry on to keep up with father and the Punch?" Froggy kept asking himself these questions over and over again as he walked silently beside her, keeping pace with her unequal steps, and holding a little bit of her gown. At last a terrible thought flashed across him, which filled his childish heart with infinite pain and consternation. Mother had gone into a public-house with father he remembered, when he had been left outside to look after the Punch. Was it possible, he wondered, that mother could have taken something then that was making her walk like this? The suspicion was too intolerable to keep to himself, and Froggy, looking up into her face with scared anxious eyes, called out –

"Mudder! Mudder, dear! haven't you been and gone and taken something too strong to drink, like Fader does?"

The voice of Froggy seemed to rouse the poor woman with a start.

"Oh no, Froggy!" she answered with a deep sob in her voice. "I'm only very, very ill! I don't know as how I shall get home, Froggy."

"Give me Benny, Mudder," said Froggy gently, ready to cry at the thought of having said anything unkind to Mother. "I've often carried 'im, that I have – he's not none too big for me;" and he stopped before her, and put out his arms for Benny.

The mother tried to speak, but her pale lips only trembled, and she let the tiny burden fall loosely from her own into Froggy's arms. Ah! Froggy knew then how ill she must be to give up Benny so quietly, for on no other occasion had she ever let him carry his little brother through the streets, for fear his head should get knocked in the crowd, or that Froggy would tumble down; for Froggy, after all, was only a few sizes larger than Benny!

Relieved of Benny, the mother seemed to get on somewhat better. Every now and then she would stop and lean against a lamp-post or a door-way to recover her breath, which she was drawing very quickly, as if it were a great labour to her, or she would pause for a moment with her hand on Froggy's shoulder in the middle of the street, as if she were trying to steady herself. Froggy continually encouraged her, using the same words that she had so often used to him when they were going home.

"We are in Soreditch now," he said once, as she faltered more and seemed to grow weaker.[3]"Only a very few steps more, and you shall be home, Mudder!"

Froggy did not know how very near his mother was to the end of the longest journey that ever man, woman, or child can take, and which ends to the good and true ones of this earth in that Eternal Home beyond the skies, about which little Froggy as yet did not understand much.

"Please, God, help Mudder home!" prayed poor Froggy aloud, as the rain came down in torrents, and the wind came cutting round the corner of the dark street. "I wish Fader hadn't run on so quick, and then I could a taken Punch, and he could a helped Mudder; but I can't see him nowhere!"

Fancy that poor little bit of a boy, already staggering under the light weight of Benny, thinking he could manage the Punch show as well! But Froggy's idea of the weights he could carry, and the things he could do at a pinch, were quite boundless.

After much toiling and stopping, they reached the house in Shoreditch at last. God had heard Froggy's prayer, you see, though it had been such a short one, spoken to Him from the crowded bustling street. Froggy opened the door of the dismal house, with its blackened front and broken windows, and ran up as quickly as he could to the top garret, where his father had arrived before them, and told him "to come down quick, and help Mudder upstairs, for she was fainty-like in the passage, and couldn't get upstairs nohow!" The father obeyed the call at once, and went down to his wife, whom he carried upstairs, and laid tenderly enough on the straw mattress which was her bed. He thoughtfully took off her wet shawl and gown, and her sodden boots, and wrapped her round in the one warm blanket which they possessed. She had been a good helpmate to him, – a simple-minded, loving, Christian woman; and the thought that he might lose her filled him with untold dread. She had often been "fainty-like before, but he had never seen her look like this. She was the first generally to bustle about and get the supper, and make everything comfortable (as far, at least, as it ever lay in her power to do so) when they returned to their garret at the end of the day. She would first minister to her husband's wants, like a faithful and good wife, and then tend little Froggy and Benny, and make them almost forget the rain and the snow, and the toil of the day that was over. But to-night things were wofully changed.[4]She lay quite still on the mattress, with her eyes closed, asking no questions, saying no word, and apparently unconscious of all that was going on around her. The father kindled a fire and made some tea, and told

Froggy to feed and undress Benny and put him to bed, as mother wouldn't be able to do it to-night.

Benny's bed was always a matter of preparation, for where do you think he slept? Why, on the top of the box which contained the Punch and the Judy, and the coffin, and the rest of the things! A little mattress and bolster were laid upon it, and there Benny used to sleep, and suck his fists, and dream his happy baby dreams, as peacefully as any little prince in his cradle! It was a matter of constant speculation with Froggy what would be done when Benny grew up and had long legs; – would he still go on sleeping there, with his legs dangling over the end, or would mother buy him a new bed? He often wondered how this would be.

Froggy had many times prepared Benny's food in the little pannikin, but he had never fed him and put him to bed before, because mother had always done that; but he managed it very nicely.[5] Seated on a low stool, with a grave frown on his brow, as if he were fully alive to the responsibilities of handling so tiny a scrap of humanity, first he fed his brother, next undressed him, and put on his little night-shirt, which was not much larger than a pocket-handkerchief, and then hushed him to rest (as he had seen mother do) on the top of the Punch and Judy box. He took care to tuck the clothing well in all round under the mattress, so that Benny could not possibly fall out during the night. After he had done all this, he approached his father very softly, and said.

"Fader, dear! I've put Benny to bed: what shall I do now?"

"Go to bed yourself, and be a good boy, and hold your tongue," said his father in a whisper; and Froggy without a word quietly retired to a corner, where there was another little mattress spread on the floor, and began undressing himself.

Froggy was very hungry, and would have liked some supper, but he never said so. He felt that this was no time for expressing any of his own wants with poor mother lying there so still and so pale; and father looking so grave. He must be quiet, as father told him, and go to bed, and forget his hunger if he could, in the face of the grievous trouble which Froggy felt had somehow fallen upon them. He lay down on his mattress and tried to sleep, but his eyes stayed wide open, and he grew hungrier and hungrier. It was a strange scene that the poor little boy looked out upon; – the miserable garret, with its bare damp walls, lit by a solitary tallow candle, whose flickering rays were trying hard to assert themselves in the current of air which blew from the window patched up with brown paper; the Punch and Judy show looming grimly opposite to him, in the corner where it was stabled for the night; little Benny lying asleep on the box; and, finally, the mattress on which Froggy's eyes were riveted, where his mother lay, and beside which his father sat, trying to feed her with some hot tea. He saw her take a few sips, and then, after a very long time, Froggy's eyes became drowsy, the lids dropped, and he fell asleep.

It must have been far into the night, nearly morning, when he awoke again. His father was still watching by the mattress, and he heard his mother's voice speaking.

" 'Arry, dear," she said faintly, "I don't think I shall ever go out with the Punch again!"

Froggy thought he heard some sobs, but he was not sure.

"You've bin a good wife to me, Jeanie. You've borne with me kind; and God knows I'm sorry for any unkind words I've spoke to you," said the husband after a moment; and now Froggy was sure of the sobs, and he felt inclined to sob too.

Presently his mother spoke again.

Figure 2 ' "Mudder! Mudder, dear! Are you going to a new land?" he cried with excitement.'
Froggy's Little Brother, 1875. Cas. London: John F. Shaw.

"You must cheer up, 'Arry, and take care o' the little uns. Send Froggy to night-school, and Benny," – her voice faltered here just a little, – "when he's growed up, and tell 'em of the land where I'm going."[6]

At these words Froggy threw off the clothing that covered him, and swift as a little hare darting from its form, he ran across the floor with bare feet, and stood by his mother's bedside.

"Mudder! mudder, dear! are you going to a new land?" he cried with excitement. "Tell me about it. What did I hear you say about going to a land?"

He waited for a moment with wide-opened, earnest eyes fixed upon his mother's face, then getting no answer, he turned and appealed to his father.

"Fader, dear! tell me, where is the land where Mudder's going?" he pleaded almost passionately, pulling at the poor man's hands that were covering his face.

"Is it far to go? Does it take much money? Where is it, Fader?"

"It's the Better Land, Froggy," sobbed the father, "where everybody is happy."

"Then I'll go," cried Froggy. "O Mudder! wherever *you* go, me must go – Benny and me! And if it's happier *there* than it is here, why don't we *all* go?" he asked, looking from one to the other, as if the wisdom of the proposition were unanswerable.

"Yes! all must come by and by," murmured the mother softly. "Blessed Jesus! bring them all home – 'Arry, and Froggy, and Benny!" and then, with a little sigh and the faintest sob, the mother's soul passed over to the eternal shores.

"Jeanie! Jeanie!" called the father in imploring accents; but there was no response. He uttered the exceeding bitter cry which so often goes up before God from the first agony of the bereaved soul.

"Oh, she's gone!" he sobbed aloud.

"Is Mudder in the Better Land now?" asked Froggy softly, looking up into his father's face.

"Yes, Froggy, she's there," he said, gazing blankly down upon him; "and she'll never be unhappy again, or footsore, or weary."

"Then that's good!" said Froggy. "Good-night, Fader, dear! I'm going back to my little bed again;" and he crept back and laid himself down.

For a long while after he could hear his father sobbing beside his dead mother, and little Froggy turned his face to the wall and cried too, but he seemed to take peculiar comfort to himself in the thought that mother would never be footsore or weary again.

* * *

CHAPTER II.
THE RETURN FROM EPSOM

AFTER this night came some very sorrowful days, in which every-thing seemed strange and new to Froggy. The mother was buried, and they all followed her to the grave. In times of trouble, women, as a rule, come out bravely and well; and so the women did on this occasion. When it became known in the house that the Punch and Judy man upstairs had lost his wife, offers of kindly assist-ance came from more than one quarter; and the lodger below, who had little children of her own, mounted to the garret on the morning of the funeral, and tied some crape round the father's hat, and some upon Froggy's, and prepared to follow with them herself to the cemetery, with little Benny in her arms. And when they came back, she lit a fire for them, and cooked their dinner, and did all that she could to console and to help them during the rest of the day.

The next day, after the funeral, the father rose up early, and went out with the Punch and Judy show as usual. It does not do for the bread-winner to suspend work, even though he has lost his wife; and this poor man went about the squares and terraces at the West End, beating the drum, and "Oy-oying!" up at all the windows, just as if nothing had happened, and there was no bitter grief at his heart. Froggy went with him, and took his mother's place by the side of the green curtain to keep off any little inquisitive boys who came too close. Not that Froggy could have done much, I think, if they had insisted upon having a peep, because he would have been too small to prevent them;

but he held his head high, and looked as big as he possibly could for the occasion. Little Benny was left at home. Mrs Ragbon, the landlady, in a neighbourly spirit had told the father that, if he liked to leave him behind along with her own little brats of a day, and pay for his food, while he went Punch and Judying, she wouldn't so much mind. And the bereaved father, who could not afford to be too particular in his choice of a guardian for Benny, now that his mother was gone, thanked Mrs Ragbon, and left him with her gladly, notwithstanding that it was whispered amongst the other lodgers that, when the landlady had taken too much to drink, "she thumped her own brats about awful!"

Froggy in these days often had a sore cry to himself, with a longing to see mother, and to kiss her. He did not wish mother back, but he wished he could go to mother. He never said so though, because he noticed that whenever he spoke of "Mudder," father turned away and sobbed, and it distressed Froggy beyond everything to see his father cry. He was very kind to his little brother, and if he got anything nice out with father during the day, such as a cake or an orange, he would be sure to bring half of it home to Benny at night. If he thought anybody had hurt Benny, or had not been kind to him in any matter, Froggy was very wrathful, and would plead for and protect him with all his might. It was good to see how he loved him, since he was shortly to become Benny's sole earthly protector in this great seething world, where everybody is struggling and fighting for his own, and the weak have often in worldly matters to go to the wall, unless they have some sturdy one to protect and care for them.

After mother's death, Froggy noticed a great change in father. He began to brush himself up on Sunday mornings, and to lead his little boy to the free seats of a neighbouring church, which Froggy used to think the most wonderful and beautiful place the world had ever seen.[7] And well he might; for Froggy's standard of comparison for everything was the poor garret at Shoreditch! The grand sounds of the organ and the voices singing he always associated with his ideas of the Better Land where mother had gone. He remembered she used to speak of the angels, and the golden harps, and the songs of praise in heaven, and he thought that surely this must be something like it. And in the evenings, father would take out mother's Bible sometimes, and spell out to them stories – *such* beautiful stories – of Jesus of Nazareth, and His wonderful words of gentle love and kindness, about the lilies of the field, and His care of the little sparrows, which always seemed to touch and comfort Froggy's heart more than anything else![8]

As they trudged along their weary way day by day, Froggy noticed, too, that father often stopped at the beautiful drinking-fountains, where fresh, clear water flows all day for thirsty wayfarers, and not only drank deeply of it himself, but gave Froggy many a pleasant long draught out of the common cup. Towards evening once, on a hot summer's day, father halted at one of these fountains. Father was very warm and tired, and looked just as Froggy had often seen him look when he used to say he *must* go into a public-house for a drop of something, or he'd never have the strength to carry the Punch home. A favourite resort of his on these occasions had always been the "Red Lion," the glaring signboard of which shone out in red and gold close to where he and Froggy were standing now.

"There's the Red Lion, father, dear," said Froggy, looking up wistfully into his face. The man looked up at the house, and then sighed heavily. "You are not going in to-night for your drop o' drink, are you, father?" said Froggy timidly.

"No, my boy; *this* is the best drink," he said, pointing to the fountain. "It cures the thirst, and keeps the head clear instead o' muddling it. I shall never go in there again, Froggy!"

"*Never,* father?" said Froggy wonderingly; "why not?"

"Because I've taken the pledge, Froggy; and, by God's help, I'll never taste strong drink again."

Froggy marvelled what this wonderful thing could be, – the *pledge!*[9] He had often heard his dead mother pleading with his father, even with tears in her eyes, to take it. He had never done so during her lifetime, that Froggy knew, for at their very last poor breakfast together he had heard her speak of it again. And *now*, father had taken it! He wondered whether dear mother knew: how pleased she would be if she did! Ah! yes, the pledge! what a blessed thing it is! How often Froggy's garret home was cheered now by father's loving ways and kindly care. It was frequently fragrant with the smell of hot coffee, and there were rashers of bacon occasionally on the gridiron (which made little Benny rub his hands joyously when he smelt it frizzling over the fire), which would certainly never have been there if father had not left off spending his money at the gin-shops. In these days of improvement, father sent Froggy to a night-school, which had been established in Shoreditch. It was a very large one, and there were boys of all kinds and sizes there, and some grown-up men as well. Some amongst them had been thieves, I am afraid; but everybody found a welcome at the night-school, whatever they were, and no one was turned out as long as they behaved themselves properly and tried to learn. But there was always a policeman on duty outside, ready to rush in and remove anybody who was riotous or otherwise misbehaving himself. Sometimes there were shameful scenes at this night-school. Wicked men and boys occasionally joined together, and came in for the express purpose of making a disturbance; they would whistle and laugh, and openly defy the clergyman and the gentlemen who were helping him, and it was with great difficulty that order was restored. But these scenes were happily not frequent. Froggy liked going to the night-school very much, and he learnt to read and to write. He went regularly twice a week till he was about eleven years old and Benny was six; then something occurred that I am going to tell you about, which prevented Froggy from going any more.

It was one evening in May, in the height of what the fashionable West End people call the London season. Froggy and his father were returning from Epsom after the great race of the Derby had been run with their Punch and Judy show, which had amused many a group of holiday folk on the breezy Downs during the day. Though Froggy was tired, and longing to be at home in the garret at Shoreditch with Benny, he was very happy, because his father had done a good day's business, and had given him sevenpence for himself. After having had a good, long lift with a friendly drayman, who was returning with emptied beer-barrels from the race-course, they had taken to their feet again, and were toiling along a crowded thoroughfare, amidst a mighty stream of pedestrians, cabs, carts, and omnibuses, when suddenly a shout was heard, and a four-in-hand drag, crowded with men in light coats and hats, with blue veils twisted round them, who were evidently more merry than wise, came rattling sharply round the corner.[10] Everything, pedestrians, cabs, carts, and omnibuses, all pulled up, and got out of the way, except one poor man and his little boy! This was Froggy and his father. Froggy remembered hearing a woman scream loudly, then saw the Punch and Judy show knocked down, then felt himself knocked down violently too – had a dim recollection of a policeman hovering over him – lastly, a dream-like feeling of being floated along somehow and somewhere, he did not know whither, with all London surging and murmuring around him – and then nothing more till he woke up, and found himself – where? Not in the crowded road-way returning home with father and the Punch and Judy show from Epsom, but lying in a bed in a strange, clean place, with a screen round him, and a gentle-looking woman in a white cap standing by.

"Where am I?" asked Froggy, opening his eyes wide and staring.

"You are in a hospital, my boy. You've been hurt, but you are better now," said the gentle-faced woman kindly.

"Who brought me here?" asked Froggy.

"The police," said the nurse.

"When did I come?"

"Yesterday evening," she answered.

"Who are you, please?"

"I am the hospital nurse taking care of you."

"Thank you!" said Froggy, and then he did not speak again for a few moments. Suddenly he started up in bed as a tide of recollection swept over his brain, and he asked anxiously –

"Please, ma'am, where is father?"

"He was brought to the hospital yesterday at the same time as you were, my boy," said the nurse, taking Froggy's hand in hers. "He was in terrible pain, but I think he is quite happy now."

"Then he's not much hurt – he's gone home to Benny?" said Froggy eagerly.

"Who is Benny?" she asked.

"My little brother at Shoreditch," said Froggy.

The nurse came closer to him and said, very kindly and gently, "No, that isn't the home where father's gone to. There is a beautiful home in the skies, my boy, where Jesus lives. Have you ever heard of it?"

"Yes," said Froggy; "it's called the Better Land, where mother went when she left Benny and me and father, a long while ago."

"Yes," said the nurse softly, "that is it; and that is where the good angels carried poor father yesterday when he was in that terrible pain."

"Won't he come back no more?" asked Froggy, looking at her with his pitiful eyes.

"No; but you will go to him," said the nurse comfortingly. "This is a sad world, and Jesus thought it was time to take father out of it, and make him happy."

"Then that is good!" murmured Froggy softly, not able to realise at first that he would never see his father again in this world.

"Ah! my boy," said the nurse earnestly, "*always* say that. Whatever Jesus sends you, try to say, 'That is good;' whatever He takes away from you, try to say, 'That is good;' and then, as long as you have breath in your body, Jesus will *never* leave you."

"Not never till I die?" said Froggy.

"Never! never!" said the nurse with the warmth of one who has tried and proved for herself the abiding love of Jesus.

"I must get up now, and go to Benny," said Froggy, with a great look of care coming into his face, that was painful to see in a child. "P'r'aps he's bin alone ever since yesterday, and maybe he's not got nothink to eat."

"You must wait till the doctor has been round first," said the nurse; "he won't be long now. Ah! here he comes;" and as she spoke a small, grave-looking gentleman approached the bedside, and began asking Froggy questions about himself.

"I feels quite well, sir," said Froggy, when he had finished answering them; "and I wants to go home partiklar."

"Well, I think you may, my little man," said the Doctor; "for you seem all right this morning."

"Please, I should like to see father once afore I goes," said Froggy with big tears in his eyes, looking up pleadingly at the nurse and doctor, who exchanged glances at the question, and shook their heads. "I know he's in the Better Land, and never can't speak to me no more; but I'm thinking as how I'd just like to see his face once again, and touch his hand, as I did mother's when she was gone;" and now the little heart seemed wellnigh bursting with the first keen pang of the orphan's loneliness, and he sobbed aloud, wailing bitterly for some minutes.

The nurse covered her eyes for a moment, for Froggy had made the tears start to them, and the doctor said very kindly but firmly –

"I cannot let you see your father, my little fellow. I am sorry to refuse you, but I have a very good reason for doing so indeed;" and poor Froggy did not press his wish further, for there was something in the doctor's tone and manner which impressed him with great confidence, and made him undoubtful of the wisdom of his refusal, though he could not guess the reason for it.

The fact was, the poor Punch and Judy man had been knocked down in the road, and the wheels of the four-in-hand drag had passed over his body, and disfigured him frightfully, so that it was no sight for a little boy like Froggy to gaze upon. It would probably have unnerved him, and greatly shocked him, which the doctor knew well enough, and this was why he refused Froggy.

"Please, sir," said Froggy after a minute, "where's the Punch and Judy what belonged to we? cos I'd like to take it. I'd put a chair inside it till I growed, and show it off that way for Benny and me."

"I hear it was smashed to pieces in the accident, my boy," said the doctor.

Poor Froggy! his heart sank at this. Without the friendly old Punch and Judy, which had kept the wolf from the door and fire in the grate all these years, what was to be done? How was he to get food for Benny? This was the question that had begun to trouble him from the very first moment he knew his father was dead. How was he to get food for Benny? Poor brother Benny! whose small, white face, crumpled up into a little comical smile, was so perpetually before him, and of which Froggy could hardly think without crying when he imagined Benny hungry, or hurt, or unhappy!

As he trudged along home after leaving the hospital, with the money which had been found in poor father's pockets, and which he calculated was just enough to pay Mrs Ragbon the rent which was owing to her, Froggy pondered much and anxiously over that question, which is daily exercising the brains of thousands in our great overgrown city of London, how to get bread and work to live? He must take to something which did not require much outlay in the beginning, for Froggy had only one and sevenpence in the world to call his own – a shilling the doctor had presented him with before leaving the hospital, and that sevenpence poor father had given him yesterday on Epsom Downs. When he met a costermonger, Froggy thought he would like to be one, to sell vegetables and fruit; but then there was the barrow to buy, and the stock, and he could not afford that. Then he thought he would like to be a shoeblack, but then he did not know what steps to take to get into the Brigade, and he had no friends to help him.[11]

"No friends!" some of my readers will exclaim; "why, where were his teachers at the night-school?" Alas! Froggy's night-school was no more. A few weeks ago, a great railway company, wanting more land to build warehouses upon, had begun clearing away whole streets of houses in the Shoreditch neighbourhood, and, amongst the rest, the night-school had been pulled down, and was not yet re-opened in another place. Froggy, who did not know where any of the teachers lived, but had some vague idea of their being always at the night-school, because he always saw them there when *he* was there, never thought of seeking them out elsewhere. If he had known the address of one of these teachers, and had applied for it, he would soon have got kindly help and advice in his difficulties. Froggy's ideas had to come down much lower. How would it do to sell cigar-lights or *Echoes*, or to buy a broom and sweep a crossing?[12] Ah! this was the best thing, thought Froggy. A broom would not cost much, and he would choose some crowded thoroughfare, where there were plenty of foot-passengers, and make a good thing of it perhaps.

Having chosen his trade, Froggy felt relieved, and the poor little boy turned into a shop and bought a penny meat-pie to carry home to Benny, in case Mrs Ragbon had been drinking and allowed him to go hungry. And this was not an unlikely thing to have happened; for Mrs Ragbon, I am sorry to say, during these later years had taken much more freely to drink, in consequence of which her husband had deserted her, and her temper had become very violent and bad. She let everything go, and take its chance. She neglected even her own children, and therefore it was not to be expected that she would take any particular care of Benny, who was not her child, and had no particular claim upon her.

When Froggy reached the dismal house in Shoreditch, the landlady met him with very scowling looks.

"Where have you been to?" she asked in harsh tones; "where's your father?"

Froggy then in a broken voice, with many tears, told her of the accident coming from Epsom, and that father was dead.

"Dead!" repeated Mrs Ragbon looking aghast. "*Never!* and he alive and well the day before yesterday, and starting so cheery like for Epsom! Lor! if that ain't awful!" she said, throwing up her hands.

"But I got the rent for you," said poor Froggy quickly, giving her the money.

"Well, that's a good thing; I can't afford to lose any o' that," she said roughly. "What do you intend to do with yoursels?"

"I means to sweep a crossing," said Froggy, with his cheeks getting a little red.

"Very well. Now listen to what I'm going to say," said the landlady severely, with her finger up, and shaking it at Froggy. "As long as you pays me fourpence a week reg'lar for the room up top, you may stay there, but the first Saturday as comes and you don't, I'll thrash you both, and turn you out o' doors, as I did my son Mac – recollect that, you young rascal!"

Mrs Ragbon called every little boy a rascal whom she met.

Seeing by Froggy's frightened face that he was duly impressed with the necessity of working to avoid the fate of Mac, she let him go, and Froggy ran up the steep stairs to Benny. He was playing with a little tame mouse, that used to come out of a hole in the garret and feed on the crumbs.

"I thought you was never coming home, Froggy," said Benny, jumping up from the floor, and leaving the mouse. "I feels so empty, I does!"

"Here's a nice pie," said Froggy; and his little brother snatched at it eagerly, having only had some crusts of bread that a friendly lodger, Mrs Blunt, had given him, since yesterday at one o'clock.

Benny's little face (which was rather a pitiful one, with a sort of "lost-half-a-crown-and-found-a-penny" look upon it), brightened marvellously at the sight of the meat-pie, and the rapidity with which he demolished it was astonishing.

"Shouldn't I like another!" said Benny with warmth when he had finished it. "Froggy, darling! where's Fader?"[13]

"He's gone to mother," said Froggy, putting his arm round Benny and clinging to him.

"Up in the sky where the stars twinkle?" asked Benny wonderingly.

"Yes, where God lives and the angels," said Froggy.

"And gentle Jesus, that I says my hymn to?" asked Benny.

"Yes," nodded Froggy; and then he told Benny all about the accident yesterday, and how poor father had been killed.

"Then we're all alone now, us two little men!" said Benny, looking very gravely up into Froggy's face. "Only I got you, and you got me. O Froggy! won't father never, *never* come back to take care of us no more? What *shall* we do? O Froggy, Froggy!" and the two little boys clung together and sobbed piteously for some minutes.

"No, we've got no one what'll take care of us now," said Froggy at last. "Mother's gone and father's gone, and we've not got no friends!"

What a sad reflection – motherless, fatherless, and friendless! But so it was; and this is the condition of hundreds of our poor little brothers and sisters in great London. Let us think of this next Sunday when the petition comes in our beautiful Litany, "That it may please Thee to defend and provide for the fatherless children and widows, and all that are desolate and oppressed!" and say from our hearts on their behalf, "We beseech Thee to hear us, good Lord!"[14]

* * *

CHAPTER III.
FROGGY AS BREAD-WINNER.

THE next morning Froggy was up betimes. He ran out, and got two penny-rolls from the nearest baker's for himself and Benny, and with a mug of water they breakfasted. Benny let some crumbs down on purpose for his pet, and by and by out came the little brown mouse from his hole, and cautiously approaching, with eyes very bright, came and nibbled industriously till they were all gone, and then retired quietly again without a sound. Benny did love his little mouse so! I do not know what he would have done if it had forsaken the garret. After this, Benny crept downstairs to seek with other children that which is a necessity of childhood – play; and poor Froggy, with all the cares of a bread-winner upon him, sallied forth into the busy streets to buy his broom and begin life as a crossing-sweeper. Before starting, he gave Benny twopence out of his little store, and told him to ask Mrs Blunt, the lodger underneath, to get him some dinner.

When he had bought his broom, Froggy began looking about him with a keen eye to business for a suitable crossing. He settled that it must be one where there was plenty of traffic, and in a shopping neighbourhood, so that people coming from shops would be likely to have coppers in change to throw to him. This was not such an easy thing to get as he had imagined, and Froggy found himself a long way from home before he found the kind of crossing he wanted unoccupied. At last, however, he halted, and took up his position at a point where four roads met in a crowded thoroughfare, close to a station of the Metropolitan Railway. An old woman with a cherry-stall, seated serenely under an umbrella to keep off the sun, with her feet in a basket, knitting a grey stocking, had planted herself as usual for the day at this busy point, and also a little shoeblack boy, who it appeared was in no way dependent on dirty streets for employment, as he was busy with his blacking-pot and brushes already, though it was so fine. Froggy wished the weather had been wet and bad, for it would have given him a better chance at his crossing, which was really so clean as to

require no sweeping at all. But still Froggy swept, notwithstanding the little shoeblack boy called out chaffingly, "I ses, matey,
you'll make your fortun at that, I can see!" and other boys chaffed
him as well. But Froggy did not mind the chaff. Whatever work
bread depends upon is such a serious matter, we cannot easily be
laughed out of it; and Froggy was ever mindful that little Benny's
bread depended upon his efforts at this crossing. He did not take a
penny for a long time. The road became very crowded as the day
wore on, and people passed and repassed by hundreds, all so intent
upon their own business that no one seemed to cast a thought
upon him. The old woman sold her cherries, and the shoeblack
boy was continually on his knees polishing boots; – everybody
seemed to be getting in their money but himself. He thought he
would compel people to notice him somehow, and with a view to
this he took to running in front of foot-passengers, looking up into
their faces, and saying, "Please, sir, throw us a copper!" "Please,
'm, 'member the sweeper!" One gentleman said, "Certainly not!
what do we want sweepers for in this fine weather?" and passed
on. Yes! but did the gentleman remember that poor little sweepers
want bread to eat in *fine* weather as well as in bad? One lady said,
"Oh, get along, you little bore! you as nearly as possible tripped
me up;" but she threw him a penny nevertheless. Oh, how pleased
Froggy was! How he dived in between the cabs and omnibuses to
look for it, for it had rolled, and he could not see it at first. The
shoeblack boy, who had chaffed him earlier in the day, now did
him a good turn, and called out, "I sees it, matey; there it be, nigh
to the kerb!" and following the direction of his hand, Froggy soon
spied it out, and pocketed it.

It was now twelve o'clock, and everybody seemed to be having their luncheon or dinner. Froggy saw a little girl bring something in a yellow basin tied up in a speckled handkerchief to the
old woman at the cherry-stall, and watching with interested eyes,
he soon decided to his satisfaction that it was hot beefsteak pud-
ding. Presently the shoeblack boy produced a handkerchief and
a clasp-knife from his pocket, and began eating a huge sandwich
of bread and meat. Numerous people darted into a neighbouring pastrycook's about this time, and darted out again shortly
after with their teeth buried in a hot bun or crunching a captain's
biscuit.[15] Everybody, indeed, appeared to be eating. Froggy was

getting very hungry, and every now and then looked longingly at the pastrycook's, where there were so many nice things to be got for a penny, but he could not make up his mind to part with the one he had till he had earned another. By and by an opportunity occurred. A Metropolitan train was just in, and a crowd of passengers, as usual, came swarming up the steps into the street.[16] Some marched briskly off at once, some called cabs, some hailed omnibuses, and others stopped and had their boots polished by the little shoeblack who called Froggy "matey." Amongst the passengers whom the train disgorged on this occasion was a very stout red-faced old woman, with bonnet-strings untied and gloves off, who bore the appearance of having gone through some very violent struggle underground. She was panting and blowing asthmatically, and notwithstanding a bunch of flowers, a large gingham umbrella, and a bag in one hand, she was trying to fan herself with the other by means of a pocket-handkerchief, which she had twisted somehow into a hard ball like the top of a drumstick – a very inefficient fan one would think, but it seemed nevertheless to be affording her relief.

This poor old woman, I must tell you, had been to Sydenham to see a friend, and the weather being very warm, and herself very stout, and not being an expert traveller on this line of railway, she came to the top very much out of breath, and feeling, as I have said she looked, as though she had gone through a most exhausting struggle. What with getting into the wrong carriages, losing her ticket, missing trains, and battling with the officials, &c., &c., she may fairly be said to have gone through something!

After a moment or two, recovering her breath, she seemed to brace herself up again for another tussle, and advancing to the edge of the pavement with a determined air, began watching her opportunity to cross. Several times did she leave the pavement; each time did she have to trundle back, for either a cab was coming or an omnibus was coming, or a something which threatened danger if she persisted. After her fifth endeavour, which proved as unsuccessful as the other four, she became very irate and highly indignant.

"Where *is* the p'leece?" she cried out at last quite loud, and looking about her in all directions for that much-abused body. "It's a positive scandal how they never is to be found when they're wanted. If Colonel Fraser or Colonel 'Enderson, or whoever he is as commands the p'leece, would only come by at this moment, I'd give him such a talking-to as never he had in his life before!" and she looked so extremely vindictive, that I think the Chief Commissioner would certainly have repented it if circumstances had brought him into her neighbourhood at this moment.[17]

Giving the pavement an angry rap with the end of her gingham, she was just on the point of holding forth again, when she heard a little boy's voice close to her, saying, "Please, 'm, do you wants to cross t'other side?" and looking down, she saw Froggy with his broom staring very anxiously up into her face.

"Wants to cross! o' course I do," replied the old woman, glad to have even a little crossing-sweeper to listen to her. "Here I've been to Sydenham, and comes back early, though sister-law begged me to stay tea and go to the Palice, purpose to avoid all noosances, and to get 'ome comfortable, and here I'm kept at this crossing ten minutes by the clock, and not a p'leeceman to be seen to take me over! It's a scandal!"[18]

"Here," thought Froggy, "is a fine opportunity."

"I'll take you, mum," said he; "let *me,* mum."

"Could you? would you? do you think you could now?" said the old woman, becoming quite affable at the prospect of help. "I'll give you a silver threepenny if you will."

"Ketch hold o' me, mum, and *I'*ll take you as safe as safe!" said Froggy confidently.

No need to tell her to "ketch hold!" Laying a heavy hand on Froggy's shoulder, she clutched at it with a grip of iron, as if her very life depended on clinging to him, though his little rough head barely reached her elbow.

"Wait a bit, mum; don't get flustered," said Froggy, feeling it was no light frigate he had in tow. "Let them two cabs pass, and that 'bus, and then – – *Now*, mum, step out!" and off they started on the perilous journey across. Midway Froggy pulled up. "Stop a bit, mum," he said; " 'ere's a 'bus coming."

For a moment the old woman became completely frenzied. Turning her head and seeing the pole of the omnibus in the distance, she screamed as if it had already struck her, and in her agitation she dropped her gingham and her oilskin bag, which was bulging with Sydenham carrots and cabbages, and out they rolled all over the road.

"Never mind, mum; *I'll* pick 'em up," called out Froggy in a high tone of encouragement.

"Never mind the carrots, boy; get me over, that's all I cares for!" shrieked the old woman loudly; but she altered her tone somewhat when, a minute later, Froggy landed her safely on the opposite side.

"Me carrots! me cabbages! and me bag! Lor! boy, try and save 'em," she cried.

The little crossing-sweeper needed no urging; without a moment's hesitation he darted in gallantly amongst the cabs and omnibuses, as he had done for his own penny, and began picking up the scattered vegetables right and left. The old woman stood on the pavement cheering him on, and almost waving her gingham in her excitement.

"Capital, me boy!" she exclaimed; "well done! good, good!" as she saw him rescue a cabbage from an imminent cab-wheel. "Excellent! well done!" And when at last Froggy returned to her with his arms full of carrots right up to his chin, and with her bag and cabbages as well, she dived into her pocket, and brought out her purse, saying, "You're a first-rate boy!" and gave him, not a threepenny-piece, but a shilling; and not only a shilling, but one of the nice Sydenham carrots, which she informed him would "eat very well raw."

Oh! for Froggy's delight over this shilling and this carrot. The shilling would pay for a whole week's rent, and for some food besides; and the carrot – what a nice supper he and Benny would have to-night! The carrot cut in half would be plenty for both, and with a penny meat-pie each, and some bread, which Froggy could now buy, they would have a supper fit for a king. Of course Froggy got something to eat after this, but his refreshment was a very moderate one in view of the sumptuous supper he and Benny were to have.

The day wore on, and at seven o'clock the old woman packed up her cherry-stall, and went home for the night. The shoeblack boy did the same with his box, and Froggy thought it was time for him to go home too. So he shouldered his broom and marched briskly

Figure 3 'In her agitation she dropped her gingham and her oilskin bag, which was bulging with carrots and cabbages, and out they rolled all over the road.' (Note: the description 'Sydenham carrots and cabbages' was inserted in later editions.)

Froggy's Little Brother, 1875. Cas. London: John F. Shaw.

homewards, only stopping on his way to buy the two meat-pies and the loaf of bread for supper. Thus ended Froggy's first day as a crossing-sweeper.

* * *

CHAPTER IV.
SUPPERLESS.

TOWARDS nine o'clock on this long summer's evening, just when it was beginning to get dark in the garret at Shoreditch, the two little brothers, Froggy and Benny, were sitting huddled up together on the window-sill, enjoying their evening repast. Their knees were touching to make a table, and they had a handkerchief spread between them by way of tablecloth, on which they had their meat-pies, their bread, and the carrot. Over the latter they seemed to have gone into partnership, for they were taking a bite by turns, just in the same way as they were sharing a mug of water. Poor little fellows! how they were munching away and enjoying themselves! – Froggy like a grave old man, and Benny looking like a queer little Irish beggar in a tiny suit of corduroy (which had been Froggy's once), with his hair all over his eyes, and his little bare feet dangling below the articles he called his trousers. "Froggy, when I was playin in the street to-day, I saw *Mac*," said Benny, as if it were a grand piece of news.

Mac was the eldest son of the landlady, and had been turned out of doors by his mother because he would not work. Some said he was a wicked boy, and deserved it; others said he had been treated harshly, and were inclined to cry "shame" on Mrs Ragbon for having cast him adrift. Mac was an object of the intensest interest to both Froggy and Benny, who had often played with him; and anything they could learn of his movements, now that he was cast on the streets without a home, they gathered in with the keenest relish.

"Did you?" said Froggy eagerly. "What was ee doing?"

"Walkin down the street like any other man!" said Benny.

Mac was only two years older than Froggy, and therefore not a *man* at all, but Benny called every little boy "a man."

"How was he dressed?" asked Froggy.

"Well, he had a nice little coat on," said Benny, "but his trousers was torn, and I could see his leg."

"Did he see you?" asked Froggy.

"Yes, cos I called out 'Hi, Mac!' and he came over and spoke to me," said Benny; "and Jack was with me, and he spoke to Jack too."

Jack was a playfellow of Benny's, though much older than Benny.

"What did Mac say?" inquired Froggy.

"He said he was very merry, and had lots o' grub and nice mates," replied Benny; "only sometimes the p'leece bothered him, and two times he has nearly bin took by the Board."

"The Board" meant the school-board officers, who were held in great terror by all the ragged street-urchins of the neighbourhood.[19]

"Did he say anythink more?" asked Froggy.

"No, nothink more," said Benny, " 'cept this. He put his thumb up to his nose at the house, and called out ever so loud, 'That's for my old mudder!' and then he ran away."

"That was wicked," said Froggy.

"Cos she couldn't catch him?" said Benny.

"No, cos it was rude to his mother – that's why," said Froggy. "The teacher as taught me at night-school said it was in the Bible never to say nothink rude to mother or father."

"Didn't Jesus ever say nothink rude to His mudder?" inquired little Benny.

"No, never," said Froggy.

"I wish I 'ad a mudder!" sighed Benny; "oh, I'd love her so! I'd never be rude to her, never! Look, Froggy, darlin! the little stars are 'ginning to come out;" and turning his eyes up from the dingy garret window to the blue eternities above, he began repeating the lines Froggy had taught him –

> "Twinkle, twinkle, little star!
> 'Ow I wonder what you are,

Up above the world so high,
Like a dimant in the sky!"[20]

"Now, haven't we 'ad a supper *just?*" exclaimed Froggy with satisfaction when everything was done, shaking the crumbs out on the floor, and folding up the handkerchief.

"Yes, and we not eaten too close neither," said Benny, jumping down from the window; "there's plenty for mouse. Ee's bin watchin us with his little hi ever so long. Yes, I's seen you, you dear bootiful little thing, you!" he called out in high glee as the mouse came running nimbly across the garret from under a chair to the spot where the crumbs lay scattered. "I wouldn't sell you for a shilling! I wouldn't sell you not to be the Prince o' Wales!" cried out Benny, going into ecstasies over his pet.

"It's time to go to bed now," said Froggy, giving himself a stretch; and the two little brothers knelt down and said their prayers. Froggy said his first, and got into bed; then little Benny followed with his.

"Pray, God, bless Froggy and me," he said, "and my little mouse, and take us and Deb to the Better Land when Froggy and me dies, where mudder went a long time ago, and now poor fadder's gone. For gentle Jesus' sake. Amen."

Then Benny crept quietly on to the mattress beside Froggy, the mouse ran back to his hole, and the garret was soon quite still.

"Froggy, are you asleep?" whispered Benny presently.

"No, not quite," answered the tired little bread-winner from under the clothes. "Say this thing and then don't talk no more."

"I was only thinking," said Benny, "how nice it would be, Froggy, if *every* day an old woman would want to cross, and us and mouse could 'ave a nice supper like this one to-night *always!*"

"Yes, it would be very nice," said Froggy sleepily. "Good-night! Don't speak no more."

"No," said Benny softly, and he lay very still, till, like Froggy, he fell asleep.

The next morning, and for many, many mornings long after, as regularly as clockwork, Froggy rose up early and went to his crossing. But by no means could he get shillings and carrots every day. Indeed, it was not long before poor little Froggy found out that crossing-sweeping was anything but a paying business.

Sometimes there were old women and nervous ladies wanting to be conducted across the road, like the old woman of the first day, and of course Froggy was always ready and willing for the work, but he never fell in with one who was so liberal as to give him a shilling and a carrot again. Twopence or threepence was the most they ever paid him for his services.

While the summer lasted, and the days were long, Froggy managed to earn enough to pay Mrs Ragbon her fourpence a week regularly for rent, and to keep himself and his little brother supplied with food. But when the days shortened, and the winter set in, these poor little boys entered upon some new and very bitter experiences.

The winter of '73 – which is the one I am writing about – will long be remembered by the poor of London as being one of the hardest they have ever known, because of the great strikes in the Welsh coal-mines, which raised the price of coal to such an extent, that some of the wealthiest houses in the land began to economise their gas, and to knock off any fires they were able to do without.[21] When coal went up in price, the other necessaries of life, meat and bread, went up too, so that to thousands of poor souls the struggle for bare existence became harder and more terrible than ever. Many a poor hard-working mother had the anguish of seeing the frail and delicate one of the family quietly droop and fade out of the world for the want of being properly warmed and comforted. There were empty cradles where the babies used to lie; there were empty chairs where the old folks used to sit; and there was grief, none the less deep because it was mute, in many a lowly kitchen and garret in the suffering East End. They kept up their spirits over it in a wonderful way, but the truth was that poor little Froggy and Benny were nearly starved with cold and hunger up in their miserable garret. They were often miserably off for food; and as to fire, they never thought of such a thing, even on the bitterest days, except when Benny and some other half frost-bitten little boys and girls made a pilgrimage to a rubbish heap in the neighbourhood, where, if they were fortunate, they could sometimes pick up sufficient wood and rubbish to kindle a fire large enough to fry a herring by or to make a kettle boil. But it was very seldom they had anything to cook. Dry bread and onions were what they chiefly existed upon, meat being a luxury seldom dreamed of in these days.

When there was nothing to eat, Froggy and Benny never despaired; they bore their poverty and misery like little heroes. Froggy seemed only miserable about it because of Benny, and Benny seemed mostly to care because of Froggy and his mouse. If "mouse" had no crumbs to eat, he took it greatly to heart, and had lately added this petition to his prayers – "Pray, God, make my little mouse stop in his hole. Don't let 'im think he'll go somewhere else. Please, God, tell 'im the winter will soon be over, and Froggy ses better days is coming!" It was Benny's greatest fear that the mouse would desert its hole.

One miserable December evening, after having been at his crossing all day in the snow and cold, poor Froggy was returning home without even having taken as much as a halfpenny! The weather had been such, that not even the old woman with her apple-stall had come out, and she was generally there on the most hopeless days.[22] The shoeblack boy had not been at his usual post either, and any passengers arriving by the Metropolitan trains, and coming out of the station, hailed a cab or an omnibus at once, and very few availed themselves of the neat crossing Froggy had swept in the snow. At any rate, no one paid him for it, and he shouldered his broom at six o'clock to go home without having taken, as I have said, even a single halfpenny.

I wonder whether my little Froggy was the boy of whom the writer was thinking when he wrote the following touching lines on a little crossing-sweeper for whom he could not find a copper. Likely enough!

> "Twas nothing but a vulgar little chap,
> A dirty, ragged, red-nosed, hungry wight;
> And all he did was just to touch his cap,
> When, feeling in my pocket one cold night,
> I could not find the halfpenny I sought;
> And when he saw my search was all in vain,
> With gentle tone of gratitude for nought,
> Said, 'Thank you, sir!' and turned him round again.
> And then I heard him whistling: very slow

> And feeble first his tones, as though a chill
> Had damped his music with a tinge of woe;
> Yet but a while, and he commenced a trill
> Of some street composition's jerky air,
> That grew and grew, and louder rattled out,
> Until he danced as though he tried to wear
> His very feet, if not the pavement, out!
> Then with redoubled vigour all around
> He plied his besom with a frantic will,
> As if his tune had made his soul rebound;
> And when I left him, he was whistling still.
> I met him ne'er again, but always kept
> My pocket ready with a copper store;
> For since, in musings, and whene'er I slept,
> A ragged little figure oft I saw;
> And late that winter night in easy-chair,
> Whene'er the glowing embers chanced to stir,
> I seemed to see that young face aged with care,
> And hear that little voice say, 'Thank you, sir !' "[23]

"I can't buy no bread now," thought Froggy as he trudged along. "But we've got a supper, so we are not so bad off after all."

The *supper* Froggy was reckoning upon was a piece of good, wholesome Australian meat, which Mrs Ragbon in a fit of generosity had given him the day before, and of which there was still a small portion remaining when he had started out in the morning.[24] The moment Froggy reached the garret, which was as cold as an ice-house, feebly lit by the end of a dismal tallow candle, he was met by Benny, with his hair very rough and tumbled, as if he had been rolling.

"Well, Froggy, 'ow much money 'as you got?" asked he, thrusting his little hands deep in his trousers-pockets, and looking very eager.

"Not a stiver!" said Froggy mournfully, throwing down his broom.[25]

"A stiver! what's that?" asked Benny.

"It means nothink – not a farden!" exclaimed Froggy. "But it don't matter not so *very* much, you know, Benny, cos we've got that meat."

At the mention of the meat, a very comical look spread itself over Benny's face, and when Froggy moved towards the corner of the garret to fetch the meat from where he had left it in the morning standing on a box, Benny followed close behind with his shoulders shrugged up to his ears, as if he were trying to keep in some capital joke. To Froggy's astonishment, when he got to the box, he saw that the meat was gone! There was the plate, but no meat – where could it be? Froggy stared blankly at the empty plate for a minute, then turned round upon Benny.

"I ses, Benny, the meat's gone!" he said, – "clean gone! Whoever can a taken it? Do you know anythink about it?" he asked searchingly, as he caught a twinkle in Benny's eye.

"Yes; I saw it go," said Benny, evidently with a strong inclination to laugh.

"Where did you see it go?" asked Froggy quickly.

"Out at the door," said Benny.

"Who took it out at the door?"

"The cat!" said Benny; and then his little comical face puckered up, his mouth went all to one side; he gave a jump forward with his knees bent and his shoulders up to his ears, and burst out into a perfect peal of laughter, which, however, rather abruptly ended, as he thought of Froggy's empty pockets.

I must tell you that Benny was a rare little fellow for laughing – indeed, quite irrepressible in this department; and though he had lost his supper, and would have to go to bed hungry, the idea of the cat having taken it so amused him, he was unable to keep quite grave over the fact when he had to record it to Froggy.

"The *cat* took it! But how came you to let him?" exclaimed Froggy, who was ravenously hungry, and could not see the joke of it at all.

"I didn't let 'im," said Benny; "he never give me the chance o' saying 'No,' – he was so sly, and did it so quick."

"Where was you when he come?" asked Froggy.

"I was lyin down on the bed," said Benny, trying to look grave, but not succeeding, "cos I was feelin very empty; and I lit the candle, and set open the door, so as to hear when you come home, Froggy. And while I was lyin there very quiet," said Benny in a whisper, "I saw mister Tom Cat come creepin', creepin' round the door, and all at once he made a dart, like that, at the box" – (Benny darted forward to show Froggy) – "and he took the meat in his mouth, and ran off like mad, afore ever I could tell 'im to stop. *Won't* I give him a hit when I meets 'im next!" said Benny, with a nod of his head.

"Don't never hit 'im," said Froggy.[26] "P'r'aps he was clemmed like we, and didn't know as how he was doing wrong."[27]

"Oh, but I think he did," said Benny, screwing up one eye, and putting on a little knowing look. "Fact, I'm sure he did, Froggy; for ee came round the door so soft, and made a dart ever so quick at the meat, cos he was afraid of being caught."

"Well, I wish he had left us *half*" said poor Froggy; "he might a done that. We can't have no supper, Benny, to-night, cos there's no money to buy none."

"Never mind, Froggy, darlin!" said Benny. "It's very bad, though, to be so hungry, that it is! Let's go to bed, Froggy, and cuddle together and get warm, and we'll pretend we're not hungry. It's very orkard not having no money, Froggy, ain't it?" said poor little Benny.

"Yes," said Froggy despondingly, "very orkard indeed."

"I couldn't a done it, if I had bin the cat; could you, Froggy?" said Benny pitifully. "He feeds better than we."

"Maybe he don't," said Froggy.

"Oh, but he do," replied Benny, "cos he gets all the rats and mouses, and I sees 'im get nice little bits of meat on sticks that the man sells in the streets, that I should like to get a nip at."

"Well, I think *I* could eat a bit o' cat's meat to-night," said poor Froggy. "I'm that empty, I could eat *anythink*!"

"A black beetle?" asked Benny.

"Don't be a silly!" answered Froggy; and then, staring at Benny for a moment, he said suddenly –

"I ses, Benny, 'ow big your eyes is growing!"

Ah! poor little Benny! It was not really that his eyes were growing bigger, but that his face was growing thin. It looked so small, and so white and sad, it seemed to strike quite a pain into Froggy to-night, and he clasped Benny tighter than ever in his arms when they got on to the mattress and nestled together to keep warm.

'Froggy, do you think Mudder and Fader knows we're hungry, in the Better Land?" asked Benny softly.

"No, cos it would make 'em fret like, and there's not nothink o' that sort in the Better Land," replied Froggy.

"I think I'd like to go there," said Benny with a little sigh.

"And leave me!" exclaimed Froggy, with a strange feeling of desolation coming over him lest someday he should be left all alone.

"Oh no, Froggy, darlin! I shouldn't like to go without you and Deb." (Deb was Benny's favourite playfellow, and lived in the room underneath.) "But I'd like to see Jesus, Froggy – wouldn't you? He was werry kind to little chaps like we, wasn't He, Froggy?"

"Yes, very," said Froggy.

"Maybe He'll take us afore we starve," murmured Benny half asleep. "Good night, Froggy, darlin!"

"Good night, Benny!" and they fell asleep after this, Benny sucking his fist as he used when he was a baby, and slept on the Punch and Judy box, and Froggy with a dark shadow over his face, as if in his dreams hunger and care were still pressing heavily upon him.

* * *

CHAPTER V.
MAC'S VISIT.

THE first thing Froggy saw, when he opened his eyes the next morning, was a little fluffy sparrow looking in at the window. It had a nice bit of bread in its mouth, and Froggy thought, "Oh, what a happy little sparrow! he's got *his* breakfast, and poor Benny and me's got none!"

As the bird flew away over the house-tops with the breakfast God had provided for it, some words came suddenly into Froggy's mind, which sounded as distinctly as if an angel's voice had whispered them, "Fear not! ye are of more value than many sparrows!"

"P'r'aps if I gets up, and looks about me like that there little sparrar, God'll send Benny and me a breakfast," thought Froggy.

"I'll get up quick, and see if Mrs Blunt won't lend me twopence. She did it once afore, and I paid her again quite honest."

Froggy crept quietly out of bed, so as not to wake Benny, and went softly down the stairs. The landing below was rather dark, but Mrs Blunt's door was open, and through it the pale grey light came slanting out from the window of her room. By it Froggy could see that there was a burly man stooping over a large tin can, from which he was dealing out milk to the charwoman, who stood in the doorway. Froggy heard Mrs Blunt say in a cheerful tone –

"Well, master, it ain't often we sees you. What's the matter with Peggie that *you* comes to-day?"

"Well, Peggie's had a haccident," replied the man. "Slipped down on a piece of orange-peel, and given her foot a nasty rick. But I wouldn't let you poor folks go without your milk, thinkin o' the babies and all; so master comes hisself you see. Why, who-ever is this?" he exclaimed, as the deplorable little apparition of Froggy came stealing down the stairs, barefooted and large-eyed, and very miserable altogether.

"Why, it's *Froggy!*" said Mrs Blunt. "Well, Froggy," addressing him, "what brings you down this time o' the morning, eh?"

"Please, mum," said Froggy earnestly, "I come to see if you'll lend me twopence, mum. Benny and me's got no breakfast. We 'ad no supper last night neither, and we're *awful* hungry this mornin'."

"Dear! dear!" said Mrs Blunt sadly. "Oh yes, Froggy, I'll lend it you;" and she began fumbling in her pockets.

"I'll pay it you back, mum, as sure as ever," said Froggy grate-fully.

"Oh yes, I'm not afraid o' that – I knows you're honest," said Mrs Blunt, bringing out the coppers. " 'Ere they be then!" and she dropped them into Froggy's outstretched hand.

He thanked her (evidently from his heart), and was just turning off with the money, when the milkman, who had been standing by and listening, called out benevolently –

"Stop a bit, little shaver![28] Here! what should you say, I wonder, to a bowl of milk for breakfast? Should you like it?"

Froggy was quite unable to answer for a moment, but the char-woman answered for him.

"God bless you, master! It would be a Christian thing to do," she said. "Froggy, run up and get the master your jug – he's agoin to give you a breakfast."

The words now rang out in Froggy's heart quite loudly and triumphantly, "Fear not! ye are of more value than many sparrows!" and with a joy that was almost too much for him, he ran up into the garret, and fetched down the broken thing they dignified by the name of *jug*.

"Oh, sir, *sir*!" gasped Froggy at length, as he handed it to the milkman, and saw it plunged deep down into the depths of the milk-can. "Whatever can us do? Whatever can us say, Benny and me?"

"Why, just thank God for it, that's what'll be best," said the man cheerily, with a look of extreme satisfaction on his face, as he brought the jug out, and handed it back to Froggy all overflowing and dripping with the milk. "Now you only wants twopenn'orth o' bread to make a *real* good breakfast. If I stands the bread, missus, will you boil it all up for 'em, and make it hot?" he asked, looking at Mrs Blunt.

"Yes, master, and glad I'll be to do it," she answered. "To be sure it's a hill wind that blows nobody any good! Now, if Peggie hadn't a hurt herself, Froggy, the master never would a come, and then you'd never have 'ad this fine breakfast."

"Was ever such a thing heard of?" thought Froggy, – "*hot bread and milk* for breakfast!" He was quite unable to express his thanks to the milkman, but he *looked* them; and I am quite sure that that good man would have felt himself more than repaid for his generosity if he could have looked into the garret a quarter of an hour later. There was Froggy standing by the bedside holding aloft the beautiful basin of hot bread and milk, and little rough-headed hungry Benny sitting up with, oh, such eager eyes! literally shouting for joy at the sight of it!

Froggy did not forget to thank God for the breakfast, as the milkman had told him to do. He knelt down presently, and said aloud for himself and Benny, "O God! Benny and me's *so* much obliged! We've had such a beautiful breakfast; it's warmed us so, and we feels quite comforted. It was the milkman that give it us, but we know, God, it come from you, cos you put it into his heart to be kind just as it's put into the hearts o' people to throw out crumbs for the little sparrars, so that they don't starve. Please, God, Benny and me's *very* much obliged!" and little Benny said heartily –

"Yes, please, God! Amen."

Then Froggy rose up from his knees, and went out to his crossing quite comforted.

One Sunday afternoon, about four o'clock, just when London was getting dark, and the lamps were being lighted in the gloomy streets, Froggy and Benny were busy over a handful of fire made up of odds and ends from the rubbish heap, trying to toast a herring for their tea. They called this meal *tea,* because it was the time when most people had it, but there was no real tea in the matter. Water was the only beverage these little boys knew, and instead of a teapot they had a jug of water, and instead of teacups, little mugs set out on a chair without a back to it, which served as a table, and on which there was also a broken plate, placed in readiness to receive the herring as soon as it was done. Froggie was on his knees holding the small fish close to the bars,[29] at the end of a short fork, with his grave old man's face looking much interested over the cooking of it; and crouching close by was Benny, with his rough head bent forward, and a pair of very eager eyes fixed on the herring, in which he was evidently as much interested as Froggy.

"I think he's getting done, Froggy," said Benny, meaning the fish, "cos ee's 'ginning to frizzle!"

"Well, it's a'most time," said Froggy. "He'll eat splendid, I know. I'll just give 'im a toasting t'other side, and then we'll enjoy 'im ever so much!"

Froggy spoke with warmth, as if he were very hungry, as indeed he was, and knew Benny to be the same. There was a sharp frost outside, and the prospect of getting anything hot to eat was very grateful to them.

"I wish we 'ad somethink nice to drink," said Benny; "the water's so cold, it makes my little inside have a pain. Don't you wish, Froggy, we 'ad some beer?"

"Beer!" exclaimed Froggy. "No, I'd sooner have some hot coffee, like what they sells at the stalls a penny a cup. But whatever do you know about *beer*?" he asked, because he could not remember when Benny had ever tasted it.

"Oh, I often gets a little sip," replied Benny. "When Jack goes for his mudder's beer, I meets him sometimes, and ee tips up the jug, and I gets quite a nice little drink at it!"

"You shouldn't never do that," said Froggy, looking severely at Benny. "That's what they calls in the Catechism 'pickin' and stealin',' cos the beer don't belong to you or to Jack; and, 'sides that, it's very bad for boys to drink beer. Mother always said so when I was little, and said she hoped I'd never drink it, never – not even when I was a man and growed up – cos it was beer that made poor father always poor, and kept us so short in the garret. I thinks when I'm a man, I'll take the pledge; they says it's capital for savin', and makin home comfortable!"

How wise of Froggy! If every boy and every girl would make the same resolution to take the pledge of temperance, and keep to it, what a good thing it would be! Those who go amongst the poor, and have opportunities of studying London sorrow and London sin, will invariably tell you that beer and strong drink are at the bottom of it all.

"Froggy," said Benny, moving closer and speaking confidentially, "shall I tell you somethink Jack has told me?"

"Yes," said Froggy.

"Who do you think it's about?" asked Benny, liking to keep Froggy expectant.

"I guess its about Mac," said Froggy.

"Yes it is," replied Benny; and then lowering his voice mysteriously, and speaking almost in a whisper, he said –

"Well, Froggy, do you know Jack says Mac drinks beer, and *he gets tipsy just like a man!*"

Benny looked at Froggy, and nodded his head to confirm what he had just announced, for Froggy looked as if he scarcely believed it.

"And somethink else too," added Benny; "he smokes real bacca-pipes!"

"He'll suffer for it some day," said Froggy, with the air of an old man; "boys that does them sort o' things always does. That's p'r'aps why he's never growed, and ain't so tall as me, though he's older."

"I nebber knew boys could get tipsy like men, did you, Froggy?" asked Benny, looking up into Froggy's face.

"No, I don't know as I did," said Froggy ponderingly; then, as the herring began to frizzle furiously, he cried out, "Now then, Benny! the dish! the dish! ee's done prime now!"

And in another minute or two the little brothers were seated opposite each other, with the broken chair serving as table between them, devouring the hot herring and some dry crusts of bread with the eagerness and rapidity of half-famished beings.

It is terrible and painful to see hungry dogs taking to their food in this way, but thrice painful is it when we see hungry boys doing so. They had not proceeded far in their meal when they were startled by hearing a footstep coming cautiously and very quietly up the ricketty stairs outside. Visitors to the garret were so unfrequent, Froggy and Benny could not imagine who it could be coming up to see them. Mrs Ragbon came occasionally for her rent, but then she always mounted with a clatter, and the stairs were only creaking now under a very light weight. Froggy and Benny paused in their eating, and fixed their eyes steadily on the door, waiting to see who would enter.

"It may be only the cat!" said Benny beneath his breath; but as he spoke the handle of the door turned softly, plainly showing it was not the cat, and in another minute a two-legged visitor entered. It was a ragged boy of stunted growth, with yellow hair, that looked as if it had never been combed or brushed for months, and with a red dissipated countenance, sadly suggestive of unlimited beer-drinking and low companions. He was dressed in the shabbiest of clothes, having alarming gaps in the legs of his trousers, showing his bare leg at the knees, and with large holes at his elbows. He came in on tiptoe with his boots in his hand.

"Lor!" cried Froggy in great astonishment; "why, its *Mac!*"

"Hold your tongue!" whispered Mac, putting his finger to his lips as a sign to them to be quiet, and jerking his thumb over his shoulder to indicate downstairs. "If the old mother catches me, there'll be no end of a row. I've just stole up without my boots to see 'ow you two chaps is getting on this weather, and to put you up to a wrinkle or two in case you're a'most starved."

Froggy and Benny stared at him in great alarm, for they knew what terrible risk they were running by having Mac in their garret. They knew that if Mrs Ragbon came up, and found him there, she would not only turn Mac out "neck and crop," but she would turn *them* out also.[30]

"Don't come, Mac," pleaded Froggy imploringly; "we'll all catch it if you do."

"I heard a door bang then," said Benny, clinging to Froggy in fear lest the landlady had already started on her way upstairs.

"Now don't be afeared," said Mac, relapsing into a broad grin. "I watched the old woman out in her bonnet and shawl afore ever I come. She's gone round to see a friend, same as she allays did Sundays. *I* knows her ways, bless you! I came up dark cos o' the other lodgers – they might tell on me if they see'd me; but I didn't run up against no one, so we're 'all serene'!"

Froggy and Benny were by no means satisfied, but they saw it was no good urging upon Mac to leave, for he had evidently made up his mind to stay. He put down his boots, thrust his hands into his pockets, and seated himself with an independent bump close to the grate, where there was still a slight blaze visible, as if he had every right to be there, and had not the slightest intention of leaving for the present.

"Well, now," he began, "I come to see how you two chaps is getting on. I've often thought on you this cold weather – ain't it cold just?" he said shivering, – "and wondered what you was doing all along o' yourselves; for Jack told me you was a shifting now alone. How are you off for food and that of a day?"

"Oh, middling," said Froggy, not at all comfortable in his mind yet about Mac, and wondering how it would be possible to hide him if Mrs Ragbon did come up.

"We gets on very bad indeed," declared little Benny earnestly, thinking Froggy had not been half strong enough in saying they got on "middling." "We gets emptier and emptier, and all our little ribs is sticking out. I've got a mouse, Mac, – a dear little bootiful thing, that I loves next to Froggy; and sometimes we can't gid him not a crumb, cos we've got nothink to make the crumbs with."

"What 'ave you got there?" asked Mac, nodding at the tea-table.

"A nerring!" said Benny.

"Have some, Mac, if you're hungry," said Froggy, generously preparing to share his portion with Mac.

"No, thank you," said Mac, looking rather disdainfully at the frizzled up tail-end of the little fish. "I knows where I can get better tackle than that. Lor' bless you! *I'm* never hungry like you chaps. I'm leading a reg'lar merry life, and gets as much beer and grub as ever I could if I was a royal dook. But *I* don't go crossing-sweeping, tho' I did try it first when I went on my own hook.[31] I very soon left it off, and took to somethink more paying, and I'm getting on capital now."

"What do you do?" asked Froggy, looking earnestly at Mac, thinking perhaps *he* might be able to follow the same paying business, if he knew what it was.

Mac looked as if he were uncertain what to answer exactly, but said, after a moment's consideration, "Well, I lives on my wits."

"What is wits?" asked Benny.

"Well, wits is wits," said Mac, unable to furnish a better explanation. "I goes about keeping my weather-h'eye open, and turns my hand to anythink that'll bring me in a penny, and never loses a chance. For hinstance," he said, "me and a chap went last Derby Day to h'Epsom, and made a capital day of it. Him and me, we dressed oursels up in billycock hats put on large paper collars, blacked our faces, and played the bones, and sang 'Slap bang 'ere we are again!'[32] It took capital. We chaffed the swells and sang to the ladies –

> 'Some lady's lost her chi-non,
> All plaited and the pin on!'

and did the cheeky wherever we had the chance. We got no end of coppers from parties just to get rid of us, and one gent as was having lunch on the top of a coach, ee threw us a bit of a fowl, and another gent gave us half a cake and some rich pie stuff – lor'! how good that was! – and Chick and me, we got a drink o' water, and did as well in the eating line as the Prince o'Wales hisself!"

The idea of Mac going about in a stick-up paper collar and a billycock hat, with a blackened face, seemed much to entertain Froggy and Benny, and they were all eagerness for Mac to tell them some more of his doings.

"Tell us some more what you've done?" said Benny.

"Well," said Mac, "there was that grand to-do of the Thanksgiving, when the Queen went to St Paul's after the Prince was took so bad and got well.[33] We did a tidy business that day, though Chick got into trouble with the p'leece, and was took to the lock-up."

"What did he do wrong?" asked Froggy.

"Oh, nothink at all," said Mac, evidently unwilling to enter into the particulars of his companion's disgrace; "ee was let free the next day. We got enough Thanksgiving Day to keep us in plenty the whole winter. Now wouldn't you sooner come along with me, and do the same as me, than go standing at that crossing all day, taking nothink?"

"Yes, Mac, if I'd get some money along with you," said poor, half-starved Froggy.

"Then come along then!" exclaimed Mac encouragingly. "There'll be a fine chance for doing some business, Wednesday; and you shall come along with me that day, and we'll share everythink we gets; only you must promise to do everythink I tells you, without asking no questions – do you hear?"

"Yes, Mac," said Froggy. "I won't ask you nothink. But what's going to be done, Wednesday?"

"Why, you knows Victoria Park, don't you?" said Mac. "Well, the Queen is comin to the h'East End purpose to see it, and drive through it, along with one o' the Princesses, and there'll be no end of a crowd and fuss."

"And will Froggy have to wear a billycock and stick-ups and 'ave his face black?" inquired little Benny hoping very much he should have the fun of seeing Froggy start out in this guise.

"No, nothink o' that," replied Mac. "P'r'aps he'll have to sell some cigar-lights, and be ready at this kind o' thing, cos it comes in useful sometimes;" and as Mac spoke he got up from his sitting posture, and quick as lightning went across the garret throwing somersaults one after the other, as if he had not an atom of bone in his body. He looked like some curious species of firework, with his yellow head and bare knees and elbows visible at intervals in his quick evolutions about the garret; and little Benny opened his large mouth, and fairly shouted with laughter. And Froggy laughed too, in a soberer fashion, more indeed out of sympathy with Benny, than from any real mirth he had in his heart. He was so glad to see Benny laughing, for Benny had not laughed heartily like this for a long time, and Froggy had been pondering very sorrowfully of late over the fact that "Benny didn't seem as merry as he used, cos he never laughed."

They had forgotten all about Mrs Ragbon, and Mac was in the middle of a somersault, when suddenly a great noise and slamming of doors was heard downstairs, and Mac paused to listen with a leg in the air, just as he would be before turning right over, and one hand on the ground. A deep silence fell on the whole party, for the landlady's voice was heard scolding loudly below, and in another minute her heavy footstep was heard unmistakably creaking upstairs. She was calling out in a tone of hottest anger, as step by step she ascended, "I'll catch you, you young rascal you! *I* knows where you are – don't you think I don't know where you are now!" and it was evident she carried a stick with her, for she was sounding it against the stairs, in order, no doubt, to strike terror into the heart of the "young rascal" whom she was promising to catch, and who, of course, was Mac.

Froggy and Benny became white with terror, absolutely at a loss to imagine the dreadful scene that would occur between the wrathful mother and her son; but Mac was as cool as possible. He gazed at the door fixedly for one moment, to make sure she was coming, in an attitude of defiant impudence, with his thumb to his nose, and his tongue out; then, with the quickness of his class, so accustomed to outwitting the police and dodging the School Board officers, he jumped on to the mattress whereon Froggy and Benny slept, pulled the clothes over him, and lay so still and flat that no one entering could possibly have imagined there could be a human being lying underneath. In another second the door flew open, and in burst Mrs Ragbon. Glancing rapidly round the garret, and seeing no Mac, she became furious.

"The young rascal!" she exclaimed; "if he hasn't give me the slip after all. He's in the house, I know he is! Thompson said he saw him come in not ten minutes ago, and if he's up the chimney, I'll fetch him down, as sure as my name's Sal Ragbon!" She delivered herself of this speech apparently unmindful of the two poor little boys cowering close together over the fire, upon whose privacy she had thus abruptly intruded.

The garret was so bare of furniture and hiding-places of any kind, that Mrs Ragbon, after taking the first searching look around, became satisfied that she was on the wrong scent, and that Mac could not be there, but must be down in one of the other rooms. The mattress was spread close to the floor, so that there was no bed to look *under,* and *in* it, fortunately, it never occurred to her to look though Froggy and Benny were literally trembling-with fear lest she should suddenly take it into her head to stalk forward and give the mattress a sounding rap with her stick, which would have roused Mac with a start and a scream, and then what a scene there would have been! How Mac would have fought! and how Mrs Ragbon would have fought! and who can tell what might have happened?

Such a scene would indeed have been painful and dreadful to witness between mother and son between whom Christ Himself has taught us, both by precept and example, that there should ever be the deepest reverence and the holiest love. Christ never preached what He did not practise; and mark, little children, how kind He always was to His mother; how, when He hung bleeding on the cross for our sins, almost His last thought was for her when He said to that disciple whom He loved;"Behold thy mother!" thus providing an earthly home for her after He was gone. There is no sin more grievous in Christ's eyes than that of rebelliousness towards parents. Whatever may be our parents' failings and short-comings, we are bound to love, honour, and succour them.

Mrs Ragbon was not a good mother; her passion for drink, and her constant indulgence of it, had drowned all her better feelings, her love for her husband, and the duty she owed to her children; but then Mac should not have been rude and disobedient to her. That was not being a good son. He should have worked hard, and tried to win his mother back again by leading a good life himself, and being kind; and who can tell that, with God's blessing, he might not have succeeded?

Having satisfied herself that Mac was not in the garret, the landlady, anxious not to lose time, turned on her heel directly, and went scolding down to the lower regions in search of him. The moment the door closed, down went the clothes, and up jumped Mac.

"Slap bang 'ere we are again!" he said, springing to his feet, and laughing as if he thought it a capital joke.

"O Mac! however will you get out?" exclaimed Froggy, not laughing at all, but very grave and frightened.

"Well, I must watch my chance, same as I've often done before," replied Mac, moving towards the door and cautiously opening it. "Listen!" he said, with his finger up, and peeping down the dark stairs, "she's gone into mother Blunt's now, and lor'! what a row she's making! She wants to look in the saucepan for me, and they won't let her, and there! she's just given one of the brats *such* a knock, don't you hear him squealing? I must make a dash in a minute. 'Ere, Benny, give me my boots."

Benny handed them to him tremblingly, with his poor little white face looking quite scared at the danger Mac was in.

"O Mac! do take care!" entreated Froggy. "If she finds out you've bin here, she'll come up and beat Benny and me – I knows she will, Mac!"

"Don't be afraid. *I* won't get you into any hobble, not me!" returned Mac assuringly. "Now don't forget Wednesday. Be up early, and meet me at the top of the street, mind."

With these words, he rubbed his hands as if bracing himself up for action, and then suddenly dashing forward, took a flying leap downstairs, past Mrs Blunt's door, down some more stairs, along the passage, and out at the street-door, before Mrs Ragbon could possibly catch him, though she was just in time to see his yellow head disappearing from her premises. She ran out into the street calling out loudly "Police! police!" but Froggy and Benny, watching from their garret window, saw Master Mac turn the corner, and they knew then that he had made good his escape, and that neither Mrs Ragbon nor the police would be able to catch him.

* * *

CHAPTER VI.
FROGGY GOES OUT WITH MAC.

ON the morning of the day on which our gracious Queen did an act of kindness which sent happiness and sunshine into the hearts and homes of thousands of her poor subjects in the toiling East End, by coming amongst them, and driving through their Park, there was a great stir going on in the garrets and kitchens and first-floor backs and fronts in Shoreditch.[34] The inhabitants of this neighbourhood are habitually early risers, but they were earlier than ever this morning, and seemed to be unanimous in their desire to get some extra time before the work-a-day world usually awoke, so that they might be free later. They all felt that this was to be no ordinary day. There was a widespread and a very happy feeling abroad that the Queen was coming to see them each personally, and therefore it behoved them, as affectionate and loyal subjects, to go forth into the streets and greet her, as many as could. For this reason, fathers were content to make shift at their breakfasts, and to help in a great many little household matters which they generally left to their wives to do, because they knew that Mary Anne or Betsy Jane was busy tidying up the children, and giving them an extra wash under the pump in preparation for the holiday. And oh! how happy the children were because mother was going to take them to see the Queen! They were to be lifted out of the gutter for one short day, and taken out into the open streets, away from the wretched alleys and close courts and passages, into lighter and purer air; and oh! delight of delights! – mother had told them that when the Queen went by, they might "Hip-hip hooray!" as loud as ever they liked, and make as much noise as they could!

The cold grey light of the dawn was just stealing in at the garret window when Benny, rubbing his eyes with his small fists, woke up, and was surprised to find no Froggy lying by his side. Rising up on his elbow, he looked out upon the garret, and then discovered Froggy in one corner, standing over a tub washing himself, with his little thin spider-like body shivering with cold, and his head looking like the top of a mop, as he kept plunging it in the water, and then bringing it out again with a jerk.

"Froggy, 'ow quick you is up!" exclaimed Benny.

"Yes, cos I've got to meet Mac, don't you know?" said Froggy, burying his wet face as he spoke in a tattered thing he called a towel. "This is Wednesday morning. I'm glad you've woke, cos I want to practise my tumbling;" and forthwith he began throwing somersaults as fast as he could about the garret, and making Benny laugh and rub his hands with delight.

"You do it cap'ly," said he when Froggy had done, and stood panting with the exertion, "as well as Mac did. I wish, Froggy, *I* was going to see the Queen too."

"Do you?" said Froggy. "Well, go along with Jack – ee's sure to be going."

"I'll try," said Benny in a tone that showed he was a little doubtful of Jack's taking him. "I *would* like to see her, and the soldiers, and hear the music and everythink, that I would! Do you think, Froggy, she'll be in a gold carriage, and wear a crown, and look like the queen on the pennies – do you, Froggy?"

"I think she'll wear a bonnet, same as the grand ladies does in the parks," replied Froggy, "but I'm not quite sure o' that. You must take care you isn't run over in the crowd. We've got nothink of a breakfast to call a breakfast," said he, regarding the few dry crusts which represented the larder; "but you know what Mac said; we was sure to get on to-day, and he'd share everythink with me. So we shall 'ave a good supper to-night, Benny, and p'r'aps be able to 'ave a fire and get warm."

After this the two boys ate their crusts, and Benny having dressed, threw himself on the ground, and coaxed the mouse out of his hole to eat the crumbs he had taken care to leave. Froggy gave his little brother a kiss, and told him to be a good boy if he went out with Jack, and then sallied forth into the streets to meet his companions for the day. Froggy wandered up and down for a long time before Mac appeared. When at last he did appear, he was not alone, but was accompanied by two boys, whom Froggy scrutinised with great interest. They were curious-looking individuals, possibly of thirteen or fourteen, with apparently boy's bodies and men's heads. They wore their hair closely shaven, and they had shrewd restless little eyes, that seemed capable of taking in a thousand things at once. Froggy thought at one minute they *must* be old men, grown down from age; then again that they must be boys after all, because of their small hands and feet, and their little chests and backs. Mac called one Chickabiddy and the other Dandy. They eyed Froggy sharply when they met, as if they would like to get inside of him if they could, to see what he was made of.

"Is he pretty quick?" asked Dandy of Mac, regarding Froggy as if he were some new little animal brought into market to be discussed.

"Yes, middling," said Mac. "He'll do for what we wants."

"He's quite fresh, ain't he?" said Chickabiddy in an undertone.

"Yes, *very*," replied Mac with emphasis; and then the three turned abruptly with one accord, and walked together straight ahead, because Chickabiddy intimated the approach of a policeman, and they all seemed anxious to get out of his way.

Froggy followed them silently down a great many streets and through crowded courts and alleys, and many queer places where he had never been before, wondering to himself a good deal the while where Chickabiddy and Dandy came from – how old they really were – whether they were brothers, or only "mates" – how Mac had come to know them – what they did to earn their bread – and a thousand other things. He heard them talking together as they went along in rather mysterious language at times, using expressions he did not understand, and which evidently had reference to the day's proceedings. They seemed to be marking out a plan of action for themselves, in which Froggy soon saw he was intended to play a part; for Dandy kept alluding to "that there!" and Chickabiddy to the "colt!" with various signs and nods, which left no doubt in Froggy's mind that he was the "that there" and "the colt" indicated. Whenever a policeman came in sight, Froggy noticed they avoided meeting him if possible – sometimes by crossing to the other side, or slipping down a side street. Now and then they parted company, and each went different ways, as if they did not desire to be seen together, but always meeting again shortly afterwards, and continuing their conversation.

By and by they got into the line of streets through which the Queen was going to pass on her way to Victoria Park. Everywhere along the royal route there was a tremendous crowd assembling, though it was yet early in the day. Men, women, and children

lined the kerbstones, jostling one another for a front place, determined to stand there till they dropped rather than not get a sight
of their Queen. There were policemen keeping order amongst
the crowd, and directing the traffic – now battling with a refrac-
tory costermonger who wanted to go his own way, now helping a
heavily-burdened mother with a perambulator across the road –
now collaring a pickpocket – now telling a suspicious character to "move on," &c., &c. There were ragged men with greasy
hats and shoeless feet pattering up and down the muddy road
in and out of the crowd, calling out in sharp, metallic voices,
"Only *one* ape'ny! portrait of 'er Majesty Queen Victoria in her
crownation robes! *honly* one ape'ny!" and there were others of
the same unwholesome fraternity selling rattles and whistles,
and cardboard carriages, and "Jump Jim Crows" dangling at the
end of elastic, and hosts of other wares, all at the same tempting
price of "*h'only* one ape'ny!"[35] There were the provision sellers
too – men with trays full of brandy-balls and penny packets of
ginger-nuts, speckled profusely with almond; and at the corners
of the streets, wherever the police permitted them to be, there
were Punch and Judy shows, and "happy families," and acrobats
in velvet dresses and spangles, and many other performances,
which seldom exhibited in these parts except on such a rare
occasion as this, when the Queen was coming, and there was a
large crowd to amuse.[36]

The poor East End seemed to be quite agog with excitement,
and every moment the crowd became greater.

About an hour before the Queen was expected, Chickabiddy,
Dandy, and Mac pulled up at a point where the crowd was dens-
est, and Froggy heard Dandy say approvingly, "Yes, I thinks this'll
do as well as any!" There was evidently the fullest understanding
between these three, and though Chickabiddy and Dandy now
nodded to Mac, and went off in different directions amongst the
crowd, Froggy felt their partnership was by no means dissolved.

"Now, Frog, lookee here," said Mac; "don't you take no notice of
me, but do just as I tell you. Do you see that old party with blue
spectacles and a big chain opposite?"

"Yes," said Froggy.

"Well, now," said Mac, "you go across and begin tumbling in
front of him. Keep turning head-over-heels until I tell you to stop.

Mind you 'tract his attention, and after a bit, ask him to shy you a copper. Don't take 'No' for a hanser, but go on till he turns reg'lar crusty, or I beckons to you to leave off."

Froggy, who had promised on Sunday, you know, to obey Mac without asking questions, went across and did exactly what Mac had told him. He began turning somersaults in the muddy road right in front of the old gentleman Mac had pointed out. He was a very kind, benevolent-looking old gentleman, taking care of several children, who, when Froggy commenced his performances, called out gleefully –

"Look, grandpa, dear! look at that funny little boy. Won't he get splashed in the mud, and won't he get giddy turning over like that?"

"I should think his mother will give him a thrashing when he gets home," said the grandpapa, "for getting his clothes so dirty."

"Please, grandpa, dear! throw him a penny," said one of the little children, "because I think he's doing it for us."

The grandpapa began fumbling at once, first in one pocket and then in another, for some halfpence he knew he had, and at last flung a penny into the road to Froggy. Froggy was just in the act of picking it up, when he was surprised by feeling a very heavy hand laid on his shoulder, and looking up, he saw a tall policeman regarding him sternly over his stiff collar.

"What is it, sir, please?" asked Froggy, very much frightened, for he had never been taken hold of by a policeman in this way before.

"I can't allow you to be doing this here," said the policeman; "you must move on. You are out along with some others, aren't you?"

"Yes, sir," answered Froggy truthfully at once, "I'm out along with that chap there!" pointing to Mac, who a minute before had been dodging mysteriously behind the old gentleman, but who was now standing at a short distance from him, looking moodily out to the left, as if he were out on no particular business whatever.

"Ah! I thought so!" said the policeman. "*I*'ll keep my eye on you, you young rascals you!" and giving Froggy an admonishing shake and a push forward, he released him, and went across the road to assist at a cab accident which had just occurred.

Figure 4 ' "Well, now," said Mac, "you go across and begin tumbling in front of him. Keep turning head-over-heels until I tell you to stop." '

Froggy's Little Brother, 1875. Cas. London: John F. Shaw.

Then Froggy saw Mac beckon to him, and immediately after Chickabiddy and Dandy, whom Froggy had not seen for some time, came up and joined Mac, and together with him began interrogating Froggy strictly as to what the policeman had said to him.

"He asked me if I was out along with other chaps," said Froggy.

"And what did you say?" asked Dandy quickly.

"Yes, I said I was with him," replied Froggy, pointing to Mac.

"You *was* a flat!" said Chickabiddy, with his old man's face looking wrathfully contemptuous.[37]

"Yes, that you was!" said Mac. "Now, just recollect this: if a policeman asks you again, you are to say, 'No, you're not out with nobody;' do you hear?"

"Yes," said Froggy; but the moment he had said "Yes," he was very sorry, for it was consenting to an untruth; and Froggy was, of all things, a truthful boy. Before he had time to recall it, Dandy said –

"Well, let's come on now as we're spotted. We'd better go to old Solomon's, and have somethink to drink."[38]

Chickabiddy and Mac seemed quite to agree, and without more talking they all walked briskly off, and went down a side street, which led to a dingy quarter, where there were old tumbledown shops, and not many people about. When they were well out of the crowd, Froggy saw Chickabiddy sidle close up to Mac, and open his hand just wide enough to let him see that in the palm lay a large silver watch.

"What a lovely!" exclaimed Mac.

"Solomon'll give you a lot for that," said Dandy. "Now, Mac, what 'ave you got?"

"I'm down in my luck to-day," said Mac; "I've only got two o' these," showing the corner of a very voluminous white pocket-handkerchief.

Froggy wondered to himself very much how they had got these things, and was just on the point of asking, when they stopped at the door of a dingy little shop, over which hung three golden balls, which Froggy knew to be the pawnbroker's sign. And into this shop they all went one after another, telling Froggy he was to remain outside. Froggy could see through the open door that the shop was full of old clothes, and that there was a very old man, with a hooked nose and a hump on his back, sitting behind the counter, who was evidently that "old Solomon" whom Dandy had spoken about, for he heard Chickabiddy say as he entered, "How do, old Sol?" There appeared to be a great talking and bargaining for a few minutes, then they issued forth again into the street in very high spirits.

"Sol's behaved like a reg'lar trump this time," remarked Dandy to his friends, chinking some money in his right hand.

"Now for something to drink!" said Chickabiddy gaily.

"Here, Frog!" said Mac, handing him two shillings, "'ere's a couple o' bob for you! What do you say to that, young 'un? ain't that rather better than sweeping a crossin, eh?"

"I dunno," said Froggy rather bluntly; then, looking straight up into Mac's face, he asked, "Where did you and your mates get them things from, Mac?"

"Didn't I tell you you was to ask no questions?" returned Mac severely. "Take your couple o' bob and be thankful!"

"We picks 'em up as we goes along," said Chickabiddy with a chuckle; and then they crossed the road, and went into a public-house, where they refreshed themselves with great tankards of beer and sausage rolls. They all drank and ate, except Froggy, who said he didn't want any – he'd rather keep his money.

"Oh, I knows why that is," said Mac. "You're thinking of the little chap at home, and buyin' coals and food, and that like. But you shall 'ave another two bob before the day is over, bless you! Come, have some beer!"

"No, I don't wants it," said Froggy resolutely, and he kept true to his resolution.

Froggy was very hungry and very thirsty, and the sight of the beer and refreshment was very tempting to him, but there was an extremely uneasy feeling in Froggy's mind that his companions had not come by their gains lawfully, and that he ought not to keep the money Mac had given him. At any rate, he made up his mind not to spend any of it at present. He would keep his eyes open very sharply for the rest of the day, and try to discover, if he could, how Mac really did become possessed of such very large white silk pocket-handkerchiefs; for he was not quite so simple as to believe entirely Chickabiddy's statement, "that they picked them up as they went along." Putting two and two together, he became more than ever convinced that his suspicions were correct, for if Mac and the others had been honest, why should the policeman have said, "Ah! he'd keep his eye on them all!" and why should Mac have objected to his telling the policeman the truth?

After their refreshment, the boys walked much farther afield, and did not stop again till they got into the crowd waiting about the entrance of Victoria Park. Then they pulled up, and dispersed as they had done before, and Mac told Froggy to begin tumbling in the mud, and asking certain people whom he pointed out to Froggy "to shy him coppers!"

Froggy had scarcely begun, when there was a great flutter and movement in the crowd, everybody pressing closer to the kerb, and showing great excitement, for in the distance they could hear the people cheering, and it was evident now that the Queen was approaching! The police woke to greater activity, hustling every kind of obstruction out of the roadway, and making short work of anybody or anything which showed signs of resistance. One policeman collared Froggy, and sent him reeling on to the pavement, and it was some minutes before he regained his breath, and recovered the shaking. When he looked up rather disturbed and red in the face, he saw Mac not far off, and Mac was looking at him and laughing as much as to say, "Didn't you get a shaking that time, old fellow?"

A few minutes passed, and then the moment of excitement arrived. The sun shone out, some outriders in scarlet appeared, and then came the royal carriage, containing the Queen and the Princess Beatrice, who were smiling graciously, and bowing right and left to the crowd, in acknowledgment of the hearty salutations which greeted them. The women waved their hands, the men cheered lustily, and the children roared "Hip, hip, hooray!" till they were hoarse. Froggy had a capital view, and hoorayed at the top of his voice with the rest. He wondered where Benny was, and hoped he was seeing well too!

As soon as the Queen had passed, there was great confusion in the crowd; some people rushing to keep up with the royal carriage, others rushing off homewards now the sight was over in a contrary direction, and there were a great many old people turning about with a dazed look, as if the noise and rush had bewildered them, and they did not know exactly where they were going, or what was the next thing to be done. These of course got into the way of everybody, who had any fixed plans of action, and so everybody seemed to think it fair to give them a push, and send them on a fewsteps, whether they liked it or not.

Froggy especially noticed one old gentleman, who was moving about in this undecided sort of way, and who was getting a good deal hustled by his more strong-minded neighbours. Watching him, Froggy became aware that Mac was watching the old gentleman too. Mac seemed to be hovering at the back of him, and so were Chickabiddy and Dandy in front. Why were they all looking so keen and mysterious? What were they after? thought Froggy. He determined now to keep his eye on them and find out. Presently Froggy saw Chickabiddy go up and ask the old gentleman the time, which seemed to startle the old gentleman, and flurry him very much. While he was fumbling and diving for his watch, which lived deep down in a waistcoat pocket, Froggy observed Mac steal quietly up at the back, and sheltered by Dandy on one side, deliberately put his hand in the old gentleman's pocket, and draw out his yellow silk handkerchief! There! Froggy saw it all now – he saw what Chickabiddy and Dandy and Mac were; they were *thieves*! He had suspected it, and now he knew it. Oh, how hot and ashamed and degraded poor Froggy felt! he wished a thousand times he had never come out with Mac; he wished he had stayed at his crossing or stayed in the garret with Benny; anything would have been better than this! What would the gentleman think who had taught him at the night-school if he could know he had been the companion of thieves and pickpockets all day! and oh! what would father and mother think if they were looking down at him from their home in heaven! This thought filled Froggy's eyes with tears, and a great sorrow came into his heart; a longing to be dead, and to be with them, out of the sin and misery and temptation of this world, in that other one, where there is no struggling for daily bread, and where nobody has to pay for their lodging!

Froggy was feeling something of that craving for deep rest, which is natural for old men and old women to feel after they have been tossing on the waves of this troublesome world for a lifetime, but which is very sad to see in a child. Froggy was but eleven, and he should not have been feeling like an old tired man; at this rate, what would his heart be like at forty? London has nothing more sorrowful to show us, I think, amongst all its sorrowful sights, than its old children, with their shrewd, anxious faces, and knitted brows, on which hard Care is stamped, instead of the glad expectancy and joyous carelessness which we generally associate with childhood.

Immediately after securing the old gentleman's pocket-handkerchief, Mac and his companions walked off, and for a moment or two Froggy lost sight of them in the crowd. He had the two shillings still in his pocket, which Mac had given him after their visit to the pawnbroker's, and now he knew he ought to go to Mac, and give them back to him. They were *stolen* shillings, and knowing them to be stolen, would he not be quite as guilty of theft as Mac if he kept them? Froggy knew, of course, that he would be, and though the temptation was strong to keep them, *very* strong when he thought of Benny's white face and the empty garret at home, he resisted it, and determined to follow Mac, and return them to him at once.

He soon caught sight of Mac's yellow head bobbing in and out amongst the people a little distance in front of him, and he could see that Chickabiddy and Dandy were with him too. Froggy began to run, and got up with them just in time to see them all tumble into a public-house together, at the corner of the street. As the great door swung to in his face, poor Froggy, with a very heavy heart, took up his position outside to wait for them till they came out. Presently Dandy appeared looking rather weak about the knees, and extremely vacant, then Chickabiddy and Mac, looking quite as weak, but more cheerful.

"Lawksh!" cried Chickabiddy, when he saw Froggy. "'Ere's the frog run up!"

"Mac," said Froggy going up to him, "here's your two bob back again – I don't wants 'em."

Mac gazed at him with a stupid grin, and seemed not to understand what he said.

"Mac," repeated Froggy louder, thrusting the money into his hand, "take your two bob back again, I say. I'd rather starve than steal, and I know you've stole 'em! You're all of you *thiefs*, and I don't wants to speak to you again!"

Their understandings were all more or less clouded by drink, but they understood Froggy's words pretty well, and saw by his manner, and the set of his little shoulders, that he was saying things the reverse of complimentary to them.

They were just in the condition to enjoy a scrimmage of any kind, and so they closed round Froggy, and began knocking him about as hard as they could, waxing warmer as their blows became harder. Froggy was a plucky little fellow, and struck out gallantly with arms and legs, back and front and to the sides of him (for he was attacked by his cowardly assailants at all points), and at last succeeded in giving Dandy a tremendous black eye, and to the other two such kicks and blows, as to disable them for a moment, and then Froggy thought he would make his escape before they could renew their attack. He could not afford to fight longer, because his jacket was getting torn to pieces, being ragged already, and then he had not the strength for it either, for he had had no beer and sausage-rolls to sustain him as his antagonists had had, and he was feeling faint for want of food. So, having shaken himself free, he marched on down the street, taking very long, independent strides, and not once looking back, though he knew Mac and the others were trying to follow him. But they were all too hopelessly the worse for drinking to make much way, and in a few minutes Froggy had left them far behind, reeling and staggering amongst the crowd.

Froggy never forgot his little brother by any chance, and he began to think what he should take home to Benny for his supper. He had, alas! only one penny to spend, but that would buy something. After much consideration he decided upon buying two meat-pies which he saw in a cook-shop, marked a halfpenny each, because they were stale. Benny would not mind their being stale, and the two would make him quite a sumptuous meal; and Froggy thought perhaps he himself might take just a quarter of one, as he was so hungry! But he wouldn't take more – of that he was determined. It was quite a "catch," in Froggy's opinion, to have got these pies, and he pursued his way homewards for some time after, with a much lighter heart.

By and by a strange sensation crept over Froggy – an overpowering feeling of faintness, and the cabs and omnibuses in the road, and the people all about him, seemed to him to be whirling round

Figure 5 'He dreamed he was in his little night-shirt sitting on his mother's knee.'

Froggy's Little Brother, 1875. Cas. London: John F. Shaw.

and round. He made his way to a doorstep, where he sat down to recover himself, and there, poor little weary fellow! he fell fast asleep, and dreamed that he was a little boy again (for he thought he was an old man now) taken care of by his mother and father, as he used to be when they had the Punch and Judy show, and Benny was a baby. He dreamed he was in his little night-shirt sitting on his mother's knee, and she was rocking him to sleep with her arms round him, and singing to him a soft lullaby, as she used often to do, after they had had a long day out at the West End, and Froggy had been a good boy, and "walked out brave!" Oh! for those blessed, happy days, when mother used to sing to him lullabies! – Froggy woke up with a little sob, because he knew it was all a dream, and, opening his eyes wide, he saw the streets were now dark. The lamps were all lit, and the gas was flaring in the butchers' and green-grocers' shops. "It must be evening, and Benny must have gone home some time!" he thought. Jumping up from the doorstep with an overtaken look, he made his way hurriedly through the busy streets, never once stopping till he reached the blackened house in Shoreditch, which was his home.

* * *

CHAPTER VII.
FROGGY WRITES TO THE QUEEN.

WHILE Froggy was on the doorstep, Benny was at home, seated on the topmost step of the stairs just outside the garret, waiting for Froggy. His little heart was full of eager expectation at his coming, because he imagined such great things would result from this long day out with Mac. He was depending upon a fire for one thing to warm his poor little body by, and perhaps something hot for supper as soon as Froggy came home, and perhaps Froggy might bring money in his pocket as well to pay for some candles, and some wood, and some oatmeal, and all the other things they were so much in need of. While he was sitting there alone in the dark, the woman who lodged below came out on to the landing to fetch some wood in, and turning her head upwards, perceived by the light of her candle, that there was something seated at the top of the stairs. She paused for a moment and then called out –

"Is that you, Benny, up there, or the cat?"

Benny thought he would pretend to be the cat, so he answered demurely –

"Me-yow! me-yow!"

"Oh, you little rascal you!" called back the downstairs lodger good-temperedly. "You can't do me like that – I know its *Benny*! – Why, isn't your brother come back yet, Benny?"

"No," said Benny, patiently. "But I'm sure he won't be long now. I specs to hear 'im open the door every minute."

"Haven't you got a bit o' candle to light up with?" said the woman.

"No – we's quite out o' lights," answered the little voice from the darkness, then hopefully, "but Froggy'll bring some when he comes."

Mrs Blunt, for that was the lodger's name, disappeared into her room for a minute, and then came out again with half a rushlight, and a match in her hand, which she held out to Benny.

"There! that'll last till you go to bed," she said.

"Thank you, mum," said little Benny, sliding cautiously down the steep steps to take the gift, and then quickly mounting again to resume his seat on the top of the stairs. He was very much surprised, and very pleased, for Mrs Blunt was not in the habit of giving them things. She had a hard struggle to get on herself, with half-a-dozen children about her, and a drunken husband to boot. She went out as charwoman during the day, and took in washing as well when she could get it; yet with all her exertions, she could barely pay her rent. She was always behindhand with it, and was being constantly threatened with a visit from the brokers, by the unmerciful landlady, Mrs Ragbon. So she had it not in her power to be very generous to the two little boys above her, though she felt very kindly towards them. She knew they suffered bitterly, like all the rest of that unhappy household, and they had no mother to teach them what was right, and what was wrong, and yet they were so honest! She had never missed a bundle of wood during the whole winter, though the temptation to steal a few sticks must have been often great, for the poor charwoman kept her little store just outside the door in a small heap, in full view of their eyes, whenever they passed up or down.

Benny thought he wouldn't light up till Froggy came, "cos maybe the light mayn't last us till we gets to bed," said he to his prudent little self, as he sat there all in the dark again after Mrs Blunt had gone into her room, and shut the door.

"I wish we was like the cats, I does, cos they sees in the dark, and they don't want no candles, nor clothes neither, cos they're born with nice little fur trousers on their legs, and warm little coats on their backs, what never gets torn, and they don't 'ave to pay no rent like Froggy and me does. I wish I was a cat! I wonder if Froggy 'ud like to be a cat too. I think I'd have my tail cut off, then nobody could pull it, I'd never go after the mouses, and I'd never, oh I'd never if I was a cat, go into anybody's room and take the meat, like Mr Tom did to we, when Froggy and me was savin' a nice little bit for supper. That was so mean of Tom, so sly! I haven't give him a beating for it, cos Froggy said I wasn't, but I sure he specs one."

Benny left off thinking about cats now, for he heard the street door go, and he made up his mind it was Froggy come at last! He jumped up from his perch at once, and ran into the damp dark garret, where he struck the match, and set it to the rush-light, which cast a feeble gleam down the ricketty stairs, up which Froggy was slowly labouring.

"He's comin' very slow!" thought Benny, with his little heart quite beating with happy excitement; "but maybe he's weighed down wid all the coals and meat and things, and can't get up quick!"

Another moment, and Froggy appeared. At the very first sight of him all the joy fled out of Benny's heart! What was the meaning of his torn jacket, and his pale dejected face, which looked like that of a suffering old man when the yellow gleam of the rushlight fell upon it! Benny eyed him gravely for one moment, and then said anxiously –

"Froggy, darlin', you've not never bin fightin', has you?"

"Yes, I has," said Froggy mournfully. "I've had a reg'lar big fight with Mac, and two other chaps;" and then he sat down on the mattress, and Benny could see that large tears were trickling down his cheeks, which greatly distressed Benny, because Froggy so seldom cried, and he knew he must be very unhappy to do so.

"Don't cry, Froggy," said little Benny comfortingly, making a very funny face as he spoke, with his nose and eyes and mouth all working at different angles in the effort to keep back his own tears, which were rising in sympathy with Froggy's;"I's *so* sorry! Hasn't the day bin good, Froggy? didn't you tumble to please Mac? what made 'im fight you, and them others – eh, Froggy?"

"Cos I wouldn't *thieve* like they!" answered Froggy scornfully. "Mac and his mates they're pickpockets. I found that out, and cos I wouldn't touch none o' their money, they began cuffin me about, and then my monkey got up, and we fought, and they've tore my jacket between 'em!" looking ruefully over his shoulder, where his little shirt was bulging from a great rent in his jacket.

"Poor Froggy!" said Benny in profound pity; "you shall have *my* coat, Froggy – the coat what's in the box. It's too long and too big for me, ain't it? Don't you know you always says I looks like a little old man Punch in it?" and he laughed out, in the hope of cheering Froggy into a laugh too; but Froggy was far too sad to laugh even a little to-night.

"I'm not cast down cos o' my jacket," he said, looking out into the dreary garret with wide-opened anxious eyes. "I'm thinkin as how I can't get food for you, Benny, and we shall have to go into the House."[39]

He covered his face with his hands, and Benny knew he was shedding bitter tears. Benny gulped down a sob himself at the thought of going to that terrible place, the workhouse, of which he had always heard the neighbours speak with such horror and dread, as if being driven to "the House" would be the very last sorrow and degradation they could know in their poor lives.

"There's nobody what'll help us – we've got no friends," said Froggy. "We may starve up here, and nobody'll care!"

"Oh yes, Froggy, darlin' – Gentle Jesus will care," said Benny. "I know He will, and He'll never let us starve if we ask Him. Don't you 'member, Froggy, about the little sparrows in the Bible? how God takes care of 'em, cos they can't take care o' themselves, and maybe He'll take care o' we!"

"Yes," said Froggy, beginning to dry up his tears at the thought of that Father in heaven, who clothes the lilies of the field, and who will not let even a little sparrow fall to the ground without Him. "Mother used to say that to father often when times was bad, and he talked o''the House,' and they was never driv to go there after all, never! God always took care of 'em."

Froggy was evidently comforted, and gaining heart again.

"I got you two pies," said Froggy, bringing them forth, and giving them to his little brother.

"I couldn't eat *both*," said Benny, nodding his head; "deed I couldn't;" and he was so determined upon taking only one, that Froggy was forced to take the other.

Benny sat himself down on the floor close to Froggy, and for a few minutes they were silently engaged over their pies, as if satisfying such hunger as theirs was a very serious matter indeed.

"Did you see the Queen?" asked Benny when he had finished his pie and fed his mouse.

"Oh yes," said Froggy, "and the Princess, and the h'outriders in red, and everythink. Did you get a good sight out along with Jack?"

"I didn't go," said Benny, "Jack wouldn't take me; he said I must be like the little pig what didn't go to market, but stayed at home, and cried out wee! wee! wee! What is the Queen like, Froggy?"

"Oh such a kind-looking lady," said Froggy, "not a bit grand like, nor stuck up, but quite smiling and haffable, as if she war quite pleased to come, and 'ave a look at us. Oh my! how the people did ip! ip! ooray her!"

"Did she wear a crown on her head?" asked Benny.

"No – she wore a black bonnet, something like the ladies wears in church Sundays," said Froggy. "And, lor', she did look kind in it! A sort of a lady that with all the hearls, and lords, and dooks about 'er, wouldn't be too mighty to think of little chaps like we, if she knowed we was hungry and put to it!"

"O Froggy!" cried Benny, his face lighting up with a sudden inspiration. "Can't we write to the Queen, and tell 'er all about it?"

He waited breathless for one moment to see what Froggy would say.

"I wonder if the postman ud take it," said Froggy, ponderingly, and colouring up a little at the audacity of the plan.

"Oh yes, if we was to wrap it up neat, and put Bucknam Palace on the outside, and wrote it was for the Queen, and slipped it in the box, it ud sure to go," said Benny, as if there couldn't be a doubt about it.[40]

"Then we'll write afore ever we goes to bed," said Froggy. "It's a good job I went to night-school and learnt how to write, ain't it?"

Benny's face clouded over for a moment, as if he had thought of some great obstacle.

"But, Froggy," he said, "whatever are we to do for paper and the hink?"

"Oh, I knows," said Froggy; and he crossed the garret to a dark corner, where there was a small square box standing, which had belonged to Froggy's father and mother. He untied the string which fastened it, and opening the lid, told Benny to bring the light, because he was going to hunt for something. He dived right to the bottom, and brought up a little blue bottle, in which there was some dried ink, then he found an old steel pen, and lastly between the leaves of his mother's Bible (which he used to read to Benny on Sundays) a sheet of white paper and an envelope which had grown yellow from long keeping.

"There! we've got everythink" said Froggy, shutting down the box, and making it fast again. "A drop of water to the ink is all we wants now."

The drop of water was soon got, and in a few minutes the little brothers were seated over the rushlight in the middle of the garret, with their heads close together, and their minds wholly engrossed, writing their letter to the Queen.

There were many difficulties at starting; first to know how it would be proper to address her Majesty, Froggy being dreadfully afraid of being "too famillar." Then there were words to spell, which puzzled Froggy greatly, his learning having become a little rusty, since he no longer went to the night-school, and he had great trouble in forming some of the letters. But each difficulty was overcome in its turn, and at last, after much toil and perseverance, the following letter was written. It began –

LADY QUEEN, – We are two little brothers what lives in Shoreditch. We've got no money, and no friends. We lives in a garret. Mothers dead, and fathers dead, and Froggy, thats me, doesn't know how to get food for Benny, whos a littler chap, and my brother. Unless it was in the Bible about the little sparrows, we should amost think God was agoin to letus starve. They say you are a kind lady, and you looks kind, cos I seen you in your potograts in the shop-winders, and I sees you to-day agoin to the Park, along with the Princess, a-smilin quite as if you knowed us all, and was a-askin us how we did about coals and vittals and things, now that them things is so dear. Benny and mes quite out of em, and we've got no breakfast to-morrow, nor no money neither, and we're afraid as how we shall have to go into the House, which some folks says is worse than prisons. If you ask Mrs Blunt, she'll tell you it's all true – she's the lodger what lives underneath.

Here the letter ended, because the rushlight began to sputter and to shew signs that it intended to go out shortly, and Froggy had yet to put the letter into the cover, and direct it.

"Do you think, Froggy, the Queen will come herself?" asked Benny.

"No – I think she'll send p'r'aps one o' the footmans," said Froggy, trying to make the cover stick with a very grimy little fist pressed down upon it.

"This hanvelope won't stick, Benny – we shall have to tie it round with a bit o' string. It won't look so well, but that don't matter."

Of course Froggy had string in his pocket; all boys have string about them, whatever else they have not; and from a tangled mass of thick and fine, Froggy selected the finest piece, and tied the letter across and across. Then he wrote in large letters in one corner – "The Queen, Bucknam Palace." And then it was all ready for posting.

The little fellows were quite joyful over it, gazing at it, and turning it about with delicious awe, as a thing that would shortly be handled by royalty!

"I can't wait till morning to post it," declared Froggy, putting on his muddy boots which he had taken off. "You go to bed, Benny, and I'll just nip out and do it."

There was no such thing as locking up for the night in Mrs Ragbon's house; the lodgers came and went at any hour they chose; so Froggy was not afraid of being stopped or questioned. He ran out into the silent dark streets, which now only echoed back the steady tramp of a policeman going his rounds, or the hoarse shout of some drunken man or woman beating the air in imaginary conflict with some one. Froggy found a pillar box before long, and into it he slipped the letter, full of a new and burning hope that good would come of it, as he let the flap fall again with a sharp metallic ring. When he got back, he found the narrow little passage stopped up by Mr Blunt, the charwoman's husband, who had come home in a drunken fit, and was calling down vengeance on the head of his hapless wife, who was trembling upstairs in her night dress. He let Froggy pass with an oath, and Froggy mounting the stairs, said to himself, "If ever I marrys a wife, I'll treat her different to that!"

The garret was quite dark now, the rushlight having subsided after a good deal of sputtering and fuss; but Froggy did not mind getting into bed in the dark, he was so accustomed to it. Little Benny lay in a deep slumber, dreaming impossible dreams of splendid scarlet-coated footmen appearing in the garret, with messages and gifts from the Queen, and a new coat for Froggy, with tails and buttons.

* * *

CHAPTER VIII.
THE POLICEMAN'S VISIT.

EARLY the next morning Froggy rose up full of a new plan for obtaining money, which had come into his head during the night. Lying awake, he had heard little Benny beside him, murmuring unconsciously something about "only a little bit o' bread," which showed Froggy that he must be suffering the pangs of hunger in his sleep, and Froggy determined to get him food somehow. He remembered what father had done on one occasion when he was pressed for money to pay for mother's funeral; he went out and pawned some things, and then when he had had some good days out at the West End with the Punch and Judy show, he had called at the pawnshop again, and redeemed them. Froggy thought he would do the same.

Their stock of worldly goods was very limited, Mrs Ragbon having seized most of them to make up for deficiencies in rent, but there were still a few things remaining, which Froggy could pawn. There was the little mattress on which Froggy used to lie when he was Benny's age, and an old waistcoat of father's, and a fur cap, and some shirts in the old deal box, and something else, wrapped up very carefully in a cotton handkerchief, which was very, very sacred, and over which Froggy sometimes shed a flood of tears. This was mother's Sunday best bonnet; the one she had always worn, and which Froggy cried over, because he said, "It looked so like mother!" It brought back to him with a vivid recollection her dear face as he remembered it on Sunday evenings in the good old lullaby days, when Froggy used to say his prayers at her knee, and tell her all his little troubles. Froggy wouldn't have pawned this for the world; the coat off his own back would have to go before he parted with that, which did the work of the rich boy's photograph for him. It grieved him to part with the other things, but he consoled himself with the thought that it would only, perhaps, be for a few days. As soon as their letter reached the Queen, he was confident help would come, and then he would be able to redeem them.

He told Benny what he was going to do, and bade him lie quiet in bed till he came back. Then he tied the things up into a bundle, and crept forth in the cold, grey morning to seek a shop whose sign was three golden balls. Trudging along Froggy made up his mind to go to old Solomon, where Mac and his wicked companions went yesterday with their stolen goods. He remembered Dandy saying he had behaved "like a reg'lar trump," and Froggy thought himself that the old Jew looked like a kind old man, who would be likely to give him the worth of his things.

Not many people were abroad yet; the dust-carts were going their rounds, and Froggy met some watercress-sellers, and some milkmen, but not many others. There were policemen about, of course, who all seemed to look suspiciously upon Froggy, staggering under the weight of his big bundle. One stopped him at last, and questioned him as to what he had in it, and where he was going.

"Please, sir, h'I'm only going to the pawn-shop," said Froggy, opening his bundle with great alacrity for the inquisitive policeman to peep in.

The policeman thrust his hand down, and satisfied himself I suppose, for after a moment he nodded to Froggy, and let him pass on. Then nobody interfered with him again, till he reached old Solomon. Froggy came out of the shop very much delighted, for the pawnbroker gave him more liberal prices than he had ever expected, enough money indeed to last Benny and himself at least six days if they were careful, and at the end of that time, he was sure they would hear from the Queen, if the letter only reached! He was very hopeful, though not quite so sanguine as little Benny, whom he found on his return keeping watch at the garret window, looking for the postman, in case, as he said, 'de letter was already reached, and de Queen had wrote back quick!' Froggy had laid some of the money out on his way home. He had bought some oatmeal and some bread, and a small supply of charcoal and wood. The little fellows kindled a fire at once, and put some water on to boil, and then Froggy made for himself and Benny a nice large basin of hot porridge, which they shared in common with a wooden spoon. Froggy said they would have some "taters" for dinner, and some more porridge for tea, and altogether they felt quite rich and comfortable in their poor garret to-day. Froggy said he shouldn't go crossing-sweeping any more; he should mend up his jacket, and comb his hair, and make himself look as "spry" as he could, and then to-morrow he would try for a place at the shops as errand-boy.

After their dinner of hot potatoes, Froggy seated himself, tailor-fashion, on the floor before the fire, and with a very grave air, began mending his jacket, which had been torn in the scuffle yesterday. He was very handy with his needle, and could patch and darn almost as neatly as a girl, but he made the mistake which most men and boys make when they work, of taking too long a thread. He sat in his shirt sleeves with his hair over his eyes and his lips pouting a little, drawing the needle out over his shoulder, with such very long thread that each stitch seemed quite a laborious effort. Benny climbed up to the sill of the garret window, and there perched himself for the afternoon. He could talk to Froggy from that position just as well as anywhere else, and he could watch his dear little grey mousie, too, scampering about on the floor picking up the crumbs, and enjoying the new warmth and comfort, which seemed suddenly to have come.

There was a yellow fog rising over London, making everything look hopeless and gloomy outside. The view from the garret window over dingy housetops and blackened chimneys, was dingier and uglier than ever, but Benny seemed not to be happy anywhere away from the window to-day. At every noise in the street, at every new sound that he heard almost, he turned his little white face towards the gloom, and peered out wistfully down into the street below, to see if it were somebody come from the Queen! He quite lost himself in delight now and then picturing what he and Froggy would feel, if a rat-a-tat-tat came at the door, and a scarlet-coated footman did really appear from the Queen, with sacks of coal and beefsteak pies, and money and treacle, and the new-tailed coat for Froggy, and all the other things he had dreamed of in his sleep!

Benny got Froggy by and by to tell him everything about his day yesterday out with Mac. He listened with keen interest to Froggy's description of Chickabiddy and Dandy, with their cunning old men's faces and stunted bodies, and of how they had dodged the policemen, and talked a language of their own, which Froggy knew now was the language of thieves and pickpockets. Froggy was just in the midst of his story, relating how Mac had robbed the old gentleman of his pocket-handkerchief, when suddenly a loud ringing at the street door bell was heard, and Benny called out excitedly –

"Oh, Froggy, Froggy, I *know* it's the Queen! everybody's looking out of dere windows, and the people in the street are all lookin' up at our house! It *must* be the Queen, or one of the footmans, Froggy, or why should they be lookin'?"

Froggy threw down his jacket, and ran to the window, clambering up, without the aid of a chair, to the sill beside Benny.

"My!" cried Froggy, looking out, "there *is* somethink hup, that's sure. Whatever can it be?"

The miserable inhabitants of the squalid houses opposite had thrown open their windows, and were leaning out into the fog; some with shawls over their heads; some with aprons up to their mouths, and a few idle-looking men, less careful than the women, were without their coats, in shirts of a questionable colour. On the pavement underneath, and at the doors and areas, there were more people on the alert, and swarms of dirty little gutter-children, ragged and noisy, were taking their share in the popular excitement, whatever it might be.[41] Quite a buzz of conversation rose from the street, and all the heads and eyes seemed turned in one direction, and to be centred upon one spot, namely, the door of Mrs Ragbon's house! Froggy got very red in the face, and his heart beat almost as fast as Benny's, as he craned his neck, first this way and then that, to get a view down into the street, in high hope, poor little fellow, that if he only stretched his head far enough, he would catch sight of "a grand royal footman," or "a beautifully-dressed gentleman like the West Henders, that would turn out to be one of the Queen's hequerries!"

By and by the sound of angry voices came up from below, and after listening a moment, Froggy and Benny jumped down from the high window-sill, and went out to the stair-head to see what was going on. The house seemed to be in a state of general uproar and commotion. Doors were banging, lodgers were hanging over the banisters, confusion seemed everywhere, and above everything, the crying of the children and the noise in the street, was heard Mrs Ragbon's voice ascending from the cellar regions, indignantly protesting against some treatment she deemed "Very 'arsh," and abusing somebody or some persons in no measured terms. Poor Froggy and Benny stared at each other in amazement.

"I don't think it's the Queen *now*, Froggy, do you?" said Benny, looking woefully troubled and disappointed.

"No, that it ain't," said Froggy. "It's a row o' some kind, but I don't know what it's all about."

At that moment, Mrs Blunt, pale and trembling, with her hands all over soapsuds, came out of her room to look over the banisters.

"Please, mum," called Froggy, "can you tell us what's up?"

"Why, it's the perlice come to search the house," called back the charwoman, in a tone of horror. "It's all along o' that good-for-nothing Mac! There's bin a daring jool robbery in the City, and he's in it, and the perlice thinks as how perhaps he brought some o' the watches and things home here, and that we're hidin' of 'em, and they've come to ferrit them out; they've woke little Deb out of such a nice sleep, and she's so ill, poor lamb!"

"Poor Deb," said Benny, "I's so sorry!"

She was Benny's favourite playmate. Then he turned to Froggy with a new and sudden dread, and whispered –

"O Froggy! you don't think the pleece is comin' to take me and you up, cos we knows Mac, does you?"

"No, don't be afeard," said Froggy; "I guess they won't come nigh us. They'll search the kitchens and that, cos they be Mrs Ragbon's places, and she's Mac's mother, but they won't come troublin' no other parties, I reckons."

But Froggy was quite out in his reckoning this time. It soon became evident that the police intended visiting each apartment in its turn, for after they had searched the lower rooms, they mounted to the higher ones, and, armed with the stern majesty of the law, effected their entrance, and commenced stolidly to perform their duty, unmindful of either remonstrance or abuse. Mrs Ragbon followed them on their tour of inspection, and in each case stood at the door, with face all aflame, and arms folded in an attitude of angry resignation, levelling sarcastic remarks and very unparliamentary language at the policeman, while he overhauledher lodger's goods.[42] She was very indignant at the unenviable distinction she would henceforth enjoy amongst her neighbours, from having had her house visited by the police. Ah! if she had been a good mother, and trained up Mac in the way he should have gone, perhaps there would have been none of this sad business.

Up the policeman came nearer and nearer to the garret. In due time he reached the top landing, and went into the charwoman's room, where little sick Deb set up a feeble wail, and the other children a loud cry at the terrible apparition of "a tall live policeman," who they made up their minds at once "had come to take them and mother off to prison!"

"O Froggy! let's come in, and shut the door," said little Benny, pale with fright; "maybe de pleece will think our door's only a cupboard and won't come up!"

"There's nothink to be afeared on – we've not done nothink wrong," said Froggy, getting very red all the same, when the next minute the policeman's heavy tread was heard outside, ascending the ladder staircase step by step, and Mrs Ragbon's angry tones, informing him "he would find nothing but rats and mice up there."

"P'r'aps, missis, its the kind of rats and mice I want just now," replied the policeman sternly, turning the handle of the door, and breaking in upon the little boys.

Froggy was standing in his shirt sleeves with his face to the door and his hands thrust deep in his pockets, looking rather hot and defiant, as if he were prepared to do battle if he were falsely accused of anything, and little Benny was clinging to him with a white scared face, determined to hang on to Froggy to the very last, and go with him to prison, if the policeman had come to take him.

"Oh, you boys needn't take on – its the way we've *hall* bin treated!" exclaimed Mrs Ragbon angrily, more for the sake of talking at the policeman than from any benevolent idea of calming their fears. "He's paid us hall a visit, quite impartial, because he don't like to make anybody jealous, and now he's come to pay a visit to the rats and mice, wishing to do the civil heverywhere, polite man!"

The policeman took no notice of the landlady, but went straight to the little bed on which Froggy and Benny slept, and began examining it closely.

"Is he goin' to take our bed away, Froggy?" whispered little Benny to Froggy, who was watching the policeman's movements with a sort of scornful anger on his face.

"No, no; I'm not going to take away your bed," said the policeman reassuringly.

"I should think not, indeed!" burst forth Mrs Ragbon again. "Honester boys you wouldn't find than these two – they're as honest as yourself I daresay Mr B 59!"[43]

"Yes, missis, no doubt," returned the policeman, with a slight smile on his grim features.

"I'm sure I don't know which I likes the best – the priests or the perlice," continued the landlady, with a toss of her head; "they both begins with ps, and ones just as great a noosance as t'other, in my opinion. One o' the black-coated gentry comes yesterday a knockin' at the door, disturbin' me and a friend at a winkle[44] tea, but I soon sent him off with some words he won't forget in a hurry!"

Thus did Mrs Ragbon speak of one of those holy men, who spend their lives in knocking at the doors of the poor, with the message of the gospel on their lips, entreating them to listen to the consolations of the Tender Shepherd, in obedience to whose command, 'Feed my lambs,' they come (all honour to them!) in spite of rebuffs and discouragements and rudeness, such as Mrs

Ragbon meted out to them. Well may we pray in Dr Monsell's beautiful words –

> "O Saviour! when on life's dark main
> The gospel net seems cast in vain,
> When through the long and cheerless night
> No souls the fishers' toils requite –
> Give them the grace content to be,
> With this one thought – They toil for Thee!"[45]

"Well, now, it's no good making a noise, missis," said the policeman quietly. "I must obey my orders. Your son belongs to a notorious gang of thieves" –

"He do not!" barked Mrs Ragbon.

"Well, p'r'aps we happen to know more about him than you do; at all events, he's wanted now," said Police-constable 59 B; "and my instructions are to search this house from garret to cellar. A bundle was seen to leave your premises this morning, missis, and you are the boy who carried it," he said, turning to Froggy, and eyeing him sharply.

"Yes, sir, I be," answered Froggy, speaking up at once and returning the policeman's glance boldly in the might of conscious innocence. "They was all my things and Benny's, sir. I took 'em to the pawnshop – old Solomon's in L – – Street."

The policeman jotted down this piece of information in a pocket-book.

"Well, and what was in the bundle?" he asked.

"Well, sir," said Froggy considering, "there was Benny's great coat, and a fur cap of father's, and a mattress as I laid on when I was a young 'un, and a waistcoat and two shirts – that was them."

The policeman asked him a few more questions, the ready answers to which he committed to the pocket-book, and then he turned his attention to the old deal box, where mother's bonnet and Bible were the only things left now.

"Please, sir," said Froggy, as the policeman took it up, "lay hold on that gentle – its mother's bonnet sir, her Sunday best, and she's dead."

"It's rather sensibler than the bonnets they wears now-a-days," remarked the policeman to himself, as he shut down the box again, and rose to his feet.

"Well, now, having discoursed upon the fashions have you about done?" inquired Mrs Ragbon, in an impudent tone. "P'r'aps as you're such a man for doing your dooty, you had better take a look into the kettle before you leaves."

The policeman appeared not to think this necessary, and having finished his examination of thegarret, walked to the door. Just before leaving he turned his head round, and remarked, nodding at Froggy and Benny, "Those boys, missis, look half-starved. They'd be better in 'the House', I suspects."

"Now, just mind your own business, if you please. I know very well where *you'd* best be, Mr Policeman!" snapped the landlady, as she slammed the door behind her, and followed him downstairs.

The moment the policeman's back was turned, Benny recovered his speech.

"Ah! Froggy," he said, "the policeman didn't know we've wrote to the Queen, when he said that about 'the House,' did he, or he wouldn't a said it. O Froggy! I was just frightened when he come!"

"Was you?" said Froggy.

"Yes, and *you* was a little bit frightened too, now wasn't you, Froggy, just a little at first?" said Benny, trying to coax the admission out of his brother. "Cos your face got so red!"

"Well, I didn't much like it, no more I did," replied Froggy, beginning upon his jacket again, and drawing out a very long thread over his shoulder. "Cos I remembered what father used to say – that folks often gets into trouble by going along with other folks that doesn't do right."

"Poor Mac! I'm so sorry he's got into tubble," said Benny. "Do you think he's in prison, Froggy?"

"No, I don't think the p'lice has caught him yet," answered Froggy. "He'll give 'em a lot of trouble. He's so quick and sly."

"Shan't we pray to God not to let Mac be caught?" said Benny.

"Well, I don't know whether that ud be right to pray," answered Froggy, gravely; "God says 'Thou shalt not steal,' and Mac has stole, and God likes people to be punished when they does wrong, or He'd have to punish 'em when they dies!"

"Then we'll pray God to make Mac good, and never to steal no more," said Benny, after a minute. "That'll be better, won't it, Froggy? And we'll ask Jesus to make little Deb well too."

"Yes," said Froggy, "that'll be best."

It was too foggy now to watch at the window any more, and Froggy had finished mending his jacket, so he put the kettle on to boil, and he and Benny had their tea.

* * *

CHAPTER IX.
BENNY LOSES HIS PLAYMATES.

SEVERAL days passed – cold, miserable, foggy days, in the which Froggy trudged from shop to shop all about great crowded London, trying to get a job, but never getting one, and little Benny kept watch at the garret window with untiring zeal for the scarlet-coated footman who never came. Every day his heart throbbed quicker at the sound of a man's heavy footstep coming up the stair, but every day he was disappointed, for it turned out to be only the parish doctor come to see little Deb Blunt underneath.

The stock of money was getting very low, and things began to look even darker than before, for unless Froggy got a job soon, or they heard from the Queen, they would be without food and fuel again, and this time without anything in the old deal box to pawn. What but starvation or the workhouse stared these poor little boys in the face! Yet their courage never forsook them. Had not God said *that* in the Bible about the little sparrows? and had not God always taken care of father and mother, and tided them over many bitter troubles, and kept them from the workhouse? They were continually reminding each other of this.

"We dwells very high, you know, Froggy," said Benny once, gazing out of the window over the forest of smoky chimneys, "quite up in the roof, and none of the people in the world seems to 'member you and me's here, but *God* doesn't forget us for that, cos the little sparrows build their nests ever so high in trees and chimleys, and yet God keeps His hi on all of them."

In these days Benny had no one to play with except his mouse. Jack went with older boys, and did not seem to care for playing with Benny any more, and little Deb was too sick to crawl even about the room. Benny missed Deb as a playmate more than he did Jack. When they played at horses she never minded being the horse; when they went to the rubbish heap together, she was always content to hold her pinafore up for Benny to fill, and when a barrel-organ set up in the street, and the little dirty gutter children, God bless them! responded to its music and joined hands and danced, Deb was always Benny's partner. She was a year older than Benny, but because Benny was a boy, she gave up to him in everything, and consequently Benny thought there was no one, in the absence of Froggy, so nice and so desirable as little Deb for a playfellow.

One afternoon Benny got very dull, and longed for a game at horses with somebody. Froggy was out, and it was raining heavily, and Benny did not think there was a chance that the royal footman would come to-day, because of the rain and the mud; so he gave up watching at the window early, and began thinking about this game of horses. What was he to do for a *horse*? He didn't care for driving a chair; he must have something alive, which would prance and run, and attend to the rein and the whip when he slashed it.

While Benny was busy tying some more knots in his whip and getting the reins ready, he heard the cat "me-yowing" outside, and it occurred to Benny that perhaps Mr Tom was dull like himself this rainy afternoon, and wouldn't mind being his horse just for once. He saw a boy driving a dog in the street, the other day, why shouldn't a cat be driven as well?[46] If Froggy had been at home, he would have told Benny he must not do it, because it would probably teaze the cat. One of the earliest lessons he had learnt from his mother, was one which all little boys and girls should take well to heart, namely, that it is of all things cruel and unkind to do anything that can possibly hurt or teaze dumb animals.

Benny opened the door, and called out in a high tone of encouragement, "Tom! Tom! Tom!" and in walked Tom, looking as sleek and almost as large as a young tiger; a very dangerous enemy indeed for any poor little mouse to meet with out walking.

Figure 6 ' "You're the nastiest, disagreeablest cat in London!" cried out Benny. ' (Note: 'cried out Benny' was deleted in later editions.)
Froggy's Little Brother. 1875. Cas. London: John F. Shaw.

Tom was quite the best-fed inhabitant of the house, inasmuch as it swarmed with rats and mice, his own particular food, which no one cared to contest with him. Benny knelt down, and began harnessing him, hissing away as if he were a groom, and saying gruffly, "Wo, Tommy – wo! Wo-back, Tommy!" just as he heard men in the streets addressing their horses. Tom was passive under it at first, but the moment he found that he was getting fettered in string, and that "*horses*" was to be the game, and he was to be the horse, he just quietly shook himself free, turned tail, and scampered down the stairs as hard as he could. Ah! the cat who stole the meat was far too knowing a hand to get caught in such a one-sided game as that! Benny was left sitting on the floor, with the string in his hand, very indignant and angry at the way in which his steed had given him the slip.

"You're the nastiest, disagreeablest cat in London!" cried out Benny as his tail disappeared round the door, but the cat took no notice and off he scampered.

Left to himself, Benny fell to wondering how long it would be before little Deb would be able to play at horses again. He remembered he had not heard her cry since daybreak, and the parish doctor hadn't been to-day, so Benny thought she must be better, but he was puzzled to know why there was such a deep, strange hush over the house, and why the neighbours kept going in and out of Mrs Blunt's room underneath, softly by turns as if there were something to see. Benny got restless and curious, and wished he could see some one to ask how Deb was. Presently he heard subdued voices on the landing below, and going out to the stairhead, he saw Mrs Blunt receiving into her apron a loaf of bread and some sticks, which a neighbour had been to fetch for her.

"Mrs Blunt," called out Benny, "how soon'll Deb be able to play at horses again?"

"O Benny!" answered back the poor mother with streaming eyes, "you'll never no more have Deb to play with, nor dance to the organs! She's gone, Benny – she went this morning, poor lamb, afore ever any of us was up."

Benny at first only dimly guessed at the meaning of those words, but gradually as he pondered over them, the bosom of his little ragged jacket began to heave up and down, he threw his whip aside, and covered his eyes with his hands. By this time all his desire for a game at "horses" had flown away. If little Deb were dead, then would he not care ever again to play at horses, or dance to the organs. "Poor Deb," he kept saying when he thought of her, "dear little darlin Deb, that I did love so much!"

He sat on the top of the stairs, crying his baby heart out for some minutes; the rain only keeping him company as it pattered down drearily on the glass skylight above him. Presently Mrs Blunt came to the foot of the stairs, and said –

"Benny, dear! would you like to see Deb in her coffin?"[47]

Benny sobbed "Yes," and with a tiny fist in each eye began slowly to descend step by step, till he reached Mrs Blunt, who took him up in her arms as if he were a very light weight, and carried him into her one poor room, where the dead child lay. The room was profoundly still, though it was full of people. There were all Deb's brothers and sisters, huddled up together and speaking in whispers, as if something very strange and terrible had happened. There was Mr Blunt sitting over the handful of fire, with an empty gin bottle at his elbow, in a state of maudlin sorrow; and there were two or three poorly-clad, dejected-looking women in one corner, gazing intently upon the small body which lay in its coffin, unspeakably still and waxen white, ready for burial the next morning. How calm and peaceful little Deb looked! – all the suffering gone out of her old woman's face, all her cries hushed, all the wrinkles smoothed away, as if for her

> "Morning's joy had ended the night of weeping,
> And life's long shadows had broken in cloudless love!"[48]

Happy little Deb! who need have wept for her? Yet the poor mother wept sorely afresh as she stood, with Benny in her arms, beside the coffin.

"Oh, my dear, I wouldn't fret about it overmuch if I was you," said one poor woman, who looked as if she had found the waves of this world very troublesome. "Life's a sad business, take it altogether from cradle to grave, and its worse I ses for women than for men. We don't likes to lose 'em when we've got 'em; no more we does, bless their innocent hearts, but depend upon it children's best out of it all!"

"Yes, that they be," said an older neighbour mournfully. "Robert and me, we've had seven, and we've buried 'em all, and we thank the Lord for it now, though we grieved terrible at first!"

"I shall have to go to work after to-morrow," said the bereaved mother, who would not have called her child back again if she could; she loved it too well for that! "But I must have my cry to-day," she sobbed.

"Yes – yes, my dear, have your cry to-day," said the neighbours kindly. "It'll do her good, poor thing!"

While the women were talking Benny was gazing wonderingly upon little Deb, and pondering deeply in his baby fashion over the mysterious change which had come, but not shedding many tears. He was thinking of a hymn Froggy had taught him to say on Sundays –

> "Tender Shepherd, Thou hast stilled
> Now Thy little lamb's brief weeping;
> Ah, how peaceful, pale, and mild,
> In its narrow bed 'tis sleeping;
> And no sigh of anguish sore
> Heaves that little bosom more!"[49]

"I sha'n't cry any more, I don't think," whispered Benny at length to Mrs Blunt, drying up the last tear with an end of his tattered jacket, and giving his nose a doleful rub; then laying his little dirty white cheek lovingly against her's, he whispered his sweet conviction, "Cos Deb's gone to Jesus, I's sure, that's why, and she's hearin' music more beautifuller than the organs, and will nebber be cold or have pains again!"

He leant over the coffin and kissed Deb's small, still face, saying hushfully, "O Debbie! goodbye! – goodbye, Debbie!"

Then there was a knock at the door, and some more neighbours came softly in to look at the dead child, and Mrs Blunt gave Benny a crust and told him to go upstairs again.

What do you think had happened in the garret during Benny's absence? Something that almost broke his heart, poor little fellow. He had left the door open, the cat had stolen up, and killed his mouse! Yes, there it lay on the floor, in the midst of the crumbs it had been nibbling, when the treacherous cat had pounced upon it from the back, with its small grey limbs stretched out, its eyes shut, and its tail quite cold and lifeless.

At first Benny would not believe it was dead – he called to it, he stroked it, he kissed it; he called to it again in the frantic hope that it was only asleep; but when at last he found that it responded neither to sound nor caress, but lay cold and dull and limp (so unlike his mousie that used to be so bright and nimble!) Benny threw himself on the floor beside it, and gave himself up to a passion of grief. He was lying there still and crying bitterly when Froggy came home an hour later.

"Why, Benny, Benny darlin', whatever is the matter?" cried out Froggy.

"I've lost my mouse," sobbed Benny. "Oh, I did love that 'ittle mouse so!" regarding his slain pet with the most pitiful streaming eyes.

Froggy looked as if he could have cried too. He came, full of concern, and knelt down beside the mouse, and gently laid his finger for one moment on its little heart, which had ceased to beat some time.

"Yes," said Froggy, with the air of a grave physician, "he be dead, Benny, so he be. Whatever killed him?"

"The cat," sobbed Benny. "I left the – door open when – I went down to see – Deb in her coffin, Froggy, to say goodbye – and he come up, and he did it! And he'd a eat it, too, in another minute if I hadn't come up!"

"Is Deb dead?" asked Froggy, with a blank look of sorrow on his face. "Poor Debbie! When did she die?"

"Dis mornin'," sobbed Benny, "when we was all asleep;" then turning his pitiful eyes towards Froggy he said mournfully, "Everythink seems to die, Froggy – why is it?"

"Cos it's good, I spects," answered Froggy, after he had pondered a moment.

"Why good?" asked Benny.

"Cos it comes from Jesus," said Froggy. "The nurse as was in the 'ospital, time father and me was took there, said as we was always to try and think everythink Jesus did was good, whether He took away things ever so; then He'd never leave us, she said, not never. I often thinks on her words, I do, and I does try."

Benny waited a moment as if he were thinking over what Froggy had said, then he looked up, and asked –

" 'Posin *I* was to die, Froggy, like little Deb and mouse, would you say to Jesus that was good too?"

The question seemed to startle Froggy and greatly to distress him. He gazed at his brother for one moment with a great look of pain, then a flood of tears came, and throwing his arms round Benny's thin, white neck, he hugged him tightly to him, and cried vehemently –

"Oh no, no, no, Benny, I don't think as ever I could say it was good if Jesus was to take *you* away. Don't never talk of dying again, Benny. If you was to die I would die. O Benny, Benny! however could I live here alone?"

"It wouldn't be such a bad thing if God 'ud take us both," said Benny; "but I wouldn't never like to go such a long journey all alone by myself without *you*, Froggy; oh, no!" and he tried to kiss his brother's tears away. "I's not so sorry about little Deb as mouse, Froggy; cos I shall meet Deb again in heaven, if I'm a good little boy, and gets there, but I shan't never meet my mouse any more."

"I'll get you another mouse, Benny," said Froggy, yearning to comfort him.

"I couldn't ever love another," said Benny, nodding his head dolefully. "There'll never be a mouse *quite* like him again, Froggy.

Oh, to think of his bright, merry eyes being shut, and that he'll *never* go into his little hole again!"

This last seemed a heart-breaking reflection. He sobbed afresh, and poor Froggy could in nowise console him.

Benny went to bed quite a heartbroken little boy this evening. He had his dead mouse laid somewhere where he could see it, and he put a little crumb of bread by it the last thing, in the forlorn hope that it might come to life again in the night, and eat it.

* * *

CHAPTER X.
FROGGY CALLS AT BUCKINGHAM PALACE.

THE next morning a tall, cadaverous-looking man, with a pale face and very black whiskers, who Froggy knew was an undertaker, came and carried little Deb away in her coffin. A sad procession started from the back-room, and stumbled down the steep stairs. The poor mother, as chief mourner, followed first, dressed in the black clothes which kind neighbours had lent her for the occasion; then followed all Deb's brothers and sisters, and lastly came Robert's wife, the poor woman who said she had buried seven children, and thanked the Lord for it now! She was going to follow with Mrs Blunt to the cemetery.

As the mournful party passed out at the door, a barrel organ in the street struck up a lively Scotch reel, the very tune to which the dead child being now borne along in her coffin had so often danced with Benny. Froggy and Benny were both at the window, peering down into the street with eager, sorrowful eyes, to catch a glimpse of the funeral.

"O Froggy, Froggy!" cried Benny, bursting into tears, "why does the organ play that, Froggy? It seems to be callin' to her to dance!"

"Don't never cry like that, Benny," entreated Froggy, with his arms about Benny in a moment. "Don't listen to it; it's a hugly organ." Then in a cheerful tone, he said, "Shall I tell you, now, what you and me'll do when winter's gone, and summer's come, and the evenin's is beautiful and light, Benny?"

"Yes," said Benny, nodding his head.

"Well, we'll go to the cimentery, you and me, and we'll visit little Deb's grave," said Froggy; "father and me went once to visit mother's, and oh! it was such a nice place. The birds was singin', and there was trees, and father said it was somethink like country."

"Tell me more about dat place," said Benny.

"There was buttercups and daisies growin'," said Froggy. "The rich people takes flowers and plants them on the graves, but poor people what can't afford flowers picks the buttercups and daisies, and lays 'em on. That's what you and me'll do, Benny; we'll pick a beautiful bunch, and lay it on Deb's grave."

The thought of this summer's evening visit to the cemetery seemed to comfort and soothe Benny, and he dwelt much upon it.

Benny's mouse had not come to life again during the night, and Froggy told Benny they must think about burying it somehow. At first Benny said he couldn't let it be buried, and begged Froggy not to talk about it, but when Froggy said that if Mrs Ragbon came up and saw it, she would very likely throw it into the dust-hole or give it to the cat Benny changed his mind, and became instantly anxious that his mouse should be given decent and honourable burial. So they wrapped its little dead body up in a winding-sheet of rag, and laid it in a coffin, which Froggy made out of an old rushlight box. Then they sallied forth with it to the piece of waste ground, where there was that rubbish-heap, to which Benny had so often gone with Deb, and which seemed such an everlasting joy to the children of the neighbourhood.

I am sure that these poor East End children fancied themselves on a kind of "Tom Tiddler's ground," picking up gold and silver! while they burrowed about amongst the oyster-shells and rubbish, filling their pinafores and baskets with the treasures that turned up.[50] It is true that not many things had come to the surface as yet more valuable than old boots, crazy tea-kettles, dead cats, and battered straw bonnets without their crowns, but then there was always the delightful feeling that at any moment, something more valuable *might* turn up! Their mothers had told them wonderful stories of golden sovereigns and diamond rings being sometimes found at the bottom of rubbish-heaps, and these stories had got repeated from lip to lip amongst the noisy, clamorous children, and had fired them with such hope, that they never seemed to tire of their digging and delving and burrowing. Ah! what an angel friend is Hope! How would the digging and delving and burrowing of this life be got through with, I wonder, without her!

Froggy and Benny went to the quietest corner of the waste ground, and there buried the mouse. Froggy took Benny by the hand coming home, and prattled away to him to cheer him up, for he observed that his little brother was very sad, and that the tears kept rolling down his white cheeks, though he tried to hide them, and to answer back cheerfully when Froggy spoke to him.

The next few days passed much like other days, only that Benny seemed to be quieter after the death of his playmates, and not to take quite the same interest in things that he used to do. He still spent much of his time at the garret window, but it was no longer to watch for the Royal footman. He went there now to gaze up at the foggy sky, and to speculate upon the Beautiful City that lies beyond, whither "gentle Jesus" had carried little Deb, and where she was now "hearing music more beautifuller than the organs!" Froggy continued to trudge about London in search of a place, each day setting out with more energy, and walking farther afield, as each day the money became less, and he saw little Benny's cheeks growing paler. Wherever he saw a card in the shop-windows saying "Boy wanted," in he turned, and besought anxiously the master or mistress to take him; but none of them would do so. Some said he was too small; some said they were suited, others that he was too weak or too young, and a great many bade him roughly be off out of their shop at once, as they didn't want a ragged dirty little rascal like him! Poor Froggy – how hurt and red he looked sometimes, when these unkind answers were given him! At last, when there was but one shilling left of the pawnbroker's money, and nearly eight days had gone by without any answer coming from the Queen to their letter, Froggy said to Benny –

"I knows what I shall do, Benny; I'll go to Buck'nam Palace, and ask if the Queen ever got our letter, I will. Maybe she's not wrote, cos she's at Windsor Castle, or up in that country top of h'England, that mother used to tell me about, where the folks eats oat-cakes, and plays the bagpipes, and the swell gents at the West End wears peddicoats, and goes to shoot birds, when town's hempty."

Having made up his mind, Froggy started directly after he had had his breakfast; for Buckingham Palace, he knew, was a long way off, though he did not know the road to it quite. He remembered seeing the Palace once, a long time ago, from St James' Park, when he and his mother and father had crossed it, late one winter's afternoon on their way home, and they stopped awhile by the water to watch the merry, muffled-up skaters on the ice, and Froggy went on with father, and had a nice little slide like all the other boys who were there. Froggy knew there would be no skaters to-day, for the weather was not quite frosty enough for ice, though there was a bitter wind abroad, and as soon as he got out of the poor Shoreditch neighbourhood, he met gentlemen, muffled up in warm winter coats, and ladies in sealskins and furs, just as he saw them when there was snow on the ground. Froggy shivered along, with his shoulders up to his ears, and a hand in each sleeve, trying to keep the cruel wind from cutting down his poor little neck at the back, and from stealing up his arms in front. He had no warm flannel jersey and drawers on like most of the little boys he met trotting along by the side of their mammas; Froggy's clothing was of the thinnest and scantiest, and it was impossible to keep the cold out.

Early in the day's journey he inquired of a policeman whether he was going right for Buckingham Palace, and the policeman, bending low down to listen to him, answered very good-naturedly –

"Oh yes, you're all right for it, though you are not near it yet, you have still a goodish step to go;" then he directed Froggy as well as he could, though Froggy was yet so far from the Palace, he found it extremely difficult to follow the policeman in all his directions about turning first to the right, and then to the left, and then to the right again, and so on. By the time he had done waving his long arm about, Froggy was staring up at him in a state of hopeless bewilderment, having failed to take in anything. The policeman perceiving this, finished up by saying –

"Well, I tell you what it is, little chap – you see that timber cart there; follow that as long as it keeps straight ahead, and then ask your way again."

Froggy trotted briskly off, having thanked the policeman, and walked along by the side of the timber cart for some time. By and by his feet grew very weary, and he thought how nice it would be to get a ride on the timber, which was high in the air in front, but low down, almost touching the road at the back. The carter would perhaps never turn round, and if he did, thought Froggy, well, he could jump off quick, before he had time to give him a cut with his whip. So Froggy ran out into the muddy road, and giving a slight jump backwards perched himself safely on the end of a plank, which was waving gently up and down with the motion of the sturdy horses in front. It made Froggy quite an easy, springy seat, and he rode along in high contentment for a mile or two. He only wished Benny was beside him, having a ride too! Presently, like most good things, it came to an end, for some boys passing, shouted out to the carter, "Put the whip behind! Put the whip behind!" and the man, suddenly rousing himself, and becoming aware of the two little strange legs dangling from the plank at the back, began lashing his whip round; but not in time to catch Froggy. On the first alarm, he jumped nimbly to the ground, and was on the pavement again before the whip could touch him.

This little ride had helped him on his way nicely, and enabled him to walk out bravely afterwards. He constantly asked policemen and cabmen if he were going right for the Palace, and they all assisted him, in pointing out the way, and setting him right when he was wrong. At length, after much weariness, and rather late in the day, Froggy found himself on the broad open road, outside the gates of Buckingham Palace, which looked very grand and vast, with its long rows of windows and stone figures on the outside, and large inner entrance embellished with the Royal monogram in gold. Froggy looked up at it with great awe, and wondered whether it were possible that his and Benny's letter, written in the poor garret in Shoreditch, could have passed through those splendid gates into the presence of the Queen! His heart sank a little when he remarked that there was no flag flying from the Royal roof, and that the windows were all closed like the windows of the houses in the West End when London was empty; Froggy thought the Queen could not be there! He resolved, however, to ask, and he began looking about the majestic iron gates for a bell, or a knocker, but he could not see one anywhere. There was a sentry box close by, and a tall soldier was on duty keeping guard over the Palace, taking rather brisk turns backwards and forwards to his box, as the weather was so cold. It required some courage to do so, but Froggy made up his mind, as his business was so important, to ask this tall soldier where the bell was. Accordingly Froggy approached him, and looking up into his face, said softly –

"If you please, sir" – –

But the soldier continued his march, with his chin up in the air, and his eyes well to the front, as if he never saw Froggy. He was so accustomed to being stared at and admired by little boys like Froggy, that not having heard him speak, he took no particular notice of him, and passed on. "P'r'aps as he's milingtary, he don't like being called *sir*," thought Froggy. "I'll try somethink else" – and he planted himself straight before the soldier, and addressed him again by a new title –

"If you please, captain," he said, "can you tell me where the bell is?"

The soldier pulled himself up short now, and glanced down over his stiff collar at the small red-nosed urchin beneath him. If Froggy's face had not been so grave and anxious, the soldier would have thought he was quizzing him, for the soldier's rank in the British army was not that of captain, or anything like it.

"The bell?" he repeated. "What bell do you mean?"

"Why, the bell as people rings that wants to go into the Palace, captain," said Froggy. "I wants to send a message into the Queen, by one o' the footmans."

"Her Majesty's at Windsor," said the soldier, with a little smile which Froggy did not see, as he was so very low down. "What is your message?" he asked, as Froggy looked very crest-fallen and sad.

"Why, it's just this," said Froggy, "it's to ask if she ever got the letter as two little chaps wrote her from Shoreditch, eight days ago. She'd remember it, she would, cos it was a letter tied up with string, tellin' her all about theirselves, and how poor we was, and everythink. We think she can't never a got it, or she'd a wrote back afore this, and I've come over just to see."

"The letter hasn't reached, I suspects," said the soldier kindly. "You had better try again – p'r'aps you'll have better luck next time."

He commenced walking up and down again, for it was cold standing, and poor little Froggy, with a weight of disappointment at his heart, crossed over into St James' Park, where he perched himself on the edge of a seat, and began shedding a few quiet tears.

There were not many people in the Park; those who were seemed principally to be making short cuts across it from one gate to another, with parcels in their hands, and business in their faces. They were all too intent upon their own affairs, to cast a thought on poor miserable little Froggy, who sat there in the damp and gloom, till the lights on Constitution Hill and in Piccadilly began to twinkle and glimmer through the leafless trees. Then Froggy, frozen almost into an icicle, took to his feet again, and began his homeward journey, choosing the line of streets where there appeared to be the most gas, and traffic, and warmth. How he envied those people whom he saw eating hot chestnuts, and drinking hot coffee at the stalls! Presently he saw a great crowd in the distance, and he hurried forward with a boy's irresistible curiosity to join it, and see what was going on. Perhaps it was a fight, or a cab accident, or a show of some kind; at any rate, it must be something interesting, he thought, to attract such a crowd. As he got nearer he could see that it was assembled round and about a large public-house, which stood commandingly at the corner of a street where two busy thoroughfares met. The gas was flaring conspicuously from showy burners and glass chandeliers inside, and through the windows there streamed enough light to light up every face in the crowd. The people in the road were pushing and jostling one another to get nearer the pavement, and those on the pavement were pressing close up against the public-house door, as though they were expecting it to open shortly, and that then something exciting would issue forth, which would be all the better seen from a front place.

Figure 7   ' "I wants to send a Message in to the Queen" said Froggy.' (Note: This caption was replaced in later editions with 'Froggy approached him, and looking up into his face, said softly – "If you please, sir".')

Froggy's Little Brother, 1875. Cas. London: John F. Shaw.

"What's the row, matey?" asked Froggy of a newspaper boy who was wedging himself in, on the outskirts of the crowd.

"Why, the p'leece has gone in there to fetch out a chap as they've bin wanting ever so long," returned the newspaper boy with a chuckle; "and there's no hend of a row. 'E's tryin' to hide, they ses, though there's two p'leece."

"What's the chap bin doing?" asked Froggy.

"Why, he's the one as throwed the snuff in the City jool robbery last week," answered the boy, as if he expected Froggy to know all about the audacious young thief, who had thrown snuff in the jeweller's face to disable him while his confederates sacked the shop.

At the mention of the jewel robbery, Froggy pricked up his ears; for the recollection of the policeman's visit to Mrs Ragbon's house came suddenly into his head, together with those words of the charwoman:"It's all along o' that good-for-nothing Mac! There's bin a darin' jool robbery in the City, and he's in it" – etc., etc.

"What if it should be Mac?" thought Froggy, and his heart began to beat with a strange and painful excitement. He knew there was no chance of seeing from where he was, for everybody towered high above him, and he was too small to force his way into the crowd, like the newspaper boy, who was taller. So he determined to climb a lamp-post that was near.

He got a man standing by to give him a "leg up;" then he worked himself to the top with the agility of a young monkey, and clung there, looking right over the heads of the people, and able from his superior height to get a better view of the public-house door than any one. At last the moment of excitement came; there was a great noise and movement amongst the crowd; the great swinging doors of the public-house burst open suddenly; a flood of light streamed forth, and two policemen appeared, holding on sternly to something that was kicking and ducking and struggling, and being dragged along between them. At first Froggy could not see who it was they had got, whether it was a boy or a man; but when in another minute they turned sharply to the right and passed close under the lamp-post, followed by the murmuring tramping rabble which always accompanies a prisoner to the station-house in London, Froggy caught his breath, and uttered a sharp cry of dismay, for the gaslight showed beyond all doubt that it was none other than the landlady's son, Mac Ragbon! It was a terrible sight to see. He had no hat on, his hair was rough, and his face was ghastly pale with marks of blood on it; his shirt was torn, and his jacket was being carried by one of the policemen. Evidently he had been resisting his capture to the last.

Froggy slid soberly down from the lamp-post after they had passed, and regained his feet with a heavy sigh. "That's what comes of leading a bad life and thieving," thought he, looking very grave and depressed by what he had seen. "I sha'n't tell Benny nothink about it, I don't think, cos he's so down now, poor little chap, about Deb and his mouse. And he'd fret ever so about Mac, if I was to tell him he's gone to prison!"

At this moment a gentleman's brougham piled up with luggage, on its way to the Great Eastern Railway station, passed slowly through the crowd, and Froggy's quick eye perceived that there was a place at the back, on which he could seat himself for a ride! He jumped on, and had a long undisturbed lift homewards, for the course of the carriage was (luckily for Froggy) exactly his, and passed the very end of the street where he lived.

* * *

CHAPTER XI.
BENNY HAS 'THE STAGGERS.'

FROGGY never forgot his coming home this evening. In after years it was as indelibly impressed upon his mind, as that other coming home long ago on the bleak December night, when mother was taken "fainty-like in the passage, and couldn't get upstairs nohow!" Benny was generally on the top stair waiting to greet Froggy on his return home, but he was not there to-night. Benny generally lit a light in the garret, to make it look warm and cheerful for him when he came home, but there was no light burning to welcome Froggy to-night; everything seemed strangely dark and silent, and when Froggy called out "Benny!" and again

"Benny!" no answer came. Froggy, much puzzled, groped his way up the stairs. As he did so, the thought struck him that perhaps Benny was playing him a trick, and was going to jump out upon him suddenly, so he paused on the threshold of the garret, and said, "I say, Benny, where be you? Come out, Benny!" No answer. "I knows where you be, Benny, you're behind the door," said Froggy, getting rather uneasy, and advancing a few steps in order to bring matters to an issue, if Benny really were hiding. Froggy waited anxiously for a moment. At first he could only hear the sound of his own breathing, but presently a little sigh caught his ear, and a slight movement coming from the direction of the bed.

"Benny, do speak!" cried Froggy. "Where be you?"

"I's here," said a very faint small voice from the darkness.

At that moment a great black cloud, which had hitherto obscured the moon, drifted right away from her, and a long beautiful silver moonbeam came slanting in through the window, lighting up the whole of the garret, and falling full upon what looked like a desolate little heap of corduroy lying on the floor between the window and the bed. Froggy started forward, for it was Benny.

"Benny! Benny! what's the matter? ain't you well?" he said with a great cry in his voice.

"I's not very," said Benny, trying to rise.

The moonlight fell on his face, and such a poor little face it was! white and drawn, and without an atom of colour on the lips.

"Do you feel fainty-like? What is it you feels, darlin'?" questioned Froggy with a terrible look of anxiety in his face, as he pressed it close up into Benny's.

"I think I's got what the cab-horses has," said Benny, staring at Froggy as he stood with great haggard eyes. "I's got the staggers, Froggy!" and as he spoke, his little legs, which were trembling and knocking together beneath him, gave way, and he fell to the ground.[51]

"Oh dear! oh dear! oh dear!" moaned Froggy aloud in the extremity of that deep loneliness which the strongest of us have all felt at times, when sudden danger has overtaken us, and there has been none to help.

But he was only dismayed for a moment. Was not God above, watching over them still? His lips did not move, but his heart went up instantly to God in the short ejaculatory prayer – "O God, I'm quite alone; teach me what to do!" The moment he had said it, he felt stronger to act, because he was sure God would guide him. Mother had always prayed in times of sickness and peril, and God had never failed mother; she had always said that, even through the darkest times, and the remembrance of this greatly comforted and strengthened Froggy.

O mothers and fathers! how your words and examples come back to your children, and influence them either for good or for evil, long after the grave has closed over you, and you are alike powerless to impress deeper that which is good or to recall that which is evil.

Froggy gathered his wits together, and lit a candle. Then he lifted Benny in his arms, and carrying him to the bed began to undress him: much as he had undressed him years ago, on the sad December night when mother was so ill, and father had told him to put Benny to bed, because mother would not be able to do it. Benny was a baby then and slept on the Punch and Judy box, now he was six years old and slept on the mattress; but it seemed to Froggy that his little brother was quite as feeble and helpless and dependent to-night as ever he had been then; Benny lay very still with his eyes closed, across Froggy's small lap, now and then sobbing, but not shedding any tears.

"Cheer up, darlin'!" Froggy kept saying softly, while he took one thing off, and then another in nervous haste. "I knows all about it, I do, and I'll soon get you better. I knows of a medicine that I'm agoin' to buy, Benny, that'll warm you ever so, and make you better. Mother always gave it father and me when we was ill, always."

This last was added by way of comfort to himself; for anything mother used to do, Froggy thought, must be right to do in any case.

When Benny was undressed, Froggy laid him on the mattress, and with great care and anxiety tucked the scanty clothing well in about him to keep him warm.

"I'm going to the chemist's now, darlin'," whispered Froggy leaning over him. "I sha'n't be away not two minutes, I'll be back afore ever you can count three, Benny!"

He kissed his little brother's white face, as if he were loth to leave him even for two minutes; then he took the last remaining shilling of the pawnbroker's money (the only money he had in the world!), and ran out into the streets to find a chemist's shop. The tears streamed down his cheeks as he fled along. "O God, make Benny better," he kept praying. "Pray God, make Benny better!"

He had not to go far; at the end of the next street he discovered a chemist's shop, and into it he ran breathlessly, and inquired of the man if he kept "Keating's Lixy?"

"Keating's Elixir? – oh yes, we keep it; there you are, seven-pence-halfpenny to pay," said the chemist, handing him over the counter a tall, narrow bottle with a seal at the top, and a very large label upon it.[52]

Froggy grasped it eagerly as the thing that was to make Benny well; then, having paid for it, he ran out again into the streets to go home. But it suddenly struck him that there was no food for Benny in the house, and no fuel either, except one or two knobs of charcoal. He had still fourpence-halfpenny left; this, he reflected, would buy some oatmeal and a bundle of sticks to make a fire. He ran to an open green-grocer's shop a few doors farther down, where the gas was flaring lavishly amongst cabbages and vegetables, and great sacks of potatoes. The man who kept the shop dealt in other commodities besides, and here Froggy was able to buy both the oatmeal and the sticks. For these things he gave his last penny in payment, scarcely realising it was his last, and then home he hurried as fast as he could fly.

On entering the garret he ran to the mattress the first thing, to have a look at Benny. He was lying just as he had left him, apparently not having moved, but his teeth were chattering now, and he looked whiter than before. He did not speak, but he opened his eyes, and looked pitifully at Froggy for one moment, as if he were appealing to him, like some poor little dumb animal, for help.

"Yes, Benny! I knows all about it," responded Froggy soothingly. "You're agoin' to be warmed d'rectly, Benny, and have some beautiful, comfortin' medicine that I've bin and bought."

He left the bedside, and set to work energetically to light the fire. This was no easy task to accomplish, for a keen blast of wind came pouring down the chimney, and kept continually putting it out at first. It was some time before Froggy could get a nice bright blaze to start up, but the moment this occurred he pulled off the little jacket from his own back, and kneeling down in his shirt-sleeves, began holding it close to the bars, as if he were desirous of making it into toast. He held the jacket there till it was thoroughly warmed through and through, then he jumped up and ran with it in eager haste to the mattress, and wrapped it about Benny.

"There, darlin'! isn't that nice? Isn't that splendid?" he said, tucking it in at all corners; "and when it gets cold, I'll warm it again. Don't speak afore you're able, Benny, but just tell me when you're beginning to get a bit warmer, will you?" whispered poor anxious Froggy, who was longing to hear Benny speak again.

Froggy hurried off now, and began busying himself about the medicine. There was the seal to be broken, and the cork of the bottle to be drawn, and water to be boiled, because mother, he remembered, always mixed it in warm water, and of course he must do the same. Before long a small, muffled voice came from the bed, "I's warmer, Froggy," it said.

Benny was certain to say he was better the first moment he could; he was such a gallant-hearted little fellow by nature, and always made the best of things. When he was a baby, and fell down and hurt himself, he used to call out, "Up again!" and up he would jump at his own word of command, with a merry laugh to hide the tears if there were any. This was fortunate, since he had never had a mother to run to him,

> "And kiss the place
> To make it well."[53]

"Oh, I be so glad!" cried Froggy. "I'll warm the jacket agin, as soon as ever you've took the medicine, Benny. 'Ere it be, nice and hot!" He spoke in a brisk tone, and came running with it to the bedside.

"Is it good for 'staggers'?" inquired Benny, from under the jacket.

He had nestled so low down, that nothing could be seen of him now except his forehead, and a little bit of his turned-up nose. "Oh yes, it's good for *heverythink!*" replied Froggy warmly, stirring it round energetically with a spoon. "Mother said it ud cure colds, coughs, nooralgy, tic, 'eadache, hear-ache, toothache, and every other kind of hache that you can think of!"

Benny tried to rise, but Froggy had to lift him up and hold the cup to his lips. At the sight of the nauseous brown liquid, Benny shuddered and drew back.

"Why, darlin'! it ain't near so bad as castor oil, nor grey powder," said Froggy encouragingly, giving it another stir.

"It's badder," said Benny ruefully, returning to it, however, and putting his lips to it again. But a second time he drew back.

"Come! it's all getting cold," said Froggy, stirring it with renewed vigour. "Now, be a good boy, and take it, there's a darlin'!"

Benny regarded it for a moment as if he were trying to make up his mind, then he said pleadingly – "Take a little drop first, Froggy!"

"Well, I will – I don't mind it a bit," said Froggy and he took a taste.

"You made a face after it!" said Benny, nodding.

"Yes, that was cos I sipped it," explained Froggy."It wouldn't be near so bad in a draught. Now, I'll count one, two, three, and when I says *three,* Benny, you must take it. I always took it when mother said three."

Then he counted slowly "one – two – *three!*" At "three," Benny brought his trembling lips to the medicine very slowly and cautiously, Froggy gave the cup a little tip up, and Benny was obliged to swallow a sip. But he took no more. He turned his face away from it shudderingly again, and some of it got spilt on the bedclothes.

Froggy was in despair; he felt overcome with the weight of his responsibilities to-night, and what should he do if he could not get Benny to take the medicine? Benny must be very ill, he was sure, to look as he did, so dreadfully white and haggard, and there was no time for dilly-dallying! Froggy determined to try what scolding would do, since persuasion had no effect.

"You're a naughty boy, Benny," he said at last.

"I'm not a naughty boy," said Benny in a very doleful voice, laying his head back on the pillow.

"Yes, you is, or you'd take your medicine," said Froggy; "you ain't being a good boy at all, going on like this! Whatever would Jack say if he was to know?"

Benny did not answer, and Froggy waited a moment. Then he tried something else.

"Deb always took *her* medicine," he said.

Ah! this evidently had made an impression. Benny's large eyes turned attentively towards Froggy, and he regarded him steadily for a moment, as if he were thinking over his words.

"She knew Jesus wouldn't love her if she didn't," continued Froggy. "And she used to bear her mustard poultices, too, like a brick."

"Did she?" said Benny ponderingly; then suddenly, "I'll be a brick, too, Froggy!" he exclaimed, and to Froggy's astonishment he raised his little, frail body in bed, took the cup between his hands, and drained it to the very dregs.

"Yes, you was a brick, then!" said Froggy admiringly, looking into the cup to see if he had left any, and finding none. "It wasn't so bad as you thought, now, was it, darlin'?"

"Worser," said Benny, giving a great heave, and the tears coming into his eyes with the effort of keeping the medicine where it ought to be after swallowing it.

"I'll get you a nice basin of oatmeal, now," said Froggy. "It'll take the taste out beautiful."

"I couldn't eat none," said Benny, nodding his head.

"Well, I don't know as I'll press you to it," said Froggy thoughtfully; "cos I don't think mother give me supper when I took the Lixy. But I'll warm up the jacket agin!"

He carried it to the fire, and held it to the bars as before. While he was busy down on his knees, turning the jacket first this way and then that, he heard Benny murmur "I's so hot!" and give a little sigh. Froggy turned his head round quickly, and saw that Benny was now lying with his arms out of bed, and the clothing below his chest, as if it were a hot summer's night.

"There! wasn't I right? Ain't it a lovely medicine for warmin?" cried Froggy with enthusiasm, running to the bedside to rejoice over his patient. "Mother always said it – there wasn't nothink like it in the world."

But when Froggy came to look at Benny, he was not quite so satisfied. Benny was looking very odd and unlike himself. Froggy took up one of his little hands to feel, and it was burning hot to his touch.

"Do you feels all right, darlin'?" asked Froggy, peering anxiously into his face.

"Yes, only I got a neadache," said Benny, turning his head restlessly about on the pillow, "and I are so hot, I'd like to kick everythink off me, I would!"

"Oh, you mustn't never do that!" exclaimed Froggy gravely. "You'd catch your death o' cold."

"Froggy," said Benny staring at him, " 'as my ead growed very big?"

"Why, no, it ain't no bigger than it was," replied Froggy, examining it carefully. "Do it feel big?"

"Yes," said Benny, "I feels just like the picters the men wheels about of the hobgobblins in the pantomimes, with little funny bodies, and large big heads!"

At that moment, a small bare leg made its appearance out at the side of the bed.

"Benny, take your leg in," said Froggy, covering it up, "the medicine won't do you not a scrap of good if you tosses about like that! When I used to take the Lixy mother always made me cover up after it, and keep warm, and get into a nice sleep if I could. Don't you think if you was to try now, darlin,' you might get to sleep?"

Benny agreed to try. "But I must say my prayers first, and 'Gentle Jesus,' " he said.

"Oh yes! of course, and I'll come and sit by you while you ses 'em," said Froggy, perching himself on the side of the mattress, and looking very affectionately at his little sick brother, who now folded his hands in preparation for saying those simple prayers, that he had been in the habit of saying so regularly and easily every morning and evening since babyhood.

But, oh, what did ail Benny to-night? He seemed not to be able to say them. After the first few words, "Pray God bless" – his speech became confused, his words ran in to each other, and it all sounded like gibberish. He seemed to know, poor little fellow! that he was doing something wrong, for his countenance became distressed, and at last he stopped and gazed helplessly at Froggy, as much as to say, "O Froggy, tell me what is the matter with me?" with that irresistibly touching look in his eyes that we see sometimes in the eyes of dumb animals when they are in pain, and which is quite as eloquent as speech.

"It's cos you're not quite well, darlin'," said Froggy tenderly, answering back the look. "Don't try to say 'em no more to-night. Lie down, Benny, and I'll say 'em for you. Jesus'll take 'em just the same as if you said 'em, cos He knows you ain't well, and all about it!"

Benny lay down meekly as he was told, and then Froggy drew closer to him, and said his sweet baby prayers for him aloud, and repeated the hymn, "Gentle Jesus!"

Froggy's voice seemed to soothe Benny; he lay very still, listening, and after a time, Froggy noticed, with the quick eye of a watchful nurse, that a slight drowsiness was creeping over him, and that sleep was likely to come. In order not to break off the sounds that appeared to be lulling him, Froggy said another hymn when he had finished "Gentle Jesus!" which was one that he had learnt a long time ago, and which he remembered all but the first verse. He began at the second, which says: –

> " 'Tis good for boys and maidens
> Sweet hymns to Christ to sing,
> 'Tis meet that children's voices
> Should praise the children's King.
> For Jesus is salvation,
> And glory, grace, and rest,
> To babe and boy and maiden,
> The one Redeemer blest!
>
> "O boys, be strong in Jesus!
> To toil for Him is gain;
> And Jesus wrought with Joseph,
> With chisel, saw, and plane;
> O maidens, live for Jesus,
> Who was a maiden's Son;
> Be patient, pure, and gentle,
> And perfect grace begun!"

Benny was very nearly asleep now, and Froggy said the last verse very slowly and hushfully to complete the lullaby: –

> "Soon in the Golden City
> The boys and girls shall play;
> And through the dazzling mansions

Rejoice in endless day;
O Christ, prepare Thy children,
With that triumphant throng
To pass the burnished portals,
And sing th' Eternal Song!"[54]

"How 'appy that sounds!" murmured little Benny softly. "The boys and girls playin' in – the – Golden City" – and now almost as he spoke, his lips parted, his eyes closed, and he fell into a light slumber. Froggy waited a moment to make sure it was sleep; then he covered him up gently, and left the bedside.

Poor Froggy had had no dinner, and he was by this time ravenously hungry. Just to satisfy the cravings of hunger, he crept to the fire, and made himself a small basin of porridge; a very small one it was, because he was anxious to leave a large share of the oatmeal for Benny to-morrow. Then he crept to the stool, and sat down and ate it, silently and sorrowfully, as if he felt it to be a very lonely supper. He kept his eyes continually on the bed, in readiness to jump up and run to him, if Benny made the smallest sign. Now and then he murmured in his sleep, and seemed to be waking; then Froggy said softly, "Sh – sh – sh!" as mother did when he was a baby, and soothed him off again!

It was a long time before Froggy got into bed, he was so afraid of disturbing Benny. When at last he did, he crept in as quietly as a mouse, and laid himself down.

Two sadder little faces could not have been seen in all London, I think, than the two lying side by side on the pillow for the last time in the poor garret to-night. The world's loneliness seemed to be there, and poverty very deep, but ah! the two little brothers were not really alone; they were not really poor! For if our eyes could have pierced the darkness, we should have known that there was watching over them, that One who is the Light of the world, even Jesus, in whose dear Presence there is an everlasting assurance of joy and peace and fellowship.

Little children, pray for that Presence – pray that Jesus may come and abide with you, then you can never be very lonely, or very sad!

This night, there was a miserable yellow-haired boy sobbing his heart out in a cell in one of the City prisons, wishing that he had only kept honest and true like Froggy and Benny, "tho' they was so clemmed and hard-up." Yes! Mac had found out his mistake at last. He had been feasting often, while they had been starving, but the "reg'lar merry life" had all come to an end now, and had brought him to what dishonesty and drunkenness will always bring a man or a boy, a woman or a girl sooner or later – degradation and despair!

* * *

CHAPTER XII.
THE PARISH DOCTOR.[55]

THE next morning, Benny woke feverish and excited. His hair was wet on his forehead, and his eyes looked strained and unnatural, with a peculiar light in them. All night long he had been murmuring and gabbling in his sleep, throwing the clothes off him, and kicking Froggy, who was perpetually out on the floor, and creeping in again, but not minding in the least, "cos they was Benny's kicks!"

When morning dawned, and the light came in at the window, Froggy started up and looked at Benny wonderingly, for he did not look like Benny at all, but like some other little boy! And when Froggy spoke to him, and asked him how he felt, Benny sat up in bed, and began talking and stammering about horses and cats, and big rats and balloons, as if horses and cats, and big rats and balloons were pressing painfully upon his little brain, and he was trying to tell Froggy a long story about them. It was evident from the incoherent jumble, that Benny's mind was wandering, and that he must be worse, instead of better.

Froggy was so puzzled, that he went down and asked Mrs Blunt to come up and look at him. The charwoman came, and at once pronounced Benny to be in a very queer state.

"You must keep your brother as quiet as you just can, and try to amuse him," said she impressively to Froggy, after she had laid a hand on his burning forehead, and felt his feverish hands. "Mr Brown'll be here before long (Mr Brown was the parish doctor); he's acomin' early to see my Jemmy, who ain't as bright as he ought to be, and then I'll ask him to step up and take a look at Benny. He ain't well – no, that he ain't!" regarding Benny sorrowfully, and nodding her head.

"Please, mum, are you goin' out a charin' to-day?" inquired Froggy, full of that anxiety which seems so deeply implanted in men's breasts, to keep a woman in sight when there is sickness about.

"No, I ain't agoin' charin' to-day," said Mrs Blunt. "I'm goin' to be busy at my tub. Have you got anythink to make a fire with, Froggy?"

"No," said Froggy; "we've no sticks, nor yet coals."

Mrs Blunt answered nothing, but went downstairs. In a moment she returned with some coals and sticks out of her own little store, which she could ill spare, poor woman; but which, with the generosity of her class, she was so ready to give!

How many a beautiful lesson can we learn from the poor – for sufferings nobly endured and heavy burdens bravely borne, where can we look better than to them, but what *generosity* they teach us! They show us how to be truly and greatly generous in their willingness to share the last crumb of comfort, whatever that may be, with a neighbour, kindly and ungrudgingly, without hope of return or reward. Theirs is not a generosity which costs them nothing – it often entails going without a meal or sitting by a fireless grate, but a self-sacrifice of some sort, *always*. It is of the highest and truest order, because the nearest to our great Pattern, whose generosity only reached its sublime perfection on the cross at Calvary, when the most perfect self-sacrifice was made that the world has ever known, and which nothing could go above or beyond! We are not called upon to lay down our lives, but we *are* called upon to make very great sacrifices, not only once, but daily and hourly, for one another; and in the homes of the poor, I think, we see this call answered as a rule more obediently and absolutely than anywhere else.

Mrs Blunt went down on her knees, and lit the fire for Froggy, out of sheer pity for his poor troubled face, that she guessed would soon be looking more troubled still. She had seen much of illness, and in this case something told her from the first that "God was going to call a little child" again, and that Froggy would shortly be alone, and brotherless. She bade him once more keep Benny quiet, and not to let him talk; then having lighted the fire, and told Froggy to give her a call if he wanted her, she went downstairs to wait till the doctor came.

As soon as she was gone, Froggy took a seat beside Benny, and began thinking what he could do to amuse him, to carry out the charwoman's injunctions to keep him quiet.

"Now, if you are a good boy and doesn't talk," said Froggy, "I'll tell you all about what I did out yesterday" –

"The big rats" – began little Benny again on the old theme, starting up and looking excited. But Froggy interrupted him.

"You're not to talk," he said, putting up one finger severely. "If you do, I sha'n't tell you nothink, Benny, and you'll be a naughty boy!"

After this Benny kept still for some minutes, gazing intently up at the ceiling, as if he saw something there which riveted his attention. Froggy commenced his narration of yesterday's doings, beginning with his beautiful ride on the timber cart, and ending with his interview with the tall soldier on guard at Buckingham Palace. Benny was generally a delightful little fellow to tell a story to, so quick to take in the smaller points, and so ready to laugh at all the funny ones, and if there happened to be anything about a *soldier* in it, Froggy had noticed that he was generally doubly pleased and interested. Yes, generally, but not to-day. He seemed too restless and too feverish to listen, and though poor Froggy laboured so hard to interest him, and to make him laugh, he could not get Benny even to smile! This struck more fear and apprehension into Froggy's heart than anything else, I think; for Benny had always been so merry; and there must be something strangely wrong, argued Froggy, when Benny ceased to laugh. "Oh, that the doctor would make haste and come!" that was his longing now, but it was still so early, there was scarcely a chance of his coming yet.

As a last resource, Froggy took to tumbling about the garret in front of Benny, remembering how he had laughed and clapped his hands that afternoon when Mac came and tumbled previous to the Queen's visit. Though he had such a heavy heart, Froggy went at the performance bravely, turning first the most rapid som-ersaults one after another, then pausing with a leg or an arm out-stretched like a windmill in the air, and his head on the ground, as if standing upon it, or else in some other impossible position. It did not matter how daring or uncomfortable these positions were; Froggy was not thinking of himself – his one object was to try to astonish, and amuse Benny if he could, and to make him smile and clap his hands, and be only as he used to be for a few short minutes!

"Did you see *that*?" called out Froggy triumphantly from the floor once, after he had gone through a series of acrobatic feats with such lightning rapidity as to make him feel he had outdone himself, and thinking that Benny would surely be sitting up, and laughing now. But there was not a smile on his little flushed face, as he stared at Froggy, and said –

"The balloon went up such a long way, Froggy, till the cat drawed it down!" – which made Froggy stare back, for what had this about the balloon and the cat to do with the tumbling? What was Benny talking about? Truly he was a very strange little brother to-day!

As he was regarding Benny with a puzzled air, Mrs Blunt entered the garret, and said gravely, "Still talking of cats and balloons! Poor Benny; he ain't much better then."

"If I could only make him laugh once again!" said poor Froggy mournfully.

"Well, p'r'aps Mr Brown'll be able – he's comin' up the stair now!" said Mrs Blunt kindly, and as she spoke, the heavy footstep which had so often excited Benny's hopes while little Deb was ill, came creaking up the stairs, and in another moment the parish doctor entered.

He was a very tall man, with a serious face and broad stooping shoulders, and a general air about him of being a hard worker. It was evident that with him, "Life was real; life was earnest!" and I who know him, children, can tell you that he was a worthy fol-lower of that One who went about "healing all manner of sick-ness," and who has made, for all time, the calling of doctors so honourable and so beautiful!

I am anxious to pay here a tribute to doctors, for it seems to me that, as a class, they shine out more brilliantly than any other men. Their patience, their kindness, their zeal, their devotion, their courage – who has not proved it for themselves at some time or other in their lives, or else heard of it from others! How the poor invariably speak of them, and who better than they can testify to their real worth? I often think what a bright array of doctors there will be in that day, when all the great things done in the dark shall be known in the light, and the army of the world's true heroes shall appear before the great White Throne in heaven! How many a poor obscure country doctor, whose homely gig and hop-and-go-one horse have been the laugh and joke of the squire and his friends, when they have met him going his weary round on a sunny September morning, while they have been striding over the stubble with dog and gun, will be found in that day the better man of them all – amongst the little band "who are unknown here, but well-known *there!*" for deeds of gallantry and true heroism which this world passes by, but which will gain the highest honours and the brightest crown in the Paradise of God![56]

> "Where loyal hearts and true
> Stand ever in the light,
> All rapture through and through
> In God's most holy sight!"[57]

The Doctor as he bent forward his head, and came in at the door of the garret, cast a rapid searching glance all around, as if he were struck by the cold and the misery and poverty of the scene upon which he had suddenly entered. He was accustomed to poverty and misery; he was in the habit of witnessing both the one and the other daily, in all its worst forms; hence, perhaps, his serious face, but *this* garret – well, it did strike him as being worse than anything he had seen for a long time! He followed Mrs Blunt at once to the little mattress whereon Benny lay, and beside which Froggy was standing.

Froggy gazed up anxiously into the doctor's face to see what sort of a gentleman he was; would he be kind to Benny? Would he be at all like that doctor who was so kind to him in the hospital? Dr Brown's very first words assured him on these points.

"How long has your little brother been ill?" he asked kindly, producing a very big watch, and taking Benny's tiny wrist to feel his pulse.

"Why, sir, since yesterday," said Froggy. "I come home from callin' at Buck'nam Palace at seven, and I finds him in a heap like on
the floor, and when I raises him, he says, 'Froggy,' he ses, 'I thinks
I got what the cab-horses has, the 'staggers,' and he couldn't stand
up nohow! That was just how it all was, sir."

"And he's bin talking wild and strange ever since," put in Mrs
Blunt standing by.

"Who takes care of you up here?" asked the doctor looking
round.

"Please, sir, Benny and me takes care of ourselves," replied Froggy;
"father and mother's both dead, and we shifts along o' ourselves."

The doctor now asked many questions, to each of which Froggy
spoke up and answered promptly, like a little soldier standing at
attention. He told the doctor all about the Punch and Judy show,
how mother had died, then how father had died, and how very
bad times had been ever since for Benny and himself; lastly, of the
letter they had written to the Queen, and of how he had trudged
over to Buckingham Palace yesterday, to see whether she had got
it, which brought him back again to his coming home, and finding Benny in a heap on the floor.

The doctor looked very grave over the story; so grave that Mrs
Blunt felt it due to herself to explain that "she was out charing
most days; had a hard life of it herself to keep her own from the
workhouse, and hadn't much to give away, though she had given
what she could!" – which was all true, poor woman.

"I only wish this had come to my knowledge sooner," said Dr
Brown; "there is little to be done now, I am afraid."

"Couldn't you give him some medicine as 'ud do him good?"
cried Froggy imploringly, looking first at Benny and then at the
doctor, with great tears in his eyes. "I ain't got the money to pay
for it, but I soon will have, and then I'll pay!"

"He's so fond of his brother!" murmured Mrs Blunt gently, for
the doctor to hear.

"I will do all I can for him," said the doctor kindly, "and you
need not trouble about the paying, my boy."

He closed his eyes for a moment, and Froggy felt sure he was
praying. Yes – the doctor was a wise, Christian man, and he knew
well enough that the physician's art would be all unavailing
unless God's blessing was with him; so he just lifted his heart in

prayer for one moment, that if it were God's will, the little sick boy now lying before him might be raised up again, but if not, that He would take care of Froggy, and comfort him exceedingly.

He then took out a pocket-book, and began writing on two pages, which he presently tore out and folded up. On one he put a large mark to distinguish it from the other.

"Now, my boy," said he to Froggy, "I want you to run with this to the chemist's in J – – Street," handing him the marked paper. "Leave it with the chemist, then run on to the red brick house next the church, in the same street, you know, ask for Mr Wallace, and give him this," handing him the other; "then, on your way back, call at the chemist's again, and he will give you some medicine. Do you understand, now, what I mean you to do?"

"Yes, sir," said Froggy, and he repeated his instructions over to show that he did.

"That is right," said Dr Brown, "now run, and we'll look after your brother while you're gone!"

Froggy needed no urging. He clattered down the stairs, and ran out into the street in hot haste to do what the doctor had told him.

* * *

CHAPTER XIII.
"OH CALL MY BROTHER BACK AGAIN!"

Having left the prescription at the chemist's shop, Froggy ran on to the red brick house next the church. He was on tiptoe, straining to reach the bell, which was rather high up, when a voice said behind him, "Good morning, little man – you needn't ring, I've got a key!" and turning round he saw that a gentleman in a black coat had gained the doorstep with him, and was just about reaching over his head to insert a small key into the hole.

"Where do you come from?" asked he, as he swung the door back on its hinges.

"I come from B – – Street to see Mr Wallis, sir," answered Froggy.

"I'm your man, then," said the gentleman. "I'm Mr Wallace. Come in, my boy – you look very cold."

Froggy followed the clergyman (for such he was) into a small room, rather bare of furniture, and with no carpet, but there was a bright fire burning, and a nice smell of hot coffee pervading the apartment, which gave it an atmosphere of comfort. A woman had just deposited, on the end of the square wooden table, a small tray, bearing Mr Wallace's simple breakfast of coffee and bread.

"The doctor said as I was to give you this, sir," said Froggy at once, handing him the paper.

The clergyman, as he took it, noted the sorrowful face of Froggy, and his own became very grave while he stood and read what the doctor had written to him, which was shortly this – "Dear Wallace, great misery in top attic, number I B – – Street. Case perhaps for Orphanage. Come as soon as you can. Yours, C. B."

He looked down kindly at Froggy after he had read the words, and said –

"Tell me a little about the trouble that is at home, my boy?"

"Please, sir," – – began Froggy, but that was all he could say. In another moment he was sobbing.

Mr Wallace, however, seemed to understand all about it; he had that "priestly gift of sympathy," without which, a good man has said, "we can never attain to the Christ-like distinction of being true sons of Consolation." It is a precious gift, rarely to be got except by going through very deep waters of suffering; those who have never suffered, can never have it as Christ loves to see it in His people.

"There, there," said Mr Wallace soothingly, laying his small gentleman-like hand on Froggy's little shoulder, "I've been through a perfect furnace of trouble myself, so I can feel for you."

"Did ever you have a little brother ill, and not know where to turn for bread?" asked Froggy, looking up with his streaming eyes.

"Not quite that, but something very like it," he answered. "I lost a little sister once when I was about your age, and later I lost other things which seemed to make me very poor till I saw God's hand was in it, and that He was leading me to happiness, though it was by a path I did not know. You've no father or mother?"

"No, sir," said Froggy; "Benny and me's quite alone."

While the clergyman had been speaking, he had poured out a cup of hot coffee which he now handed to Froggy.

"Here," said he, "drink this, little man. It will do you good."

"I'd rather not, sir – I couldn't wait, sir," said Froggy in a great hurry, drying his tears up with the sleeve of his jacket. "I must run back to Benny, sir; he'll be callin' for me."

"But drink the coffee first," urged Mr Wallace, "and you shall have the loaf to carry home to your little brother."

Froggy drank the coffee after this. The promise of the loaf made him feel he could take the coffee, since the bread would be an equivalent to Benny. It had been always so! Froggy could never enjoy a good thing unless Benny had his share of it!

"I shall be round to see you in less than a quarter of an hour," said Mr Wallace kindly. "Stop one moment, though," he added, as Froggy, having finished the coffee and got the loaf, was about to run off.

"Tell me, isn't *Ragbon* the name of the person who keeps your house?"

"Yes, sir," answered Froggy. "That's she; – Sally Ragbon she's called."

Then, as he remembered what the landlady had said to the policeman about her dislike of "the long-coated gentry," he added quickly –

"But she don't like parsons, sir; she won't never let you in, I guess; she's terrible fierce."

"Oh, but she will have to do so, I shall insist," said the clergyman.

"She's awful strong!" said Froggy gravely. He looked at Mr Wallace measuringly, and thought he was not tall enough to grapple with such a giantess as Mrs Ragbon; but Froggy measured him wrongly. Mr Wallace was a man of small stature, but with great breadth of shoulder, and a look of quiet, reserved power about him as if he could hold his own against any number of infuriated landladies.

Froggy had yet to learn that small men are quite as well able to grapple with strength, both morally and physically, as tall ones. It would have surprised him very much if you had told him, what is undoubtedly true, that some of the world's greatest warriors, who have led her armies to victory, have been quite small men, such as Napoleon, Wellington, and Havelock. Like Zaccheus of old, who you remember, was small of stature, and triumphed over hindrances when he wanted to see Jesus, by climbing up into the sycamore tree, little men, as a rule, I think, overcome the obstacles and difficulties of daily life more determinedly and effectually and gallantly than taller men; perhaps, because they are generally more strongly made, and are possessed of greater physical energy. I suppose Mr Wallace guessed what was passing in Froggy's mind, for he smiled and said –

"You think Mrs Ragbon is stronger than I am? Well, we shall see shortly. In a few minutes I shall be round."

"Thank you, sir," said Froggy gratefully. And now with the loaf under his arm, and feeling all the better for the hot coffee, he left the friendly red brick house, and ran down the street to the chemist's again, according to the doctor's instructions. Having got the draught, he hastened home.

To his great surprise, when he reached the doorstep he found Mr Wallace already standing there (how true he had been to his word, and how very quick he had been over his breakfast!) in conversation with Mrs Ragbon, who had opened the door to him.

The landlady was actually smiling, and the clergyman was looking very pleasant, but resolute. Froggy heard her say as he came up –

"Please to walk in, then, your reverence. Here, Froggy," as she caught sight of him, "show his reverence the way." Froggy wondered why she was so civil! The fact was, Mrs Ragbon had taken a correct measurement of the small, square-shouldered gentleman before her, and felt that he was quite as determined to enter upon this occasion as ever she could be to keep him out. There was, moreover, another reason for her yielding to him, and yielding pleasantly too. The policeman's visit lately, and Mac's disgrace, had naturally brought her house into great disrepute, and she thought it would look rather well to the neighbours now, if they saw that she was on terms with the clergy. I fear she had no higher or better motives for behaving properly. Froggy led the way, and Mr Wallace followed him up the steep stairs to the garret, where Doctor Brown and Mrs Blunt were still watching beside Benny. He looked more flushed and excited than ever, as if he were puzzling himself to comprehend who this strange, tall gentleman was, sitting so close to him, and hushing him when he talked. The doctor had got one hand across his little chest, keeping the bedclothes on him, for Benny was still restless and inclined to kick them off.

As soon as Mr Wallace entered the garret, the doctor rose up and met him. Their greeting, quiet and undemonstrative, was evidently that of men who were in the habit of meeting constantly, and between whom there existed a perfectly good understanding. Theirs was, indeed, no common friendship. Begun as happy schoolboys on the play-ground at Winchester, and continued in all its warmth and freshness, it had survived the wear and tear of years until now, when as men, we find them standing like faithful soldiers in the breach, "heart within and God o'er-head," working and fighting and striving together to stem the mighty tide of human misery and sin, which is everywhere abroad in this great city.

Froggy saw them shake hands and then begin to talk earnestly together with Mrs Blunt, but he did not wait to listen to what they said. He ran eagerly to the bedside, and showed Benny the bread.

"Look, darlin'!" he cried holding it aloft, "a beautiful loaf, crusty and hot, all for we!"

Such a sight had not been seen in the garret for many a day, but, alas! it had come too late for little Benny to enjoy. He took no notice, but asked if Froggy would soon be back?

"Why, Benny, he *is* back," said Froggy. "Look, Benny, 'ere he be – 'ere's Froggy. I'm Froggy, don't you see, darlin'?" peering anxiously into his face.

" 'Es bin away such a long while!" murmured Benny with a sigh, evidently not recognising his brother.

"He don't even know me now!" said Froggy sadly, as if this were the very climax of all his sorrows.

At this moment a friendly hand was laid on his shoulder, and Dr Brown's kind voice said –

"Don't lose heart, my little fellow, God has sent you friends at last; and now we are going to see what we can do for you!"

Looking up, Froggy saw that the doctor and the clergyman and Mrs Blunt had now drawn close to the bedside.

"I am going to send a lady to you," said Mr Wallace gently, "who will look after you, and nurse your little brother, and bring him all that he wants."

At the mention of a *lady,* Froggy felt disturbed. His thoughts instantly flew to the grand fly-a-way ladies, whom the boys chaffed in the streets, with large chignons and Grecian bends.[58] How, thought he, would one of these do in the garret? But Mr Wallace's next words reassured him.

"She is a very kind, good lady," continued he, "accustomed to nursing and sickness, and she will do for your brother all that his mother would have done, if she had been alive. Miss Goff," he said, addressing himself to Mrs Blunt, "is one of the matrons of our Orphanage, so she will know exactly what to do in this case."

"Please, sir, when will she come?" asked Froggy.

"As soon as she is able – I'm going off to her at once," said Mr Wallace. "It may not be possible for her to come just yet. In the meanwhile, Mrs Blunt has promised to do all she can for you."

As he spoke, he slipped some money into the charwoman's hand.

"There, that will keep a good fire here and buy anything that is necessary till Miss Goff comes."

Mrs Blunt curtseyed and thanked him, and then they all quietly left the bedside, and went out on to the landing, where they talked together for a few minutes in hushed tones. It was likely that Mr Wallace and the doctor were giving Mrs Blunt some last directions as to what she was to do for Benny, till the lady from the Orphanage came. Froggy heard them go downstairs, and then Mrs Blunt came back into the room with her face very grave and her eyes full of tears.

"Mrs Blunt," said Froggy, looking up into her face, "do you think Benny'll soon get well?"

"The doctor'll do all he can," said Mrs Blunt kindly, "but he's very ill, Froggy, very ill indeed. He's to have his draught now, and the doctor thinks that p'r'aps he'll go to sleep, and if he do fall off, Froggy, mind you're not on no account to wake him. We wants 'im to go to sleep – that's his best chance."

She poured the draught out into a mug, and brought it to the bedside. Froggy feared that Benny might object to it, as he had objected to his medicine yesterday; but to his surprise Benny sat up and drank it with avidity, for he was feverishly thirsty, and the draught felt cool and pleasant to his lips. This done, Mrs Blunt laid him down soothingly, and covered him over, telling Froggy to be sure to watch, and see that he did not throw himself about. "I shall be up and down," she said, the last thing, "to see how he's getting on, and I'm going to bring you something to eat, Froggy. The clergyman said he'd send some fresh meat in for us all to have a good dinner, God bless him!" Then she made up the fire and went downstairs, leaving Froggy alone with his brother. We all know what it is, do not we? to be sitting by the bedside of some beloved one after a night or day of feverish tossing, and to be watching and praying for the blessed repose of sleep to come to them. How long it seems in coming, but when it does come, like many another good thing earnestly prayed for, and at last given, how unspeakably blessed it is!

It seemed a *very* long time to Froggy before Benny showed any signs of sleeping. He continued to murmur and to toss about as restlessly as ever for some time, after Mrs Blunt left the garret, and Froggy was continually occupied in the hopeless task of keeping him covered up. But at last, at last! a delicious change came, something like the lulling of waters after a great storm; for Benny got suddenly quiet, and Froggy became aware that his eyelids had drooped, his lips were parting; and listening, his ear caught the sound of short, regular breathing. If nothing came to disturb him, he would assuredly be asleep in a few minutes. Froggy sat like a grave little sentinel beside him, holding his breath, and stirring neither hand nor foot, on very tenter-hooks lest something should break the happy spell. The street outside was full of turmoil and noise. There were costermongers with their barrows crying their cheap wares, dustmen going their rounds, calling out at intervals, "Dust ho-a, dust ho-a!" and cabs and carts rattling past in a continual stream. And inside the house, there were noises too. Now and then, a door banged sharply, or a child screamed, or a lodger called down to a neighbour below; there was never anything of peace or repose in Mrs Ragbon's house. At these sounds Benny sometimes stirred, but he did not wake.

After a time Mrs Blunt came softly up the stairs and put her head in at the door.

"Asleep?" she whispered.

"Yes," nodded Froggy.

Then she entered cautiously, and crept to the bedside with a plate of meat and bread, which she deposited on Froggy's lap.

"Eat it," she whispered, "it will do you good, Froggy. It's fine butcher's meat."

She waited one moment with her eyes fixed steadfastly on Benny's face.

"Ain't he red?" said Froggy, following her eyes, "and don't he look small, mum, and funny?"

"Bless him!" was all she could say, for the poor mother was thinking of another little suffering face that had lain looking just like his lately in the room below; and it is possible that just then a vision arose before her of two little playmates meeting on the shores of a heavenly land, which filled her eyes with tears, and blinded her for the moment. She turned and poked up the fire; then she softly left the room.

Froggy sat with the plate on his lap for some time after she was gone, looking down at it, but not eating.

By and by he took the bread and began munching it solemnly, but the meat he did not even taste. It would be so splendid for Benny, he thought, when he woke up, and cried for something to eat.

"He'll be ever so hungry, I guess, when he wakes," said Froggy to himself, and he stretched out one hand, and put the plate down noiselessly on the floor beside him.

As the morning wore on, and Benny still slept, an overpowering sense of fatigue came over poor Froggy. The walk to Buckingham Palace and back had been a long journey for him yesterday, and he had gone through anxiety and trouble enough since yesterday evening to try a strong man even, let alone a little weak, half-fed boy like himself! It was not to be wondered at, then, that he was worn out, and tired to a degree which bordered on pain. He did all he could to shake off the drowsiness which he felt was stealing over him; for if Benny woke and wanted something, what would Benny do if he (Froggy) were asleep? Every now and then his heavy lids would, in spite of himself, close over his weary eyes and compel him to doze for a few minutes, till, in a vague, dreamy, troubled sort of way he realised what he was doing; then he would start up, and open his eyes wider than ever, and stare fixedly at some object, till the same thing happened, and everything had to be done over again. By and by an organ came, and droned away in the next street, and Froggy began silently to follow the tune in his own mind. He had heard the boys singing it in the streets –

"When Johnny comes marching home!"[59]

and the poor old organ seemed to be saying very distinctly in its dull old voice, "Hurra! hurra!" and to be never tired of declaring –

"And – we'll – all – be – happy when –
Johnny comes marching home!"

Suddenly – Froggy found that he was drifting away to the music of that tune; that somehow he was in a boat, drifting out to sea, with Benny standing on the shore beckoning to him. He tried to drift back, but he could not, and away he floated farther and farther, unconscious of everything except that he was resting deeply, and that God was with him in his little boat on the broad waters. Of course, we know what had happened. Froggy had fallen fast asleep, and was dreaming. Yes! there he sat, with his head bent forward, and his limbs dangling limply from the old broken chair, in a deep heavy slumber.

The day had grown a good deal older by the time Froggy awoke. Dark shadows were creeping over London, and reminding every poor toiler in the vast city once again that –

"Be the day ever so long,
At length it ringeth to evensong."[60]

The rough bawling cries of "Dust ho-a!" and cheap vegetables of the morning had given place to those of the water-cress and periwinkle sellers. The poor, unhappy women whom all Londoners know so well, were slipshodding along in woful garments, close to the area railings, with their baskets hung loosely on their arms, crying out in doleful trebles, "Any fine water-cre-sees!" and the old men with their periwinkles, keeping up a sort of duet with their baser cries of "Periwunks! periwunks!" were a sure sign that four o'clock, the poor people's tea hour in the East End, was nearly approaching.

Froggy woke himself with a long, deep-drawn sigh, and would have rubbed his eyes, only that something seemed to prevent him from raising his hands. Opening his eyes wide to make his vision clear, he looked to see what was the impediment, and found, to his surprise, that his body was packed up in a *shawl* that was a total stranger to him. Whose shawl could it be? How had it come, who had brought it, and who had packed him up like this? wondered Froggy, greatly amazed. It was not one of Mrs Blunt's shawls. It was far too thick and good a garment ever to have come out of *her* poor wardrobe, of that he was sure; but, then, whose could it be?

He turned his eyes to the bed, and there, over the tattered counterpane, was another strange wrap spread, so as almost entirely to hide the small thin body of Benny lying underneath. He began to guess what had happened. The lady of whom Mr Wallace had spoken must have come while he was asleep and covered them up like this.

How soundly asleep he must have been, thought Froggy, never to have heard her! Was it not possible that Benny might have awakened and called for something, and not been able to make him hear?

Froggy felt keenly reproached when he thought of this, and it was with the greatest anxiety that he started up, and looked into Benny's face to discover what he could of his state. Froggy was relieved; things seemed very well with Benny now. The fever flush had left his cheek, and he was sleeping very quietly and calmly.

There is a superstition amongst Norwegian mothers that when children smile in their sleep, they are talking with angels. Well, these mothers would certainly have said that Benny was talking with angels now, for over his little thin white face there kept fleeting, as he slept, smiles so unexpected and happy, that Froggy began actually to smile too, out of sympathy! Froggy was on tiptoe, gazing wonderingly down upon him, when suddenly the small, peaceful face of Benny clouded over, the smiles all vanished, and his tiny bosom began to heave up and down with heartbreaking sobs. In another moment Benny was sitting up in bed with his arms clasped round Froggy's neck, crying as if his very heart were coming from him in tears. Froggy's distress was great.

"Whatever is the matter?" he said, clasping Benny tightly in his arms, and looking out with startled, troubled eyes at the wall. "What's the matter, darlin'? what *is* the matter? Oh, I thought you was well – I did think you was better, Benny! Why, a minute ago you was laughing, and now you're cryin' like this!"

"I 'ad – a – dream," sobbed Benny, "a beautiful – appy dream" – – but he could say no more.

"What was it all about, darlin'?" asked Froggy rocking him to and fro. "It'll do you ever so much good to tell me, that it will. I always told mother whenever I 'ad a dream and didn't like it. Once I thought she was drownded in the sea, and I woke up a-cryin' just like you, and she comforted me ever so, cos I told her just hevery-think all about it!"

Benny now raised his head from Froggy's shoulder, and without loosening his arms from about his neck, he looked up into Froggy's face, and said in broken whispers –

"Froggy darlin', I dreamt I was dead and gone from here. I think I was in heaven, cos there was angels, and all the little children's faces was bright, and there was no tears. Nobody seemed hungry, and nobody seemed thinkin' about their rent. Little Deb was there, and she took me by the hand, and we listened to the angels singin'. And we went into fields and played, – and we was quite happy till Deb said – she'd go and see her mudder, and I said I'd – go and see you, Froggy! I come, and I looked in at the window, and, O Froggy, you was sitting all alone – in the dark cryin'!" and Benny sobbed again as if his very heart would break at the pitiful vision he had had in his dream of poor Froggy sitting alone and forlorn, with his head bowed in the empty garret, crying because he was dead.

"It was only a dream, you know, darlin'," said Froggy falteringly, clasping him very tight.

"Yes – yes!" murmured Benny, but he still continued to sob softly with that grievous, grievous pain with which we have all,

God help us! awakened out of sleep sometimes after an intensely real and sorrowful dream.

The two little brothers remained locked in each other's arms for some minutes. At last Benny's sobs grew gradually less, and Froggy felt that by degrees Benny's little arms were loosening about his neck, as if he would shortly fall away from him.

"Benny, do you feels a bit comforted?" asked Froggy gently.

"Yes, Froggy, I can hear the angels singin' again!" said Benny faintly, and a peculiar light shone over his face. His hands unclasped, and he laid his little rough head back on the pillow. For a moment he was very still, then he said –

"Froggy – what's the time?"

"I've bin asleep, darlin', and don't know *quite*," said Froggy, "but I should think it's a'most four, cos the cresses is being called."

"Then it's near evening – everybody's going home," murmured little Benny, and Froggy heard him sigh deeply, but that was all! There was nothing else to tell that in London's sorrowful army of starving, struggling people, another little sufferer had fallen out of the ranks, because there seemed no room for it here, and had gone with its pitiful face and bleeding heart to lay its head down, and to be consoled and comforted for ever more in the bosom of its Saviour! A look of unspeakable rest and satisfaction settled on his features, something that Froggy had never seen before, though Froggy remembered it in his mother's face after she was dead, and he thought Benny looked very like mother now, though not so old! He stooped down and kissed Benny; his face was very cold; he touched his hand and that was very cold too. He took the tiny limp hand between his own, and rubbed it, but he could get no warmth into it. How was it that Benny was so cold? But still Froggy did not guess the truth. He chafed the little hands more vigorously, he spoke to Benny, he kissed him again and again, at length he called to him, but he did not answer. Froggy grew uneasy, and was just thinking he would call Mrs Blunt, when he heard footsteps on the stairs. Somebody was coming – what a relief! He would be able to tell them of this strange deep sleep of Benny's.

A minute later the door opened, and two people entered. In the dusky light Froggy perceived that one of them was Mrs Blunt, and the other was evidently the lady whom Mr Wallace had said would come. She was tall and gentle looking, dressed in quiet black clothes, and carried in her hand a basket full of the food and necessaries, which she had discovered were so sadly wanting when she had visited the garret earlier in the day. She had found both little boys asleep then, and (as Froggy guessed) had covered them up softly with the wraps she had brought with her; then she had left to fetch the things with which she was laden now.

"Mrs Blunt," said Froggy in an anxious tone, directly they appeared. "Benny's gone so dreadfully asleep I can't wake him nohow, nor yet warm him neither. Just you feel his hand, how cold it be!"

Both women hastened to the bedside; Mrs Blunt with a look of grave apprehension on her face, as if she feared what she might see. She took Benny's chilly hand, and held it for a moment, but only for a very brief moment. The first touch satisfied her of what had happened, and she laid it down quietly, from whence she had taken it, on the counterpane. Miss Goff also took it, and without a word laid it down in the same way. None of this world's heat, they knew, would ever warm that little hand again; none of its joys or sorrows bring either smiles or tears to that little, still, white face on the pillow!

"Try and wake him!" said Froggy beseechingly, as they turned and looked at him.

Miss Goff then drew him to her, and putting her hand lovingly on his shoulder, she said with large tears in her eyes –

"Froggy, your little brother is very happy, God has made him so. You will not see him about any more here, but in another world you will meet him, and know him, and love him as your own little brother again, and he will know you in heaven."

For a moment Froggy did not speak. He seemed stunned and terrified.

"Can't we call 'im back?" he cried at last, "he ain't bin gone long! he said he'd never leave me; he said he'd be afraid to go that long journey all by his-self! – He's gone without nobody to look after him! he said e'd never, *never* go without me!" and now, poor little Froggy broke down and sobbed bitterly.

"He hasn't gone *alone*, Froggy," said Miss Goff ever so tenderly, with her hand still touching him, "God has been with him every step of the way. He would not suffer him to be either lonely or afraid; oh, be quite sure of that!"

"If I'd only knowed he was goin', I'd 'a kissed 'im more! I'd 'a said good-bye! I'd 'a told 'im more how I loved 'im!" wept Froggy. Then covering the little dead body with frantic kisses, he sobbed, "O Benny! Benny, come back! Benny, my brother – my dear little brother – O my brother, come back! I can't live without you, Benny! Benny! Benny!"

His words rang through the empty garret with a wail of sadness, which struck painfully into the hearts of the women standing by.

"You will not be left to live here alone," said Miss Goff tenderly, "you must come home with me."

Froggy looked round the poor garret, where he and Benny had been starving so long – the scene of so many struggles, so many tears (but with all its poverty it had a friendly home look to him) and he said mournfully, "Oh, let me stay!"

"You'll be ever so comfortable, Froggy, if you goes with the lady," said Mrs Blunt.

"I don't wants to go anywhere comfortabler," wept Froggy. "If only Benny 'ud come back just once again, and speak to me. O Benny! Benny!" he cried, "my dear little darling brother, come back! Benny, come back!"

It was vain to try and console him; the same frantic cry went up for a long while after, and no entreaties, no persuasions would induce him to leave the bedside on which lay the cold, lifeless, little body of Benny. When at last his strength was thoroughly spent, and he could sob no more, he threw himself down on the bed which Mrs Blunt had prepared for him in a corner of the garret, and Miss Goff heard him murmur as he closed his eyes, "Mother said we was all to come by and by – and now all's gone – 'cept me!"

So poor Froggy fell asleep. Miss Goff did not leave him. She knew what it would be to the broken hearted little brother to wake up in the morning and face his sorrow alone, so she did an angel's work, and stayed with him all the night through, God bless her!

* * *

CHAPTER XIV.
FROGGY COMFORTED.

I NEED not tell you how sorely Froggy cried when the day came for Benny to be laid in his coffin, and carried to the grave. When he kissed his little brother for the very last time, and looked upon his meek white face, and whispered to him his last passionate appeal to wake up before they came to carry him away, his grief was such that I care not to dwell upon it.

The funeral was much like little Deb's, only that there were not so many followers. Benny had no mother to weep for him, and no sisters; Froggy was his chief and only mourner. Miss Goff came very early in the morning, and when it was time took Froggy by the hand and followed with him through the maze of busy streets, out to the quiet cemetery, where so many tired citizens had entered into their rest. There were no butter-cups and daisies yet, but the little spring flowers were beginning to come up, and in the stillness and solitude about the silent graves, there seemed to be the Shepherd's voice sounding over all, reminding the poor mourners who came to weep there, of that sweet and most consoling promise, "And they shall be Mine, saith the Lord, in that day when I shall make up My jewels."

When all was over, Miss Goff took Froggy by the hand again and led him back to Shoreditch. Not to the old house with the blackened front, but to a large, clean, red brick one, standing near to the church, with the words printed over the door, in large letters, "Suffer the little children to come unto Me."

This was the Orphanage of which Miss Goff was under-matron, and where Mr Wallace had arranged that Froggy should be sheltered for a time, till another home could be provided for him. There were twelve little children, altogether, in the Orphanage. Very noisy and very happy seemingly, but poor Froggy felt strangely sad and lonely amongst them. He was very quiet and tearless after the funeral, doing all that was told him, and being a good little boy, but not joining in the children's games, or laughing with the rest. He was too sad to do that for many a day after Benny's death.

You will like to know what became of poor little Froggy, will you not? Well, he was removed from the Orphanage shortly, and sent, through the kindness of Dr Brown and Mr Wallace, to a Home for little boys in the city, where he is learning the trade of a carpenter. I must tell you of something which happened soon after Froggy entered the Home.

One winter's night, near Christmas time, Mr Wallace and several gentlemen of the Committee were busy at the Home auditing the accounts, and looking into the many matters which required their attention at this season of the year. They were seated round a wooden table, a gas burner overhead, and a roaring fire in the grate; in a small room off a much larger one, also gas-lit and warmed, where there were a number of boys (inmates of the Home) of all sizes and ages, of all kinds and descriptions to be seen. It was a bitterly cold night outside; the snow lay thick on the ground, clean and compact like the sugar on the top of a bride-cake, without an appearance of thawing, and everybody knew it was freezing still. Skating had been going on all day in the parks, and boys and men muffled-up to their chins, were returning brisk and joyous from the ice, confident they would have another good day upon it, to-morrow. How sharp the air was, and how the voices seemed to ring out when there was talking in the streets! It was well to be indoors on such a night!

Mr Wallace was sitting with a very grave face casting up accounts, and the other gentlemen were very busy too, when they were interrupted by the porter coming in and addressing Mr Wallace.

"Please, sir," he said, "there's a policeman outside wants to see you."

"A policeman!" repeated the clergyman looking up. "Do you know his business at all?"

"No, sir," said the man. "He's got something carrying in his arms, but he didn't say what it was."

Mr Wallace looked a little worried, but quietly laid down his pen and went out into the hall, from which he presently returned looking very thoughtful, and somewhat anxious.

"Well, Wallace, what is it?" asked the gentlemen.

"Shall I call in the policeman and let you see?" said Mr Wallace.

"Yes," said the gentlemen of the Committee. "Let the policeman come in."

There was a profound sensation in the larger room amongst the youthful inmates of the Home, when a moment later a very tall policeman entered, covered with snowflakes, carrying under his wet oilskin cape a bundle, from which hung down a small bare leg and a little boot.

It was a bundle with a voice, for they heard it distinctly crying; and excitement rose to a very high pitch, as the guardian of the public peace carried it solemnly through the crowd of boys into the room where Mr Wallace and the gentlemen of the Committee were waiting. The boys followed the policeman eagerly, and pressed close up to the door of the Committee room, which was left open behind him. Foremost amongst them was our little friend Froggy.

The policeman's story was soon told. An accident had happened on his beat, a very short distance from the Home; a poor working man carrying a little boy in his arms, had been knocked down by a runaway horse, and taken off insensible to the hospital. The child crying piteously, and terrified almost to death, had been left to the tender mercies of the crowd, till Police Constable 27 X appeared upon the scene, and took him under his wing to the Police Station.

"What have you found out about him, policeman?" asked one of the Committee.

"Well, all I can get out from him, sir," said the policeman smiling, "is, that his name is Billy, and that he lives upstairs with father, and has no mammy. Where he lives, or who he is, we shan't know, sir, till the father comes to himself in the hospital and tells us. Poor little chap!" he said kindly, looking down under his cape from which little sobs had been audible all the time, "he seemed quite cowed at our Station. The Inspector sent me on here with him. Billy, speak up now, and tell the gentlemen who you are!" and the policeman exhibited him to the Committee.

Unless there had been such trouble in the matter, I am sure that at this stage of the proceedings the gentlemen would all have laughed; as it was, a very amused look came into more than one countenance, and exclamations of, "Oh my!" "Oh lor'!" "What a

Figure 8 'A moment later a very tall policeman entered, covered with snowflakes, carrying under his wet oilskin cape a bundle, from which hung down a small bare leg and a little boot.'

Froggy's Little Brother. 1875. Cas. London: John F. Shaw.

little rum 'un!" came distinctly from the group of boys peeping in and pressing up against the open door.

Billy was the tiniest thing in the shape of a boy you ever saw, and quite one of the funniest! He had a small pinched face, with a very red nose, and bright little black eyes, which, in the gaslight, he blinked very much. He sat up in the policeman's arms and eyed the gentlemen very keenly for a few moments, as if he were anxious to take in their respective characters; then having satisfied himself apparently that no one was going to hurt him, he amused and astonished them all exceedingly, the stolid policeman into the bargain, by suddenly diving into his pocket, producing a nut, and quietly cracking it with a precision that showed Billy had got some good strong teeth of his own. He proceeded to eat it, taking very small bites at a time, much after the fashion of marmozet monkeys in the Zoological Gardens, and regarding the amused faces around him with a gravity that was truly comical.

"Are you hungry, Billy?" asked the policeman, giving him a little shake.

Billy vouchsafed no answer, but went on munching the nut.

"What's to be done with him, Wallace?" inquired the chairman laughing. "He seems wide awake to the charms of a nut, doesn't he?"

"Yes," said Mr Wallace, regarding him thoughtfully; "he's too small for the Home, I am afraid. How old are you, Billy?"

Billy either did not know, or he thought this a rude question, for he gave no answer.

"Not more than four or five, I should think," said Mr Wallace. "How the light and the warmth are reviving him! We had better call Mrs Holt, and hear what she says."

Mrs Holt was the matron of the Home; a kind, motherly person, whose heart went out in compassion at once to the unfortunate little waif in the policeman's arms. But she gave it as her decided opinion that he was too young for the Home.

"You see he's really not much more than a baby," she said, addressing the Committee. "And there's not a single bed vacant, gentlemen, in the house."

"Then I shall have to take him to the Union," said the policeman preparing to wrap him up again in his cape, and to face the cold and the snow once more.[61] Whereupon Billy uttered a little wail, and called out –

"Oh, please, don't take Billy out in cold again!" with an appealing look at the gentlemen, as if he thought they could not possibly countenance such an act of barbarity.

"It does seem hard to turn him out on a night like this," said the chairman. "Wait a moment, policeman. Mrs Holt, is there, indeed, no corner you could put him in? You see he's not very big."

"No, I's quite little," wailed Billy, showing that he understood very well what was said.

"Indeed, sir, every bed is full," declared the matron, "Unless we were to put him in with one of the boys" – –

Before she had time to finish her sentence a movement was heard amongst the eager, listening group at the door, and in rushed Froggy, his face quite quivering with excitement. Unmindful of the many eyes that were instantly turned upon him, he stood before the Commitee, the matron and the policeman, and made quite a passionate appeal on Billy's behalf.

"Let *me* take him! let *me* take him!" he cried. "Give him to me; don't turn him away! he shall have half my bed, half my supper, half my clothes, half everythink I have, but don't turn him away! He's like Benny, sir, somethink like Benny, ain't he?" turning with earnest, streaming eyes to Mr Wallace, the only one present who had known his little brother.

"Yes, Froggy, something like, certainly," said Mr Wallace, laying his hand kindly on Froggy's shoulder, as if to calm his excitement; then Mr Wallace turned to his friends, and in a few graphic sentences told them what he knew of Froggy and of Froggy's little brother.

The story seemed to touch them greatly. One kind old gentleman began clearing his throat, as if he were going to speak, but he could not get out a word. Another took off his glasses and began polishing them vigorously, as if they had become suddenly dimmed, which was really the case.

"Well, now, let us consider," resumed Mr Wallace. "Mrs Holt, what do you say to this arrangement; could Billy be put in with Froggy to-night, do you think?"

"Well, sir," said Mrs Holt, "Froggy's a good boy, and if he'll promise to help me with him, we *might* manage it just for to-night."

"Or say till after Christmas," said the kind old gentleman, who had recovered his voice. "I'll double my subscription, and I know others," looking at some benevolent gentlemen with whom he had been conferring, "will do the same in order to keep Billy in the Home for a time. Eh, Mrs Holt?"

Mrs Holt, nothing loth to give shelter to one more helpless little soul, cheerfully agreed, and the policeman was just about to hand him over to her when Froggy coming close up, stretched up his arms towards Billy, and said. – –

"Oh, please, sir, let me take 'im! come to me, darlin', won't you?" speaking to him as he used to speak to Benny. "I'll cuddle you up ever so warm in my nice little warm bed, and give you half my supper, Billy, and never let anybody hurt you, Billy, never, never!" And Billy, with a curious look of newly-awakened interest and satisfaction in his face, held out both his hands so as to clasp Froggy's, and showed unmistakably that he was going to take very heartily to his new-found protector and friend.

The last thing Mrs Holt saw that night when going her rounds through the quiet dormitories after everything was still and hushed in the Home, was little Billy fast asleep on Froggy's pillow, and Froggy sitting up in bed looking down with the intensest interest and delight on his funny little bedfellow.

"Are you very happy, Froggy," inquired the matron, as she paused for a moment with the light in her hand. "Is there room for you both in your little bed?"

"Oh yes, mum," answered Froggy. "Plenty." And then she noticed there were big tears falling down his cheeks, as he said, "He *is* like my darling little brother Benny somethink; I'm sure he is!"

"Would you like to call him *Benny,* Froggy?" asked the matron kindly.

"Oh no, no, *no,*" said Froggy, "I couldn't never do that! There'll never be another Benny again, *never*! But I think Billy's a bit like 'im, I do think that really, and I'll be ever so good to 'im, mum – for Benny's sake, that I will. You don't think the gentlemen'll turn him out after Christmas, does you, mum?"

"Well, I can't say – we shall see," said Mrs Holt soothingly. "Good-night, Froggy," and she passed on.

The policeman called at the Home next morning, to say that Billy's father had died during the night in hospital, from injuries received, without having recovered consciousness. So now Billy was an orphan and destitute. The kind gentlemen of the Committee still keep him in the Home, and the last thing I heard of Froggy and Billy was, that they, with several other pale-faced, sorrowful-eyed little boys, were wondering anxiously whether enough money would come into the Home this year to give them a treat in the country! The other boys had one last year, and, oh, what a day it was! Tea in a hay-field, and games afterwards, and *such* a ride through the city in decorated vans. The smell of the hay, and the singing of the birds, and the shouts of their play-fellows visited them in their dreams long afterwards, and quickens their comprehensions still, when on Sunday they are talked to of the love of God, and the beauty of all His works. Better than all the sermons and books in the world, will a day in the country teach them of these.[62]

Parents and little children, you especially who are rich, remember it is the Froggys and Bennys of London for whom your clergyman is pleading, when he asks you to send money and relief to the poor East End! They may be street Arabs, but they have immortal souls, and they are our brothers and sisters, though we may not own them. As we hope to partake of the same citizenship in the one Everlasting City, let us take care how we disregard our pastor's pleading, for when we are arraigned at the Last Day before the Judgment Seat of Christ, and Christ asks us, "What have you done for my little ones?" the excuse, "Lord, we never knew any!" will avail us little with Him, Who made His Kingdom above all a children's Kingdom, and Who will hold us responsible for the little souls that enter into His Presence there, maimed and scarred and ignorant for the want of the care, and love and teaching, which we on earth have denied them.

We may not from circumstances be able to go and labour personally amongst them, but we can help those who are, and there are so many ways of doing it! all through the year by sending our pennies and shillings to help schools, and Homes, and Kindergartens for their benefit; in summer time by responding liberally to the appeals made through the Press and other channels for funds to enable poor little East End children to have a day in the country; and at happy Christmas time, when appeals are made for warm clothing and Christmas dinners. Let us not be dismayed nor discouraged by the apparent smallness of the returns for what we do; if we cannot *cure* the sorrow and the sin, we may at least mitigate them, and are we not told to "sow in faith beside all waters?" Let us be content to wait for our reward till that Day when the truth of the saying, "Cast thy bread upon the waters, and thou shalt find it after many days," shall be manifested to us, as, doubt not, O rich man, it *shall* be manifested, wonderfully, fully, overflowingly, with the same Divine generosity which made the lame man not only to walk, but to leap; the wine at the wedding in Cana of Galilee to be *more* than enough; and the very fragments of the miraculous feast to be twelve baskets *full*!

Notes

Jessica's First Prayer

1 The first part of 'Jessica's First Prayer' (Chapters I and II) began on p.431 of *The Sunday at Home, A Family Magazine for Sabbath Reading*, 7 July 1866. The story appeared under the title 'Pages for the Young' by 'the author of "Fern's Hollow"'. There were no illustrations in the magazine serialisation, other than the illuminated first letters of each chapter. The first characters of each chapter in the Religious Tract Society's first hardback edition were also illuminated.

2 There were no chapter titles in *The Sunday at Home*; these only appeared with the first volume publication in 1867.

3 Henry Mayhew's description of coffee-stall keepers in his *Morning Chronicle* article of 30 November 1849 is similar to Stretton's depiction of Daniel's stall: 'The coffee-stall usually consists of a spring barrow with two, and occasionally four wheels. Some are made up of tables, and some have a trestle and board.' Mayhew adds that it is from the coffee-stall keepers that the poor man obtains his breakfast. Stalls are generally at the corner of a street and pitched in front of a tea dealer's shop; the coffee-stall keeper buys his goods there and so has leave to stand nearby. Mayhew also comments that the coffee-stall keepers are also frequently termed 'vendors of saloup', saloup being an aromatic drink made from bark, roots etc., but this is perhaps an ironic comment about the flavour of coffee sold from the stalls. Henry Mayhew, 'Letter X111'. Victorian London, http://www.victorianlondon.org/mayhew/mayhew13.htm [accessed 7 April 2012]. In his 1867 column, 'A Summer Night in the Streets', in *Once a Week*, Arthur Ogilvy writes that 'the coffee [from the penny-cup-of-coffee stalls] is ... warming, ... if deficient in quality'. Arthur Ogilvy, 'A Summer Night in the Streets', *Once a Week*, 4, 85 (1867), pp.187–92 (p.190). A joke column in *Fun* of 13 November 1869 states: 'A Coffee Stall.- Too often, Horse Beans'. Anon, 'A Coffee Stall', *Fun*, 10 (1869), p.101.

4 Jessica's dark eyes are referenced twice in this paragraph and may imply that she has Jewish or gypsy ancestry. (See note 6 for a discussion of Jessica's name.) Elaine Lomax notes that in Victorian literature the East End Jew and the gypsy share the status of 'eternal' or 'mythic' outcast and that both feature in Stretton's fiction. The city poor are central to many of Stretton's texts ... [and] '[t]hese urban masses were augmented by a seasonal influx of what Mayhew had termed "wandering tribes" – tramps, beggars and diverse itinerant labourers ... .The consequences of this intermingling are apparent in [Stretton's] *Lost*

Gip (1873: chapter 1); of uncertain paternity, the infant, with her black eyes and a tangled mass of black hair, is deemed a "thorough" or "reg'lar" little gipsy.' Elaine Lomax, *The Writings of Hesba Stretton: Reclaiming the Outcast* (Farnham and Burlington: Ashgate, 2009), pp.193–7.

5   *Griped*: colic/sharp pains in the bowel. In Jessica's case, this may refer to hunger pangs.

6   Jessica may have been named after Shylock's daughter in Shakespeare's *The Merchant of Venice*; in Chapter V, Jessica tells the minister that her mother used to play 'Jessica' at the theatre and the name would seem to be of Shakespearean origin. It may be a version of Jesca/Iscah (from Genesis 11:29) who appears to be Abraham's niece. Hanks, P., K. Hardcastle and F. Hodges, eds (2006) *A Dictionary of First Names 2nd ed.* (Oxford: Oxford University Press), online version 2012. However, the minister comments, 'that is a strange name,' (p.20) which further establishes Jessica as other and accentuates the issue of her ancestry.

7   Daniel is anxious that Jessica may bring or attract other similar waifs to his stall and thus presumably drive away his regular customers.

8   'Stock-in-trade' is not hyphenated in *The Sunday at Home* (p.431).

9   'both of her benumbed hands' in *The Sunday at Home* (p.431).

10   'Jessica's use of the term "Prime!"'(which she repeats in Chapter 8 when describing Daniel's coffee and buns to the minister) would seem to be a slang term for 'the best'. In the 1848 publication *Sinks of London Laid Open*, author unknown, illustrations by George Cruikshank, the volume's Flash Dictionary explains 'prime twig' as meaning in high condition. Cruikshank, G., illustrator,*Sinks of London Laid Open: A Pocket Companion for the Uninitiated to which Is Added a Modern Flash Dictionary Containing All the Cant Words, Slang Terms, and Flash Phrases now in Vogue, with a List of the Sixty Orders of Prime Coves* (London: J. Duncombe, 1848), p.120.

11   *Jade*: a disreputable woman.

12   This description of 'the snug, dark corner, with its warm fire … and its fragrant smell of coffee' is of a womb-like nurturing paradise for the child, and her feared expulsion, through her sin, is positioned as akin to The Fall. The title of the chapter , 'Jessica's Temptation', emphasises this Biblical resonance.

13   Daniel's comment that he 'could never have done it myself' is highly ambiguous. It may be that he would never have attempted to steal the money, although his look of 'strange emotion', his shaking head and repetition, suggest that he might have done so, had he also been destitute.

14   The second part of the*The Sunday at Home* serialisation (14 July 1866) begins here (p.447).

15   'Chapel' instead of 'walls' in *The Sunday at Home* (p.447). Brian Alderson suggests that the frequency of changes to do with the word 'chapel' (subsequent changes, itemized in these notes, include 'chapel-keeper' to 'beadle', 'chapel' to 'church' etc.) reflect the desire of the

publishers to secure a wide market: 'In our secular age we have lost the niceties of doctrine which served to characterise particular Nonconformist sects, or even factions within the Established Church, but the Religious Tract Society was clearly endeavoring to give *Jessica*, as a book, a more widely acceptable face than she needed to have for the fairly predictable readership of *The Sunday at Home*'. Brian Alderson,'Jessica Again', *Children's Books History Society Newsletter*, 29 (1984), pp.4–7 (pp.5–6).

16 Jessica refers to Daniel as both 'Mr Daniel' and 'Mr Dan'el'.

17 'these' instead of 'those' in *The Sunday at Home* (p.447).

18 'chapel-keeper' instead of 'pew-opener' in *The Sunday at Home* (p.447).

19 The description of the police as 'natural' enemies of the street child references a common preconception of the street arab as criminal. In Stretton's *Lost Gip* (1873), street child protagonist Sandy is apprehended by a policeman who tells Sandy's adult companion: 'He's been doing nothing that I know of now...I must take care he doesn't give me the slip. Slippery as eels all this sort are.' Hesba Stretton, *Lost Gip* (London: Religious Tract Society, 1873), pp.57–8.

20 'chapel' instead of 'baize covered' in *The Sunday at Home* (p.447).

21 The presence of the policeman suggests that attendance is only permissible to those individuals perceived as appropriate members of the congregation. In *The Quiver* (26 March 1864), a correspondent comments that '[a] good coat is unfortunately now regarded as a necessary qualification for entering a church or chapel; and this probably is one of the principal reasons why places of worship in the metropolis...are rarely filled....although a poor man has a right to a seat in any church or chapel...he is nevertheless practically excluded'. Anon, 'Progress of the Truth: The Work of the Gospel in London, No.III, *The Quiver: An Illustrated Magazine for Sunday and General Reading*, 128 (1864), pp.477–8 (p.477).

22 'barefoot' in *The Sunday at Home* (p.448).

23 In *The Sunday at Home*, this section reads: 'It was an untold relief to Daniel that Jessica did not ply him with questions about the chapel when she came for breakfast every Wednesday morning' (p.448).

24 '...while he was lighting up the chapel' in *The Sunday at Home* (p.448).

25 'The chapel-keeper' in *The Sunday at Home* (p.448).

26 In *The Sunday at Home* text, Winny says, 'Let us call the chapel-keeper', rather than referring to Daniel by name. The alteration in the text of the first hardback edition to include Daniel's full name results in a continuity flaw in Chapter VIII when the minister asks Jessica who 'Daniel' is; if the minister is unaware of Daniel's first name, it is unlikely that his daughters would know.

27 In *The Sunday at Home*, a 'not' is inserted after 'have' (p.448) which would seem appropriate for a modern reader, given the Christian resonances of Winny's statement. However, Alderson identifies this

difference as having 'much to say about the intensity with which Biblical texts were scrutinized in the Age of Doubt' (p.6). He writes: 'To the lay reader of today this seems to make perfect sense as a plea for Christian equality: "not to accept Jessica will be a failure to demonstrate Christ's ecumenical love". For Hesba Stretton, however, it represented a misreading of the passage in the General Epistle of James (chapter 2, verse 1), and when the book was published the quotation was corrected and the second negative omitted ... At first ... this seemed like a misprint, the sentence apparently running counter to Winny's enthusiasm ... [but] a close reading of the Authorised Version, and the persuasive arguments of the scholar who undertook the collation of texts, clarifies for me that James, and Winny, mean: "not to accept Jessica will be to exercise the faith of Christ according to one's respect for persons (i.e. making class distinctions)".' Alderson adds that it is 'an interesting example of a nice theological point being properly sustained' and suggests that the children of 1867 may have been as well versed in such things as Jane who comments, 'the Bible seems plain'. Alderson, 'Jessica Again', *Children's Books History Society Newsletter*, pp.4–7.

28 The third part of *The Sunday at Home* serialisation (21 July 1886) begins here.

29 Jessica's mother's former profession is described euphemistically; in the sequel, *Jessica's Mother* (1867) she states that she 'rode in [her] carriage once'. Hesba Stretton, *Jessica's Mother* (London: Religious Tract Society, 1867), p.13. As Nancy Cutt explains, this comment identifies her in nineteenth-century parlance as the former kept mistress of a wealthy man. Nancy Cutt, *Ministering Angels: A Study of Nineteenth-Century Evangelical Writing for* Children (London: Croom Helm, 1879), p.138. Already reminiscent of her mother in terms of her exposure to the public gaze, Jessica may be fated to replicate the older woman's life; the term 'play' is ambiguous and implicitly sexual. The child as performer was a phenomenon that Victorian commentators frequently deplored. For example, in the *Wesleyan-Methodist Magazine* of November 1872, writer J.V.B.S. reports meeting a child in Angel Alley: We chance upon a little pallid, golden-haired child, less than nine years old, – a child in name, a woman in address. Her *sobriquet* is " *La Petite*", and her craft is dancing in theatres, thereby maintaining her parents. At four years of age she was a "fairy" in pantomimes. Her quickness was detected and utilized by a "gentleman," who had her taught to dance, and has recouped himself by hiring her out for sensational performances. This is ..."defrauding of childhood" a precious little creature.' J.V.B.S. 'Life Among the London Lowly', *The Wesleyan-Methodist Magazine*, 18 (1872) pp.1010–14, (p.1010).See also Marah Gubar, 'The Drama of Precocity: Child Performers on the Victorian Stage' in ed. Dennis Denisoff, *The Nineteenth-Century Child and Consumer Culture* (Aldershot and Burlington: Ashgate, 2008), pp.63–78.

30 The introductory 'but' is absent in *The Sunday at Home* (p.463).

31 'Thy' was capitalised in later editions.

32 The adage that 'cleanliness is next to Godliness' would seem to be implied in Jessica's comment and is a notion replicated by other publications seeking charity for destitute children. For example, Mary Jane, a rescued waif adopted by *The Quiver*, is represented by a drawing and the editorial comments that she looks 'so sweet and clean in the brown dress and large white pinafore...that we could not refrain from giving her a kiss'; only now that she is clean can she be petted. Anon.,'The Life-story of the Quiver Waifs', *The Quiver: An Illustrated Magazine for Sunday and General Reading*, (1888), pp.1–3, (p.1–2).

33 'chapel' instead of 'church' in *The Sunday at Home* (p.464).

34 'come to your chapel' instead of 'come to hear you' in *The Sunday at Home* (p.464).

35 *Spree*: a period of fun or extravagance, but here with a suggestion of over-indulgence, given that Jessica's mother has already been identified as a frequent drunk.

36 Jessica's mother not only forbids her daughter to read the Bible, but attacks the missionary who comes to her home and so is positioned as beyond salvation, although Lomax suggests that there may be narrative mockery of institutions such as missionaries in Jessica's words and an authorial endorsement of female agency in Jessica's seemingly positive and admiring statement. Indeed, as she adds, a number of Stretton's female characters are strong-willed and so question the desirability of the passive female. Elaine Lomax, *The Writings of Hesba Stretton: Reclaiming the Outcast*, p.142.

37 'and die for us' is absent in *The Sunday at Home* (p.464).

38 The fourth part of *The Sunday at Home* serial begins here on 28 July 1866, p.476.

39 'God' instead of 'our Father' in *The Sunday at Home* (p.476).

40 'chapel lamps' instead of 'lamps' in *The Sunday at Home* (p.476).

41 'Mr Daniel' instead of 'Mr Dan'el' in *The Sunday at Home* (p.476).

42 In *The Sunday at Home*, this passage reads: ' "Yes," said Daniel, kneeling beside her, and taking her wasted hand in his. / "Did he tell you at chapel?" she asked, faintly. / "Yes," he answered again, parting the matted hair upon her damp forehead' (p.476).

43 'chapel' instead of 'house' in *The Sunday at Home* (p.476).

44 'nor did Daniel' in *The Sunday at Home* (p.476).

45 'food, and fuel, and light, and all night long' in *The Sunday at Home* (476).

46 'to God' is changed to 'of God' in later editions.

47 'sick' instead of 'ill' in *The Sunday at Home* (p.477).

48 'warning' instead of 'waning' in *The Sunday at Home* (p.477). Both words suggest that Jessica is dying.

49 Daniel evidently sees the minister as culpable for his continuing condition as a sinner and the minister appears to agree. Here Daniel also

confirms that Jessica has been chosen by God to instigate his salvation.

50   'chapel' instead of 'place' in *The Sunday at Home* (p.477).

51   An additional 'then the chapel was eighteen shillings a week' in *The Sunday at Home* (p.477).

52   'chapel folks' instead of 'chapel-wardens' in *The Sunday at Home* (p.477).

53   'God' instead of 'Our Father' in *The Sunday at Home* (p.477)

54   'chapel-keeper' instead of 'beadle' in *The Sunday at Home* (p.477).

55   In later editions, 'chillness' is replaced by 'dullness'.

56   There is an additional 'somewhat nearer the chapel' after 'little house' in *The Sunday at Home* (p.477), emphasising both Daniel and Jessica's proximity to God from this point.

57   'chapel' instead of 'building' in *The Sunday at Home* (p.477).

Froggy's Little Brother

1   In Brenda's *Little Cousins or Georgie's Visit to Lotty*, middle-class children Lotty and Georgie are allowed to 'give the nod' to the Punch and Judy men who come into the London square where they live, thus signing to them to set up their show. An illustration by T.Pym shows the girls watching the performance through the dining room window. Brenda,*Little Cousins or Georgie's Visit to Lotty*(London: John F. Shaw, 1880), pp.132–5.

2   Froggy's father evidently visits public houses on a regular basis and while this is the first reference to the detrimental effects of alcohol, later in the chapter Froggy fears that his mother has been drinking, while the family's landlady is 'given to drinking' and beats her children when drunk (see Chapter II). Brenda was seemingly pro-Temperance and her only adult book, *The Secret Terror* (London: Stanley Paul, 1909), directly confronts the consequences of female alcoholism.

3   This (mis)spelling of Shoreditch may have been intentional to suggest a childish voice and continued to appear in editions until 1896; later editions use 'Shoreditch'.

4   'Wofully' is changed to 'woefully' in Avery's 1968 edition.

5   *pannikin*: a small cup or bowl, usually of tin.

6   The night school mentioned by Froggy's mother, and presumably the same school that has been closed down in Chapter II, is likely to be based on those run by the Ragged School Union. In 'Our Week Night Schools: Who will come to the rescue? 'in the *Ragged School Union Magazine* of November 1863, the author, calling for more volunteer workers, states that there are currently 93 Night Schools in the West and South of London. The writer comments that attendants at a Night School are of a rougher class, their language less refined, of a more unwashed aspect, and more ragged in attire, than consists with a well-ordered Day School ... .the distinctive character of a Day School

is *preventative,* whilst that of Night School is *reformatory* [sic]. Anon, 'Our Week Night Schools: Who Will Come to the Rescue?'The *Ragged School Union* Magazine, 15, 179 (1863), pp.250–4 (p.250). Information of this nature may well have been the basis for the description of misbehaviour at the night school, described in Chapter II.

7   In the nineteenth century, churches often rented pews to those who could afford them, but as the century progressed, social concern for the spiritual wellbeing of the poor resulted in increased free seating.

8   Froggy is referencing the New Testament. 'And why do you worry about clothes? See how the lilies of the field grow. They do not labour or spin' (Matthew 7:28); 'Are not two sparrows sold for a penny? Yet not one of them will fall to the ground apart from the will of your Father....you are worth more than sparrows' (Matthew 10:26–31).

9   The first temperance pledge made in 1832 by Joseph Livesey of Preston (and others) read: 'We agree to <u>Abstain</u> from all liquors of an <u>Intoxicating Quality,</u> whether ale Porter Wine or Ardent Spirits, except as medicine'. Anon, 'Temperance Notes and News', *The Quiver,* 831, (1901), p.842. Concern about the dangers of alcohol, particularly in relation to its effect on the poor, increased through the century and is notably described with some sympathy by writer George Sims in Chapter 3 of *How the Poor Live*: 'Drink is the curse of these communities; but how is it to be wondered at? The gin-palaces flourish in the slums, and fortunes are made out of men and women who seldom know where tomorrow's meal is coming from. Can you wonder that that gaudy gin-palaces, with their lights and their glitter, are crowded?....The gin-palace is Heaven to them compared to the Hell of their pestilent homes'. George Sims, *How the Poor Live* (London: Chatto and Windus, 1883), p.15.

10 A 'four-in-hand drag' was a type of coach with seats on the top, driven by a team of four horses and the 'merry' men in light coats and hats with blue veils twisted round them are wearing a traditional Derby Day outfit. Prints and paintings of Derby Day between 1860 and 1880 show that white, cream or pale yellow coats and hats were worn over Morning Dress suits, either when the weather was bad or when travelling by coach and horses. The coats are likely to have been made from undyed (and thus cheaper) material as their primary function was protection. Veils or scarves around top hats were adopted earlier and protected the wearer from dust; they were also sometimes in the colours of a favoured runner. There are numerous references to blue veils in commentaries on Derby Day. In 'Notes and Sketches' in *The Morning Post*, 4 December 1854, the correspondent writes: 'If, on the Derby-day or Oaks Day of 1853, one had walked into St. James's-street about 11 o'clock in the morning, there were to be seen the young men of fashion with their admirably appointed carriages, preparing for the sports of the day, and most of them with blue veils tied round their hats, intended to be used as guards for their complexion, when

encountering the sun and dust of the road' (p.2). *The Leeds Mercury* of 30 May 1872 in 'The Derby Day' (from our own correspondent) tells how '[y]oung men in the Guards and "men about town" were mounting to the roofs of their drags and four-in-hands at a time which on any other day would not be dreamt of in their philosophy. The clerks in the city were now sitting on the roofs of 'buses marked "For Epsom Downs", jauntily arranging their green or blue veils round their white hats when they should have been vaulting on their stools and opening their ledgers' (p.5).

11 The Shoeblacking Brigade (also known as the Blacking Brigade and Boot-blacking Brigade) arose from the Ragged School Shoeblack Society, established in 1851 to provide work for those being trained at Ragged Schools, although increasing numbers of 'rough' boys meant that discipline and instruction became part of the training. See Rob Roy, 'Rise, Progress, and Results of the Ragged School Shoeblack Societies', *Ragged School Union Quarterly Record*, 3 (1878), pp.1–15. Froggy dismisses ideas of becoming a shoe-black because he lacks knowledge of how to apply, but such an occupation would have provided him with a respectable means of earning a living.

12 *Echoes*: refers to the London *Echo*, a halfpenny daily newspaper first published in 1868.

13 Brenda's attempts to depict colloquial speech are sometimes problematic and often inconsistent. Here, for example, Benny talks about 'Fader', but eight lines later refers to 'father'.

14 Although the chapter ends at this point in the first edition, all subsequent editions carry an additional, significant paragraph: 'The owners of the drag, which had caused the death of Froggy's father, called at the hospital the next day to make what reparation they could for the accident which their reckless driving had brought about. But alas! too late. They were greatly dismayed to learn that their drunken carelessness had cost the life of a fellow-creature, and that the orphan boy had returned to his desolate home, without leaving any trace behind him.' This addition, believed to have been written by Brenda, confirms that the men of the 'merry' party were drunk, but also suggests that some moderation to the text was deemed necessary to counteract the seemingly uncaring recklessness of the group as depicted in the first edition. While the incident may not reflect an actual accident, the Derby traffic was evidently dangerous in the 1870s. In 1873 there were several accidents as the crowd returned from that year's Derby Day; a cart and wagon collided and a man died in the ensuing fight, a child was 'jerked out of a wagonnette under the wheels of an omnibus and killed and a young man injured his spine when his "velocipede" [bicycle] was hit by a "gaily-equipped wagonette" [sic]'.Anon, *The Dundee Courier and Argus*, 6191 (1873), p.3.

15 *Captain's Biscuit*: is a hard biscuit related to ship's biscuits that can be dipped in warm liquid and softened.

16 The Metropolitan (underground) Railway opened in January 1863 and ran from Paddington to the Farringdon Street terminus.

17 The woman is confused by the way in which police districts are organized at that time. Colonel Sir Edmund Henderson was Chief Commissioner of the Metropolitan Police from 1869 to 1886 and Colonel Sir James Fraser Chief of the City Police from 1863–90.

18 The old woman's reference to 'the Palice' is likely to be to the Crystal Palace, erected to house the Great Exhibition of 1851 and later moved to Sydenham Hill.

19 Mac is evidently avoiding school, but the narrative offers no explanation as to why the school-board officer is not also pursuing Froggy and Benny. The 1870 Elementary Education Act made provision for the elementary education of all children aged 5–13 and established school boards to oversee the network of schools. A number of school boards required compulsory attendance, although there were exemptions. See Derek Gillard,'Education in England: A Brief History', www.educationengland.org.uk/history (2011) [accessed 5 January 2012]

20 Benny recites a verse from Jane Taylor's *The Star* (1806).

21 Although the narrator stresses that the poor suffered as a result of this strike, there were evidently some sympathies for the action of the miners. In the London *Examiner* of March 8 1873, correspondent 'Y.Z.' stated: 'The strike in South Wales...has, within the last few weeks, assumed the importance of a conflict of principles. On the one hand, the men have been making proposal after proposal for the resumption of work on definite terms...and the masters have consistently declined to discuss these terms....They have treated their workmen as headstrong children who have petulantly broken loose from authority....It is for this reason that we regret the approaching termination of the strike, and the triumph of the baneful principle which is represented by the masters'. Y.Z.,'Current Events', *Examiner*, 3397 (1873), pp.248–51 (p.250).

22 The old woman sells seasonal fruit: cherries in the summer and apples in winter.

23 The author of this verse is unknown.

24 The fact that Australian meat is offered to the boys is a highly topical comment at the period of publication. Cattle plague and rapid population growth reduced cattle herds in the mid-nineteenth century in Britain and by 1867 Australia was said to be exporting some 30,000 lbs of beef to England every month. However, it was not always welcome or perceived as authentic. In 1871, a writer in *The Sporting Times* commented: 'Some of the papers are setting up a cry in favour of the horrible stuff they call Australian meat. I do not believe it all comes from the Antipodes, but is manufactured here from the refuse and offal of Smithfield [London's meat market]. There may be good meat in Australia, but precious little of it comes here'. Anon, 'The Woman About Town', *The Sporting Times* (1871), p.348.

25   *Stiver*: generic term for a coin of very little worth.

26   Brenda comments further on cruelty to animals in *Uncle Steve's Locker* (1888), linking this with adult cruelty to children: 'How often we see mothers and guardians...not confined by any means to the lower strata of society, allowing to pass unnoticed the reckless stamp of the small foot on the worm in its path...[societies such as the NSPCC] are good, and do a noble work; but if we want to pluck the evil they fight against out by the root, we must aim at the *young* of the land, inculcate early in the well-to-do nurseries...that it is a base...thing to hurt, to harass, to hunt, to render unhappy anything that has *life* in it, of whatever degree.' Brenda, *Uncle Steve's Locker* (London: John F. Shaw, 1888), p.209.

27   *Clemmed*: starved.

28   *Shaver*: small boy.

29   A misspelling of 'Froggy' that appears to have been replicated in all subsequent editions.

30   'Neck and crop' is similar to 'coming a cropper'; both expressions derive from falling from a horse and indicate a tumbling fall.

31   *On my own hook*: by himself.

32   Mac and his friends dress as minstrels for their Derby Day outing and sing a music-hall favourite, composed by Harry Copeland (c.1865) and popularised by the 'Great Vance'. Information from JScholarship https://jscholarship.library.jhu.edu and Mudcat.org: Traditional Music and Folklore Collection and Community mudcat.org., (n.d.) [accessed 7 March 2012]. There are variants of this song, but the following extract from one early version would seem to be particularly appropriate for Mac and his companions:

> We're jolly dogs who take our ease,
> And never take things cross.
> We neither heed laws or police,
> And spree about, of course;
> And we always are so jolly, oh, So jolly, oh, so jolly, oh.
> A fig for melancholy, oh.
> Rare jolly dogs are we

CHORUS

> We lark – we spree – we laugh, ah, ah.
> We laugh, ha, ha, and spree and sing. Rare jolly dogs are we. Fal lal, lal, tol, lol, lol, fol, lol, lol, Fol lol lol, tral lal lal, lol lol lol, Fal-de-riddle-iddle i-do. Slap, bang! Here we are again. Here we go again! Here we go again. Slap, bang! here we go again. Rare jolly dogs are we.

> Firth b.27 (362), Bodleian Library Catalogue of Ballads, http://bodley24.bodley.ox.ac.uk, 9 (n.d.) [accessed April 2012].

33   The 'grand to-do' at St Paul's Cathedral was on 27 February 1872 to give thanks for the recovery from illness of Albert Edward, Prince of Wales.

34   Queen Victoria visited the Shoreditch area in April 1873 when she drove to Victoria Park. The mortality rate in the vicinity had been

blamed on overcrowding, insanitary conditions and polluted air and 30,000 local residents had urged the formation of a park in an 1840 petition to the Queen. The park was opened in 1845.

35 'Jump Jim Crow', a minstrel routine song and dance, was performed from 1828 by its author Thomas Dartmouth. The toy would have been a minstrel figure that moved ('jumped') when the string was agitated.

36 There is an assumption that Brenda's readers will be familiar with the sideshow 'Happy Families', but it is puzzling that there is no narrative comment on such shows, given that Brenda appeared to deplore cruelty to animals (see note 26).Henry Mayhew describes Happy Families as 'assemblages of animals of diverse habits and propensities living amicably, or at least quietly, in one cage.' He reports the words of a man who has been connected with Happy Families for three years: 'In our present cage we have 54 birds and wild animals, and of 17 different kinds; 3 cats, 2 dogs (a terrier and a spaniel), 2 monkeys, 2 magpies, 2 jackdaws, 2 jays, 10 starlings … ,6 pigeons, 2 hawks, 2 barn fowls, 1 screech owl, 5 common sewer-rats, 5 white rats (a novelty), 8 guinea pigs, 2 rabbits (1 wild and 1 tame), 1 hedgehog and 1 tortoise. They live together in their cage all night, and sleep in a stable unattended by any one. They were once thirty-six hours, as a trial, without food … and no creature was injured, but they were very peckish, especially the birds of prey.' Henry Mayhew, *London Labour and the London Poor, Vol.3* (London: Dover, 1861), pp.215–6.

37 Mac and his friends speak 'a mysterious language' of their own which is incomprehensible to Froggy, both literally and metaphorically, because it is the language of thieves. In *Passing English of the Victorian Era*, James Redding Ware lists 'Flatty' as thieves' dialect, explaining: 'A greenhorn. An endearing diminutive of flat, who would be more despised than the less contemned flatty'. James Redding Ware, *Passing English of the Victorian Era: A Dictionary of Heterodox English, Slang and Phrase* (London: Routledge, 1909), p.134.

38 'Old Solomon' is likely to be a reference to real fence, Isaac (Ikey) Solomon, thought to be the inspiration for Dickens' Fagin. There are clear resonances with *Oliver Twist* (1837–8) in this chapter as innocent Froggy unwittingly joins with pickpockets.

39 *The House*: the workhouse.

40 *'Bucknam Palace'* : Buckingham Palace, the official London residence of Britain's queens and kings since 1837.

41 'Gutter children' are here presented as different to Froggy and Benny, although they are as destitute as the street children. The narrative thus separates Froggy and his brother from the hordes of street urchins and positions them as the more acceptable 'other', implicitly worthy of sympathy and assistance.

42 *Unparliamentary language*: language deemed inappropriate for use in the House of Commons, and here suggesting that Mrs Ragbon is abusive.

43   *Mr B59*: B59 is the identification number on the policeman's uniform.
44   *Winkle tea*: Winkles are small edible sea snails, popular in the nineteenth and early twentieth centuries, and eaten using a pin to hook the snail out.
45   The author of this verse is John Samuel Bewley Monsell (1811–75) who wrote eleven volumes of poetry encompassing 300 hymns.
46   Benny has seen a dog cart, often used by pedlars.
47   It was customary to keep the body of a dead relative in the house prior to the funeral, and although Debbie's body is buried the following day, the destitute poor were not always able to arrange burial so swiftly. George Sims describes how the dead of the poor can remain in the house for some time after death: 'let the reader in doubt ask any sanitary inspector or officer of health to whom he can get an introduction if it is not an appalling fact that the poor have grown so used to discomfort and horrors that they do not look upon a corpse in the room they live, and eat, and sleep in as anything very objectionable! It often happens there is no money to pay for the funeral, and so, with that inertness and helplessness bred of long years of neglect, nothing at all is done, no steps are taken, and the body stops exactly where it was when the breath left it'. George Sims, *How the Poor Live* (London: Chatto and Windus, 1883), p.37.
48   From the hymn, 'Hark, Hark My Soul' (1854) based on Psalm 30:5.
49   Hymn written by Hohann W. Meinhold (1835) and translated by Catherine Winkworth in 1868. 'Hymnary.org: a comprehensive index of hymns and hymnals', www.hymnary.org., (n.d.) [accessed 2 April 2012].
50   Brenda's depiction of Froggy and Benny's scavenging for survival is couched in images of childhood play and so emphasises their 'natural' impulses as children. Tom Tiddler's Ground is a traditional children's game. 'A line is drawn on the ground, one player stands behind it. The piece so protected is Tom Tiddler's ground. The other players stand in a row on the other side. The row breaks and the children run over, calling out, "Here we are on Tom Tiddler's ground, picking up gold and silver." Tom Tiddler catches them, and as they are caught they stand on one side. The last out becomes Tom Tiddler'. Alice Gomme, *The Traditional Children's Games of England Scotland and Ireland in Dictionary Form, Vol. 2*, London: David Nutt and Company, 1894), p.398.
51   Benny aligns himself with animals in his observation that he is suffering from 'staggers', a fusion that highlights the child's innate comprehension of and allegiance with the natural world. Benny has witnessed cab-horses with 'staggers' on the London streets and is naively assuming that he is suffering from a similar illness, although this is unlikely. Staggers in horses is a nerve and muscle disorder and in *The Modern Horse Doctor*, Richard Dadd suggests that staggers is

caused by poor dietary management and that hay and grain of inferior quality are likely to cause the illness. The dull, sleepy appearance and staggering gait of the animal are, he states, 'symptoms not to be mistaken'. Richard Dadd, *The Modern Horse Doctor: containing practical observations on the causes, nature and treatment of disease and lameness in horses* (New York: Judd, 1883), p.38.

52   Thomas Keating was a pharmaceutical chemist in St Paul's Church Yard, London, offering medicines for coughs as well as flea powder and other insecticides. An advertisement in *The Athenaeum* (January 5 1867) for Keating's Cough Lozenges states that they cure coughs, asthma and incipient consumption.

53   'And kiss the place / To make it well' is a line from the poem 'My Mother' by Ann Taylor from *Original Poems for Infant Minds* (1804).

54   The hymn is 'Come, Sing with Holy Gladness', words by John J. Daniell (1868).

55   The parish doctor, appointed by the parish to tend the poor and destitute, generally worked for a meagre salary and was likely to have been responsible for workhouse inmates. Anne Digby reports that a successful London practitioner, writing of a 'country cousin' who practised in Norfolk, commented: 'I bade adieu to my kind and intelligent...brother practitioner, heartily wishing him better luck in his laborious and ill-regulated office of surgeon to a Union of sixteen parishes, for which he receives the paltry sum of twenty pounds a year'. She adds that some medical men were unwilling to take on this office because they feared that their contact with the poor would rebound adversely on their practice with more affluent patients. Anne Digby, *Making a Living: Doctors and Patients in the English Market for Medicine, 1720–1911* (Cambridge: Cambridge University Press, 2002), p.120.

56   Brenda's effusive praise of doctors displays personal experience of such a level of devotion and was gratefully acknowledged by correspondent 'M.D.' in *The British Medical Journal* of 30 October 1880. Under the title 'A Generous Tribute', he writes: 'I send enclosed an extract from a child's book recently published by J.F.Shaw and Co., Paternoster Row, as it contains a deserved tribute to our profession, which I think is rarely now to be found, for insertion in the Journal, if you consider it acceptable.' The extract from *Froggy's Little Brother* ('I am anxious...the Paradise of God' pp.145–146) was published under the letter. M.D., 'A Generous Tribute', *The British Medical Journal*, 1035 (1880), p.728.

57   A verse from the hymn 'O Paradise, O'Paradise' by F.W.Faber (1862).

58   Froggy's anxiety as he imagines a lady visitor would seem entirely valid; contemporary fashions could certainly have made entry into the garret problematic. A Grecian Bend was a style of posture or walk in which the body bends forward from the waist, the result of rigid 'cuirasse' bodices and high-heeled shoes.

59   'When Johnny Comes Marching Home' (1863) was a popular song of the American Civil War.

60   A variant of a sixteenth-century Christian proverb.

61   *The Union*: abbreviation for the Union Workhouse.

62   The text ends at this point in the 1968 Gollancz Revivals Series edition of *Froggy's Little Brother*, edited by Gillian Avery. Avery explains in her Introduction that 'two or three passages have been removed from the book because they have seemed so out-of-date as to be irrelevant – such as the original two concluding paragraphs which begged readers to send money and relief to the ragged schools and children's homes of the East End'. Brenda, *Froggy's Little Brother*, ed. Gillian Avery (London: Victor Gollancz, 1968), p.12.

Printed in China